Borrowing Time

a sequel to

The Other World

D. D. Riessen

Borrowing Time - Fantasy

Copyright © 2017 by D. D. Riessen
Cover design by D. D. Riessen and Phelan Riessen

Library of Congress Control Number: 2016959372
ISBN 10 - 0991663071
ISBN:13- 978-0-9916630-7-1

ddr
books

San Diego, CA 92119

They would smile and nod hello in passing, each wondering where they had seen the other before, a kind of endless Deja-vu.

Prologue

Sam *glanced down at the slip of paper that the cabbie had given him, a phone number to call when he was ready to leave. He tucked it into his pocket and headed up the dirt path to the small house nestled into the side of the hill. The gate was open.*

Sasi, a petite elderly woman with fine features and graying hair pulled back into a bun, met him at the door. She shook his hand, stepped aside to let him in and checked to see if he was followed before closing it. They sat in a small room, doors open to a balcony that overlooked the street leading up to her house. She served tea and biscuits.

"Your journey went well?"

"Very well. Thank you."

Sasi smiled, her laugh wrinkles showing her age. "Thank you for taking the trouble to come see me." She leaned back into her chair and studied Sam. "Mushin was your great, great, great, grandfather's brother, my great, great, great grandfather."

"I'm not even going to try to figure out how many distant cousins we are."

"As you know, the entire family was wiped out when Krakatoa erupted in eighteen eighty-three."

"Yes."

"They were preparing a welcoming celebration when Krakatoa erupted. My great, great grandfather and his wife were away when that happened. That is the only reason that I am here today."

"I see. Lucky for you."

"Joko, my brother, and I have always been curious as to why there was going to be a celebration."

"In preparation for my family's arrival?"

"We think so. But, then we have to ask why your entire family was traveling here. For them to make such a dangerous journey, we think that something of great

They would smile and nod hello in passing, each wondering where they had seen the other before, a kind of endless Deja-vu.

Prologue

Sam glanced down at the slip of paper that the cabbie had given him, a phone number to call when he was ready to leave. He tucked it into his pocket and headed up the dirt path to the small house nestled into the side of the hill. The gate was open.

Sasi, a petite elderly woman with fine features and graying hair pulled back into a bun, met him at the door. She shook his hand, stepped aside to let him in and checked to see if he was followed before closing it. They sat in a small room, doors open to a balcony that overlooked the street leading up to her house. She served tea and biscuits.

"Your journey went well?"

"Very well. Thank you."

Sasi smiled, her laugh wrinkles showing her age. "Thank you for taking the trouble to come see me." She leaned back into her chair and studied Sam. "Mushin was your great, great, great, grandfather's brother, my great, great, great grandfather."

"I'm not even going to try to figure out how many distant cousins we are."

"As you know, the entire family was wiped out when Krakatoa erupted in eighteen eighty-three."

"Yes."

"They were preparing a welcoming celebration when Krakatoa erupted. My great, great grandfather and his wife were away when that happened. That is the only reason that I am here today."

"I see. Lucky for you."

"Joko, my brother, and I have always been curious as to why there was going to be a celebration."

"In preparation for my family's arrival?"

"We think so. But, then we have to ask why your entire family was traveling here. For them to make such a dangerous journey, we think that something of great importance was about to take place."

"Such as?"

"I was hoping that you might provide some answers."

"You know that my ancestors were murdered?"

"Yes. We had heard that."

"Sameer had two sons, Musheer and Kashif. Musheer's daughter, Mahin, escaped the night of the attack. Kashif was away checking on Musheer, who had become sick and later died. Kashif and Mahin were the only survivors."

"And they stayed in Mogadishu?"

"Yes."

Sasi sipped her tea, slowly, thoughtfully, looking over the rim of her cup. "Do you know that you have the cheekbones of your line, our line?"

"I've been told it was my eyes." He held up his hands, palms outward. "And these, working man's hands, I'm told. I guess that means I'll never be rich."

"Money does not make your life rich. What do you do in America?"

"I'm an instructor in martial arts." Sam smiled. "So, I will always be poor but my life is rich. And you? What do you do?"

"I make a small stipend translating, a bit more teaching at the university on occasion and a small pension from my deceased husband's work. I get by."

"And yet, something was important enough that you paid my way to come here."

"We will talk about that soon enough. For now, I have prepared a meal. Shall we retire to the back of the house?"

Sam followed Sasi through a tiny kitchen to a shaded courtyard in the back. Hot coals were already glowing inside of a small rock pit. The grill above, burning off oil from some previous meal, smoked thinly. Sasi removed the skewers of meat from a container in the cooler, turned them in the marinade and placed them on the grill. "Satay, grilled chicken, cooked with a hot pepper sauce."

"Smells wonderful."

"I serve with nasi goreng, fried rice. And...," she

reached back into the cooler, "Gado, gado, salad with peanut sauce."

"All of it looks delicious."

Sasi turned her attention back to the satay, rotating the skewers in and out of the heat, turning occasionally. "Have you ever heard of Animism?"

"That animals have a spirit?"

"Yes. Do you feel that they do?"

Sam nodded. "Yes…, all animals."

"Plants?"

"I think we're only beginning to understand plants. A spirit? I don't know if we can call it that. I think we don't know what it is."

"What about the wind, rivers, mountains?"

"I don't know if those things have a spirit. Certainly some cultures believe that they do."

Sasi placed a small pan on the grill, poured in a bit of oil and spooned several scoops of fried rice into it. She turned the skewers, brushed chili sauce over the meat and then began to stir the sizzling rice around in the pan. "Do you believe that the spiritual world can visit this one?"

"I believe that there is always a fluid interaction. I don't know if the barrier between these worlds is thin enough that one can break through."

She looked up with a smile. "Do you believe in magic?"

"I've read of many accounts that have no logical explanation. If magic was the cause, I don't know. What about you? What do you believe?"

Sasi dished rice onto Sam's plate in silence, added salad and two skewers of chicken. "I believe that there are many worlds, all of them touching each other on the fringes. On occasion, our worlds overlap and we are left to deal with the unknown. Please eat while it is hot. After that, we have much to discuss."

"The problem with today's society," said Sasi, leaning back into her chair, "is that they have a very simplistic view of what the spiritual world consists of. They think it's all about a God, or Gods, or they are atheists, whatever else us humans can conceive of, mostly in our own image. If everyone understood that we are a tiny part of a much larger existence, we'd all be better off."

"How so?"

"We consider dreams as a consequence of our daily lives. Our brain is sorting out the details of the day, discarding what isn't needed and putting everything else in neat little packages, storage for later use. Does that seem simplistic to you?"

"I never really thought about it. I suppose so."

"Consider instead..., our dreams are interacting with other worlds. Our spirit is exploring and our dreams are the playback."

"You're saying that we live in two worlds?"

"We live in this one. We interact with several. Sometimes, and you were right when you said that the barriers could become thin, it's possible for the two to merge. And it may not even be limited to two. Three worlds could interact simultaneously."

"Interact. You mean that our worlds are physically connected?"

"Yes, from time to time."

"How?"

"I don't know how. But I do know that occasionally barriers break down. Surely you've felt that you've seen something or someone before? Even though you know you never have."

"I suppose so. Deja-vu?"

"We categorize our thinking in terms of time. But, that's a limiting concept. It has no meaning when it comes to dreams. That moment of Deja-vu exists forever. It's out there. Your spirit just passed through and collected it.

1

You're seeing the playback."

"That would mean that I've actually had that experience before."

"Or, you will. Not you, as Sam necessarily. Your spirit has had the experience at some point in its existence."

"If I die in this one, what happens to my spirit?"

"It will find another outlet for its energy. Either by joining with other spirits to become something different, or by adopting another life form on its own."

"How do you know this?"

Sasi smiled, a twinkle in her eyes. "Because I have been there. All of this time, Sam. And not once have you mentioned the firestone. I have danced around the subject for hours and not one word out of you. Do you think I would invite you here for anything less?"

"I suspected as much."

"I've had the firestone..., thirty years now. It's been a slow process, learning what it can do."

"Why are you telling me this?"

"I am going to die soon. I have cancer. I have seen it and I accept it. I have to pass the firestone on to its new owner."

"I held it once. If you're offering it to me, I don't want it."

"When did you hold it?"

"In a dream, eighteen eighty-three."

"And you don't think you have enough power? The stone was calling you."

"It is not my mission to possess the stone. I have other goals. I do not want it."

"You don't get to choose, Sam. You've been training for it all along."

"My mission was to return the stone to its rightful owners. That was accomplished."

"And you think it's over? No. This is only the beginning."

"OK." Sam set his tea down. "Why bother? The stone has been with us for, how long? Has it done anyone any good? Why keep it?"

2

"That gets us back to why your side was coming to visit. Joko and I think that they were intending to leave the stone here."

"And here it is."

"But, if true, why were they going to leave it? Did my family have some kind of special knowledge about the stone? And, since my side was wiped out before your family arrived, who did they give it to?"

"Someone brought it across later. It's here. What does it matter?"

"Something's missing."

"Give me the stone. I'll take it down to the ocean and throw it in. It's over."

"No. It cannot end like that."

"Have you been working with anyone? Joko? What does he know?"

"He's my brother and I love him. But he's a fool. Spends most of his time in different towns, has a girl in every one of them, spends all of his money. He's harmless and doesn't care about the stone."

"Anyone else?"

Sasi sighed. "I started training someone, Hamza. But as innocent as he was when he was young, I never imagined what he has become. I stopped training him a few years ago, told him the stone had been stolen. Don't know if he believes me. And he knows that I'm ill."

"Give me the stone. I'll destroy it."

"It's not that simple. And you have the wrong philosophy. We are not here to keep the stone. Our mission is to keep it from getting into the wrong hands. Can you imagine someone with evil intent getting into someone else's dreams? Especially when the walls break down."

"Then..., what do you suggest?"

"Before you decide anything, let me show you what I've learned."

Capn was acting strangely. Even Paul, busy with his homework, took note. "You see that, Mom? How many times in the last hour has he gone topside?"

Kathryn looked up from her book. "I watched him. He wanders up to the bow, sits at the pulpit and sniffs the air, like he's waiting for something."

"Does he have to go? I need a break. I'll take him for a walk."

"That's not it. Scares me. The last time he acted like this was just before the island."

"Another adventure? Cool!"

"No. We're done with that."

"It was amazing, wasn't it?"

"I don't ever want to go through that again."

"Have you had any more dreams of..., what's his name?"

"Bardolf. No. But I still have nightmares of you getting shot. That was horrible."

"Yet here I am, in all of my glory."

"Speaking of that. I see you got an A in Science."

"You were right. Make Mr. Cobb *do* the work. I caught him on an error in one of his equations today. He thanked me, but I could see that it bothered him. That was cool."

"Don't be vindictive. That's not cool."

"I'm not being vindictive. I'm being super-attentive. No malice. Satisfaction, more like."

"That's just about the same thing. But at least your grades are up. Talked to Melissa lately?"

"Saw her in the library today. She's working on some kind of investigative program. I think she's going to be a detective."

"What does that mean, investigative program?"

"Something about predicting outcome. She inputs whatever facts she has and this program is supposed to analyze and come up with the most logical conclusion."

"Does it work?"

4

"Says it has a few bugs. Where did Sam go?"

"Some place called Lampung."

"What's he doing there?"

"He got a letter from a distant cousin. She wanted to meet with him."

"What about?"

"She didn't say."

"And, on that, he went?"

"She paid his airfare. How could he refuse?"

"Anything to do with the firestone?"

"No idea. But this whole thing is starting to freak me out. Capn acting the way he is. And now this letter comes out of nowhere. I want all of that to go away. I'd rather believe all of that was just a dream."

"Can't do that, Mom. You've got the book, the dog and the boat that he rode in on. We got the firestone back to the owner. Way I see it, the stone owes us."

"Don't even think like that. We want to keep that thing out of our lives."

"Here it is. Found it. Lampung. It's in Indonesia. If Sam's in Indonesia, it's probably got something to do with the firestone."

"Get back to your homework. Stop thinking about it."

"Especially if she wouldn't talk about it. What was her name?"

"He didn't say."

"Doesn't their culture attach meanings to names?"

"I think all cultures do. What are you getting at?"

"If you think about it, all of these coincidences are building up, just like you've been saying. There was no guarantee that everything was going to stop after the dog was saved. That just means we own it. That's all. We might be dealing with magic and stuff that happens once in a blue moon. Finding out the meaning of her name is a clue."

"And you think *Melissa's* going to be the detective?"

"You told me to pay attention. I'm on it."

"Just because Sam went there doesn't mean that any of this involves us."

"If he's in it, so are we."

"He wouldn't want to risk our lives."

"But he knows he's got a good crew. We're battle hardened."

"We're lucky to be here. Especially you."

"Maybe, in this magical world we have nine lives. I just used one, that's all."

"Capn's back. Look at him. He's just standing up there looking down at us like he's waiting for us to do something."

"Right. Back to my homework."

"Sam. Can you hear me?"

"Yes."

"Say my name."

"Sasi."

"Do you know where we are?"

"I feel like I'm standing in the middle of nothing."

"You understand that you are apart from it?"

"Yes."

"You remember the light, how it engulfed us?"

"Yes."

"It is only a short burst. When it retreats back into the stone, our conscious energy is swept along with it. Remember this place, this state of mind, because it is your only way back out."

"I don't feel my body."

"You won't. It is your spirit that you are now in touch with, nothing in-between. We are in the deepest layer of the stone. Soon, you will begin to see what looks like star light."

"I see it, dimly."

"After that, the differences."

"Shadows. I see a faint light behind all of the shadows..., everything's moving. What's out there?"

"This is a rest point. From here, you go. And it is back to here that you must come. It's peaceful, like floating in the clouds."

"I have no control over anything."

"You have control over everything. You are a warrior, Sam. You've been training for this."

"I cannot move of my own volition."

"Because you are thinking as if you have a body. Your power is your desire to be this, or that, here or there. It's all up to you. Move toward light..., or dark. You choose. Go slowly. You are now at the front end of your consciousness. You are learning new pathways. Always remember where you came from."

7

"Where do I go?"

"Wherever you will."

"Do I have to take the same path back?"

"No. Come back to here, this state of mind. Never lose sight of the beginning...,"

Kashif smiled weakly from his bed, a thin mattress on the floor in the corner of the room. Two candles lit up the half empty glass and the pitcher of water nearby. Mahin began to stand when Sam and Sasi walked past the screen, but Sam motioned for her to remain sitting and gave her a hug before he joined Sasi, who was finding a place to sit.

Oskar helped Kashif to a sitting position while Mahin moved toward the foot of the bed. Kashif coughed, a hoarse, gravelly sound coming from deep inside.

"It's gotten much worse in the last week," said Oskar. "You picked the right time to visit."

Sam frowned. "I didn't pick this time. I don't even know how I got here." He glanced over at Sasi for confirmation.

"You were drawn to this time," Sasi explained. "Remember where you came from?"

That moment of conversation, floating in the clouds with Sasi, seemed an eternity away. Yet, weren't they just there? Sam nodded yes, turned back to face Kashif and smiled. "It is good to see you. How are you feeling?"

Kashif nodded and managed a thin smile. "Never..., so good. Yes?"

"Every day is good," said Sam. He motioned to his right. "This is Sasi."

Kashif studied her for a moment and then extended his hand. "You..., from Mushin? Yes?"

"Yes."

"Eyes..., and here." He touched his cheek. "Same."

Sasi smiled, nodding. "Yes, the same. Kashif, you called us. How may we help?"

Watching Sam as he spoke, Oskar translated. "He says that the stone must go back to Teluk Betung."

Sam glanced over at Sasi. "We are in Lampung, what used to be Teluk Betung..., right?"

8

She shook her head. "Apparently not. What year, Oskar?"

"Eighteen ninety-seven."

"Where are we?"

Oskar looked puzzled with the question. "Mogadishu. Of course."

"Sasi, we are at your house in Lampung, right?"

"Sam, Mogadishu, eighteen ninety-seven. The stone is on the wrong side of the sea."

"Someone brought it over."

Kashif looked down at his wrinkled hands with a quiet smile. And then he turned his attention to his niece. "If Mahin keep, die young. Stone must go."

"Why don't we just rid ourselves of it?"

Kashif looked over at Oskar, unsure of what he heard. After Oskar explained, he began to speak. "He says that there are two stones. The other one is in Teluk Betung. He wants to bring them together. He says that will end..., conflict. I think that's the word."

"How?"

"He says each stone is only half of a dream, therefore broken. That is the reason they were going to Teluk Betung. His brother knew where the other half was."

"But then, Krakatoa?"

"Yes."

"What happened to that stone?"

"We don't know."

"Then..., there is no reason to take this one back."

"He says the stone is there. The best way to find it is to go to Teluk Betung with this one and use it to find the other."

Sam looked over at Sasi. "Have you been looking?"

"I've spent my whole life looking for something. Only now do I know what it is. I should've contacted you, years ago."

Melissa did not understand the results. Using their trip to the island on a blue moon as an example, the conclusion should be that they returned back to their own time and place safely. But the program kept classifying that information as just another clue, not a conclusion.

That just didn't make sense. She already knew the outcome. The program correctly predicted the outcome ninety percent of the time of several murder mysteries that she'd read, solved recent crimes and was pretty good, Melissa thought anyway, at predicting the ones yet unsolved. So, it didn't make sense that the conclusion was just another clue. Frustrated, she called Paul.

"Melissa, what's up?"

"I'm bored. You want to do something?"

"It's a school night."

"So? That doesn't stop you when you want to do something."

"What do you want to do?"

"Movie?"

"What do you want to see?"

"I don't know. How about bowling?"

"Now you're really getting low. What's the matter? You sound frustrated."

"My program's got a flaw. I'm tired of trying to figure it out."

"Well, at least you don't have a physics test tomorrow. What's your program doing?"

"It keeps listing our blue moon thing as another clue, not the conclusion."

"That's funny. Capn's acting strangely. Mom and I were just talking about it."

"How's he acting?"

"Like how he acted before we went to the island."

"Oh." Melissa stared at her screen. "You think the program's right?"

"Odd that you call right after our conversation. Did

10

*you know Sam was in..., where was that place, Mom?
Lampung."*

"Where is that?"

"Indonesia, I guess."

"Is that near Teluk Betung?"

"I think it's what used to be Teluk Betung."

"Why did he go there?"

*"He got a phone call. Somebody paid his way. That's all
I know. You sure you want to go bowling?"*

"Why would I go bowling? I need to get back to my
program."

"Not so bad when it proves you right, huh?"

"Thanks, Paul. See you tomorrow."

Startled, Sam did a quick take of his surroundings, sitting in the tiny underground room beneath the floor. A ventilation fan hummed quietly from somewhere while the dim light above their table cast a soft glow over the stone. His tea was still hot.

"Sasi?"

"Yes, Sam."

"What just happened?"

"You lost your concentration."

"We were speaking with Kashif."

"Yes."

"I don't understand. What happened?"

"You got confused."

"How?"

"With the impossibility of being in two different times and places at the same time."

"We were there."

"Yes."

"How do I go back?"

Sasi laughed. "You're the one that took us there. Only you know the path."

"It was real. I hugged Mahin."

"I saw you. And I shook Kashif's hand."

"And yet...,"

"Now you begin to see the possibilities of the stone? And..., now we know what we're looking for."

"You say we, as if I've agreed."

"How can you refuse?"

"Sasi," Sam fiddled with his tea cup, running his fingers across the smooth rim. "If I take this on, the odds of finding the other half are, let's just call it like it is, impossible. Krakatoa buried the stone along with whoever was holding it at the time. It's at the bottom of the sea."

"A few years back, a diver came across an unusual stone. It was reported in the paper and, from the description, sounded like he had found something similar to this one.

I immediately set off searching for him, but when I arrived at his house, I was told that another man had called and offered to buy it. The stone and buyer disappeared and were never found. Several days later the diver was found at the bottom of a cliff."

"What was his name?"

"The diver, I think his name was Dimyati. The buyer's name was Aki, my only clue. Origin of that name is from Japan. But, having no last name to reference it with, the search became impossible."

"Passenger lists of airlines? You've got the time frame."

"As far as I know, he did not come or go by air. I checked ships. No one with that name as a passenger and they won't reveal the names of their crews unless you're an official from one government or another. I got nowhere. He could have been on any one of them. He might have left by train. All you need is a ticket. No name required."

"Supposing I take the stone. What do you expect me to do?"

"If you can get it out of here? Look for the other half. Know of anyone good at snooping around on the Internet?"

"*If* I can get it out of here?"

"Hamza. I mentioned him earlier?"

"Your student?"

"He has a lot of friends. Most of them are up to no good. When you arrived, did the driver give you a phone number to call when you're ready to leave?"

"Yes."

"Did he pick you up at the airport?"

"Yes."

"Then they already know who you are and where you're from."

"And when I'll be going back. I feel like you're handing me a lit stick of dynamite."

"I've got a friend who has a car. She can take you to the airport. But you'll be on your own to board the plane."

"And the stone? How will I get that through security?"

"There's the problem. It wasn't that long ago that you could walk onto the plane with it in your luggage."

"Send it through the mail? Add a few other rocks and say it's from a dig."

"Maybe. Government might want to know what I'm sending out of the country, especially if it sets off any alarms."

"Sasi, sorry to say, I think you're handing me an impossible task. I don't want the stone. I have no way to leave with it and where do I go with it? Back to the states? That doesn't do anyone any good. Even Kashif said to look for the other stone here. Aki could be from anywhere. Seems we've reached a dead end."

"Not necessarily. We have the stone. Tell me, what were the circumstances when you held it?"

Sam pulled the rug back over the trap door in the closet while Sasi, in the kitchen, dished steaming hot soup into two bowls. The timer went off on the oven, sending a low buzzing sound into the room. Sasi cancelled it, opened the door and retrieved the rolls.

"Kashif said that you couldn't leave the island without the dog?"

"Yes, the night before Nerissa sailed."

"What is it about the dog?"

"I don't know. But, he was right. Our time on the island ended the second the dog reached the boat."

"When the whole crew was finally back together?"

"Right."

"I think there's something about equilibrium within the stone. Things have to balance out. What happened next?"

"I don't know where, when or how, but I had another discussion with Kashif. He offered me the stone."

"Because you saved him?"

"I don't know, maybe."

"Why did you refuse?"

"I was overwhelmed with the sorrow that came from it. Why would I want to own anything like that?"

"What did he say?"

"He asked what I wanted."

"He was offering you a *choice*?"

"It seems so."

"How did you answer?"

"I wished to be safe at home with my friends."

"That happened?"

"Yes."

"What about the dog?"

"They still have him. They all live on the boat."

"It sounds like Kashif had control of your destiny, all of your destinies. He let you *choose*. How did he do that?"

"All right. I understand your concerns. What's next?"

"Tell me more about the dog."

"You have to understand that when I talk about it, there are two versions, Oskar's accounting in eighteen eighty-three, the one I've read about, and my own experience."

"Separate, yet connected, two worlds coming together. Of course."

"In eighteen eighty-three, Oskar and Bardolf had gone onto the island to recapture some chimpanzees. Bardolf captured the dog instead and was taking it back to the ship when it disappeared. It was there with a rope around its neck one second and gone the next, according to Oskar."

"You remember our short discussion about animism?"

"That they have a spirit?"

"Yes. Apparently we aren't the only species that has a relationship with the stone. This confirms my thinking that language has no real effect. More like..., emotion. What kind of stress was the dog was under?"

"In our time, he was going to be put down. Don't know if he knew that. He had been living on a boat with his old owner who died."

"Have you got a picture of it?"

Sam retrieved his cell and started thumbing through the images. "What are we going to do?"

"How can a dog live both in eighteen eighty-three and now? The only thing I can think of is that, since the dog is with us now, it was dreaming about that place. Otherwise, it can't be the same animal."

"No way to tell. The only ones who saw it in eighteen eighty-three were Bardolf and Oskar. Bardolf died without seeing the dog when we were on the island. I don't know that for sure. But he did offer a trade, Kashif for the dog, so he knew of its presence. Oskar was not on the island when we were there. The only real way to know is through DNA testing. Like that's going to happen."

"Same island, disappearing dog and some kind of time warp."

"Kathryn said they read the story on a blue moon, something Oskar warned about, which just happened to be the same night that the dog was in animal control."

"Dogs have nightmares, don't they?"

Sam smiled. "This one does. He runs a lot in his sleep. We all wonder what he's dreaming about."

"OK. He's under stress, having a bad dream, there's a blue moon in effect and your friends are reading the book against Oskar's warnings. Have I got that right?"

Sam nodded.

"All of these coincidences. How did you get involved?"

"Kathryn, the dog's owner, felt she was being stalked by Bardolf and wanted training in self defense."

"Apparitions?"

"She said she first became aware of him in her dreams. After that she claims that he visited the dock where she keeps her boat."

"She has proof?"

"No. Where is the proof in any of this?"

"He was looking for the dog. If it's the same dog, it has the ability to *be* in the place of its dream."

Sasi and Sam exchanged glances. Both said it at the same time. "But only during a blue moon."

Aki quietly set the stone back down on the table. He didn't want to hold it again, just yet. But, nudging it gently with the tips of his fingers, he rotated the stone slowly, watching the light's changing reflection inside. He paused to clean his glasses.

Quartz? Maybe, except for where it looks like it's still molten. But, it's not hot. Warm? Seemed like it was warm when I first touched it.

The stone had an irregular oval shape and, moving it so that when the longer end was pointing toward his chest, he noticed a long, smooth, crack in the glass, narrow at the top and wider at the bottom, that formed what looked like a lion's nose.

Leaning forward and looking straight down at the stone, fluctuations in the material, darker areas, deep imperfections, one higher than the other but both located about where they should be if those were eyes, squinting toward some distant place.

Fascinated and curious, Aki turned his gaze down past the nose to where he spotted a horizontal crack in the stone, a crooked ledge recessed into the area above the chin, pursed, thin lips, mouth slightly turned down.

Now that he'd seen the face, something between that of a lion and human, Aki was surprised that he hadn't noticed it before. How could he have been so oblivious to its features? He was now face to face with the stone's face.

Picking it up again, the curved side fit easily into his palm and, holding it like that, the only place for his thumb was over a flat, dull, sheered off section while his fingers wrapped around and came to rest on a similar satiny surface on the other side.

A tingling sensation, feeling like his hand had been asleep, started at his fingertips and flowed like a wave up through his arm and, warming his chest with the energy, spread head to toe, much like a fog seeping into all of the

18

nuances of a dark night. Thin glowing lips moved ever so slightly.

Hello. I am Missy.

Aki was sure that he had locked both doors and closed all of the windows before retreating back to his bedroom. He knew he was home alone. But, hearing the words so clearly, he had to turn and look. The doors to both the bathroom and the spare room were closed. The place was empty. "Hello?"

I am Missy. Who are you?

"Where are you?"

We are speaking through the stone.

"I..., I'm hearing, but not seeing you."

What would you like me to look like?

"I have no idea."

Form a picture and I will be that.

"Male or female?"

Friend. May I come in?

It was such a casual request, done in such a relaxed way and so much a part of Aki's normal life that he nodded yes without even thinking about where she was going to come into.

Depending upon Aki's sudden and shifting perspective, he felt like he and Missy were sitting together in the same chair, one on the lap of the other. No matter how he moved, she was still in his head, right there with him, ear to ear, like they were sitting in his living room, his private room where only his private thoughts were known.

I will be comfortable here. Thank you.

"I didn't do anything."

You invited me in. I will stay.

"What?"

I am Missy. I am now part of you. We are as one. Your name?

Aki attempted to drop the stone but his hand refused to let go. He tried flinging it down to the floor. But the harder he tried the tighter his grip.

Your name?

Swinging his arm wildly, Aki slammed the back of his

hand against the wall. He could not let go.

My name is Missy. You invited me in and I accepted. It will take a while for us to get used to each other and we may not get along at first, but we will learn. You may now put the stone down. Your name?

"There are three types of memory, the past, present and the future. These concepts can be used to guide your experiences within the stone."

Sam moved the pillow against the wall and settled into it, still sitting within reach of his tea back at the table. "How is it possible to remember the future?"

"I am going to wash dishes when I go back into the kitchen. It is that task in the future that I must remind myself to do when I get there. You can use that technique when you plan your destination."

"But you're not really remembering the future. You're predicting what you might do. It's not for certain until you've done it. Instead, you might go into the kitchen and get more of that cake."

Sasi laughed. "Is that a hint?" She reached over the table for his plate. "I forget the appetites of youth. I'll cut you a big piece."

"Did you make it?"

"Oh, no. There's a bakery not far away."

"How does thinking about the future work with the stone?"

"Like when we visited Kashif. You can do the same with the future."

"But, we never really visited him. He died in eighteen ninety seven."

"Correct. Right after we visited him. And I say "we" because I shook his hand."

"But it didn't really happen."

Standing, Sasi shook her head and headed for the kitchen. "I'll get your cake so you can have more time to think about it."

She returned with the whole thing and additional hot tea, which she placed on a mat next to her pillow at the table after she filled their cups. "Well? What have you come up with? Still in denial?"

"I can agree that we had a shared experience with Kashif,

Mahin and Oskar. But that was not a real experience."

"We gleaned information. We had physical contact. Was it not as real as the two of us sitting here and eating cake?"

"It cannot have happened."

"And yet, it did. Think about it. Just as you channeled your thoughts to a previous time, you can also catch a glimpse the future."

"How? It hasn't happened."

"No. But it is one of an infinite number of possibilities. The beauty of the stone is that you can pick one and sneak a look. Otherwise, how did Kashif know where and when to place your destinies?"

"You're saying that it's possible to change the future?"

"No. I'm saying that the future is already out there. Had Kashif not intervened, it sounds like you and your friends were going your separate ways. He picked the path you asked for. *How* did he do that? Eat your cake."

Sam smiled. "I am embarrassed. I should never have used cake as an example. Thank you." He cut himself a piece, put it on his plate, took a bite and followed with a hurried sip of tea. "So..., what's next?"

"We have a formidable crew. Maybe if we...,"

"Crew? No. They all have lives. I can't involve them. Paul and Melissa are in school and Kathryn is busy with her new job."

"All of us are in alignment. We'll never have this much power again. Think about it, Sam. This is the impossible combination."

"I don't like to think about it. Paul was killed..., died in our encounter with the stone. I could never forgive myself if something happened to any of them because of me."

"Perhaps we should let them decide."

"How? Text them? Call them? There's no way that I can convey this enough for them to make an intelligent decision."

"Sam. You are so negative."

"Cautious."

"I agree. There's no normal way that they can know.

But, don't forget. We have the stone."

"What are you proposing?"

Sasi smiled. "We'll start with..., what's her name? Kathryn?"

"Yes."

"Remember what I said about the spirit being freed up when we dream?"

"Yes."

"We'll make contact. You and I will visit her in her dreams. The next morning we'll send a picture of us. She can decide then."

"No one remembers their dreams. How will she recognize you?"

"She'll recognize my spirit when she sees my face in the photograph. Is this idea acceptable to you?"

"She's too young."

The girl was sitting on the edge of a rock, one leg pulled up to her chest, foot flat on the rock, the other kicking the water idly. She had tied the boat to the trunk of a small sapling up on the bank. In the shallow water, tied to a stake, two captive trout struggled to get away.

"She looks like Kathryn but I didn't know her when she was this young."

"Sam, this is her dream. She can be whatever age she wants."

"She won't recognize me."

"We'll see. Think of us sitting in the rowboat, facing her. Call her by name and say hello. Introduce me."

"I don't know how to do that. I...,"

"Think back to how I explained remembering the future, dishes in the kitchen, the cake. Remember the process."

Surprised to suddenly be sitting in the front seat of the boat, Sam looked up and studied Kathryn's features while Sasi, quietly moving the oars out of the way, settled into the weathered wooden seat behind him. A slight breeze, blowing in from across the lake. Tiny waves lapped up against the flat, wooden stern of the boat.

"Hello, Kathryn."

She did not look up. "Hello, Sam. What are you doing here?"

"I came to see you."

"It's so sad. He's gone now."

"Who?"

"You don't know him. We used to lunch further up the bank. There's a little flat area."

"I'm so sorry."

"No need."

"What did he die of?"

"Die? No. He's alive, just gone. Why are you here, Sam?"

"To introduce Sasi."

24

Kathryn opened her eyes and looked past Sam, over to Sasi. "You're not like I imagined."

"What did you imagine?"

"Darker hair."

"Age does that, turns it gray."

Kathryn blushed a bit. "I thought you were younger."

"I wish I was."

She pointed to the two fish tied to the stake. "They're yours if you'd like. I was going to let them go...,"

Sitting across the table from Sam, stone in between them, Sasi smiled. "Very good, Sam. You learn quickly."

"What did I do?"

"Introduce me to Kathryn. Next, we'll send a picture of us and see what happens. It's kind of like those two fish she caught. We'll see if we hooked a dream."

Ever since she'd woken up, Kathryn was feeling fuzzy around the edges. She'd slept good, got to bed a little late, but she hadn't had too much to drink, only a half glass of wine.

That always happens. Drink less, dream more. I slept harder. Gad! I feel pooped, like I've been problem solving all night. Must be the new job, trying to figure everything out.

She poured herself another cup of coffee and, checking for messages, noticed that she had one from Sam. Seated at the table in the galley, she turned off the morning news playing on the little TV over in the corner.

Hi Kathryn,

Anything interesting happen since I've been gone? I'm staying at Sasi's house in Lampung. Seems our families go way back so we have a lot to talk about. She's quite the cook, just like you. I attached a picture of Sasi and me. See any resemblance?

Missing you guys, hope to be home soon.

Sam

Opening the image, Kathryn studied Sasi's picture. She looked familiar. Surely, living on opposite sides of the world, they would never have had any chance to meet. Yet...,

Wonder what she does. Maybe I've seen her on TV? Hmm. It's because she looks like Sam. Thought she would be younger...,

Enlarging the image, Kathryn studied Sasi's eyes. They were looking into the lens, but it was the way that her gaze met the camera, something timeless about that. Kathryn leaned back into the nook.

Anything interesting happening? Let's see. Capn's acting weird. Melissa's got some kind of program that predicts outcomes and it's saying..., not sure what it's saying. Paul's getting straight A's and you're in Lampung with a woman who's got some kind of secret..., apparently.

26

Sam looks the same but, standing there with her, he's changed. Sasi, what is it about you?

Leaning up to the keyboard, Kathryn typed:

Hey Sam,

Good to hear from you. Yep. You two look like twins. Amazing! Anything exciting happening there? I'm still picking you up at the airport Sunday night, right?

K

Kathryn got up, grabbed a sponge, soaped it up and started washing dishes. Paul left early apologizing for the mess on his way topside and saying that he'd clean up tonight.

Right. Like that's going to happen. He has practice and then he'll have homework. He already knows who's going to clean up tonight. Hmm.

Kathryn put the dish rack away and checked messages.

Hi Kathryn,

Cancelled the ticket. Will book another date and let you know when. Don't worry about picking me up. I can take a cab. I'll keep in touch.

Sam

Mysterious response, cancelled plans..., Sasi. Returning to her cleaning, Kathryn could feel a knot tightening in her gut.

They had different tastes. Aki preferred water. Missy liked iced tea with sugar which, according to Aki, made it taste even worse. Aki didn't like meat, especially red meat. Missy craved all meats. Aki liked to take walks and exercise. Missy preferred to lay around during the day.

Living together inside Aki's head was wearing him down. He used to sleep peacefully, a good eight hours, waking only occasionally, remembering nothing in the morning and almost always feeling refreshed.

Missy wanted to sleep most of the day, which made Aki lazy, something he never was before. At night, Missy spent the time stalking something in their dreams, following silently through the shadows, heart racing, waiting for the perfect moment to attack.

After a particularly brutal kill on a deer one night, Aki woke up the following morning shaking. Missy laughed.

"I don't like violence."

Get used to it.

"I used to sleep very well."

Night time is best for me.

"I need a good night's sleep. With you killing things, I don't get it, I feel crappy all day."

That's why daytime is a good time to sleep.

"We are not compatible. You need to leave."

You invited me in. I accepted.

"I'm inviting you to leave."

I choose to stay.

Ignoring her, Aki went into the kitchen, grabbed an orange out of the bowl, rinsed it off in the sink and, sitting, began to peel.

I don't like oranges.

"Shut up."

If you're going to eat that, at least have bacon or sausage and lots of eggs. That grain stuff makes me gag.

"I like my cereal."

No wonder you're so weak.

"I'm not weak. I'm in shape. At least I used to be until you came along."

You should be more careful about who you invite in.

"I thought you meant into the room. I've never wanted you inside my head."

You're not going to make coffee again, are you?

"It's what I drink in the morning. It gets me going, especially after a night with you."

You had coffee yesterday. I want tea.

"You don't get a vote."

I want tea.

"It's my body. I was here first. I have squatter's rights. I want coffee."

Fine.

Aki jumped when the sound blared into his head, something between banging on metal trash cans, monkeys screeching, water crashing over rocks and a roaring lion, everything combined into one continuous cacophony of sounds, all at ear splitting levels.

Aki held his hands over his ears and then realized that it was all in his head. Eyes shut, he clenched his fists and waited. It wasn't going to end.

"OK! I'll drink tea! But you can't control me. I am my own boss."

We shall see. Thank you, Aki. You're so considerate.

Back in the living room, Sasi opened the shutters to the balcony and waved her hand toward the view. She motioned for Sam to sit opposite her at the small table. "My house isn't much, but the view is pretty good. Don't you think?"

Sam leaned out over the balcony. "I especially like the drop-off. Nobody can build here."

"They keep trying. I remind them that there is a city easement on that strip. Goes all the way up the hill. Don't know what they're going to use it for. I just hope they leave it alone until I'm gone."

Sam seated himself across the table from Sasi. "Everything changes with time. Usually the wrong things. Why is that?"

Sasi rubbed her thumb and forefinger together. "Money. Follow the money."

"And so, it goes." Sam checked messages, hoping to see something from Kathryn. Nothing. "OK. We've sent Kathryn our picture. Is her response what you expected?"

Sasi shrugged. "Don't know. Unfortunately, we don't have much time. I suggest that we try again."

"Because of your health? Is your time short?"

"They give me six months. I give me six years. We'll see who wins. No. It's not that. We've confirmed that there was another stone and that it's from here. Where is it and what kind of power does it have?"

"It's at the bottom of the sea."

"You keep giving me reasons why we can't do something. Sam, you're a warrior. Being cautious is a great asset. But it's not going to get us anywhere."

"What are you suggesting?"

"All of this talent is aligned. All of these coincidences. Kathryn reading the story on a blue moon, saving the dog, you getting involved. I'm thinking, all by ourselves on the next full moon, which is just a week away, we can create a blue moon event."

"Is that even possible?"

"Once in a blue moon, the unpredictable. That's us, Sam."

"Like I said, they're in school. I'm not going to interfere with that."

The endless arguing between Aki and Missy was wearing him down. Sooner or later, his invitation for her to leave was going to have to be enforced, although he had no idea how he was going to make that happen.

One day. Aki relented to Missy's constant badgering, made buttered popcorn, fixed a tall glass of sweetened iced tea and sat down in front of the television.

They stumbled upon a nature program that showed a herd of gazelle bounding through the grass. Missy's impulse was to lunge through the screen. Spilling the popcorn, Aki clutched the arms of their chair.

"It's not real, Missy! You're going to get us killed. These are just pictures."

I can taste them.

"No, you can't. If I can't taste them, you can't taste them."

Sitting in the chair, feeling like he was stalking the herd, Aki began to feel Missy's passion to be free. The bickering stopped.

Nature shows became the new thing. Missy was interested in anything that moved. Close-up videos of birds and butterflies, anything within reach, and Missy tried to bat them down. Aki twitched and turned in his chair, holding back because he loved butterflies.

"Missy, you're driving me crazy!"

They're just bugs.

"They're beautiful!"

Bugs with wings.

"How come you want to kill everything? You can't eat a butterfly."

I don't want to eat them. They're just practice.

When they chanced upon videos of larger game, Aki discovered a tenseness inside his body that he never knew he had. His leg muscles cramped as she crept forward, making ready for the kill.

The next day, after watching several of these shows,

Aki noticed that his leg muscles were sore, about how he'd feel if he'd bicycled all day or had hiked up a tall mountain. And he began to notice that his reactions were much faster. Viewing the world from Missy's perspective, he was aware of every little movement, every little thing that had changed since the last time he saw it.

Seeing lions, tigers, any kind of cat or dog on the screen, brought out anger, an almost unstoppable desire to leap out of the chair and kill them.

Shaking with the adrenaline, Aki whispered, "Missy, you're going to give me a heart attack."

Then don't watch.

"I can't stop watching! You've got me hypnotized."

As I've said. You're weak.

"Let's watch something else."

Before Missy could protest, Aki flipped to a new channel, a video of a volcano erupting, bursts of red and yellow glowing lava, searing upward into the night air and disappearing into the billowing smoke. Aki and Missy sat in silence, speechless as rumbling thunder filled the room.

Aki soon forgot about the show after it was over. But, from somewhere deep inside, Missy felt the tug of some distant, terrible loss.

Sasi was careful to pull the rug over the trap door, overlapping it past the edges as she pulled it back down into place.

Seven PM in Lampung. Four AM in San Diego. With a little help from the tea, Sam nodded off into San Diego time. Sasi figured that she had a good hour before everyone started waking up over there and Sam was most likely out for three or four hours here.

Sorry, Sam. This has to be done. You don't fully understand. If you did, you'd agree.

The electrical wiring that went down into the cellar was primitive, something she'd wired in from the wall socket upstairs. It gave her two outlets, one for the ventilation fan and one for the light switch at the top of the stairs, which she flicked on, for the dim light at the bottom of the steps.

She seated herself at the table and thought of Kathryn, Paul, Melissa and the dog, remembering their postures in the images that Sam shared, the looks on their faces and especially their eyes.

Next, she carefully lifted the stone from the box and unwrapped the soft leather covering, laying it out flat as she set it down. Touching it delicately, she positioned the stone so that she was facing the beast.

She thought of it as a beast because the face changed, depending on what she termed the 'mood' of the stone. Over time, sometimes days, sometimes weeks, the face would show a slightly different reflection of light that turned the corners of the mouth up or down, or she'd spot a new variation of the nose and cheeks. The eyes always seemed to be squinting toward some distant object, although a few times Sasi thought she saw them move.

Sasi backed away from the table, sat up straight and, breathing slowly, moved her hands out to either side, keeping her palms facing the stone while she closed her eyes.

Always give the stone room. Never get too close when it's active and never hold it for too long. Sam, you should be here for this. These are important lessons.

For more than a hundred years the object of our quest has remained unknown. Finally, it is revealed. We have the opportunity to discover this source of sorrow.

Never have I seen the participants so aligned. I call upon the power to aid me in our search and, if you will, find Kathryn as I think of her and connect me with her dreams...,

She was sitting on the top of the cabin adjusting her wide brimmed canvas hat to keep out the sun and watching Paul scrub the deck. "Why does it get so dirty so fast?"

Paul dipped the brush into the bucket, moved it around a bit to shake off the black stuff, and then looked up. "It's the jets. All of that black stuff is coming from them. We're in their flight path."

"Seems like they should pay for our cleaning."

Sasi was seeing all of this from her perspective, standing on the dock, watching. Kathryn looked up. "I know you."

"We recently met. I'm Sasi."

Kathryn smiled and motioned toward Paul. "This is my son, Paul."

He would have offered to shake her hand but his were wet. He shrugged apologetically. "Sam is with you?"

Sasi nodded. "He's spoken very highly of you, says that you should be a warrior."

Kathryn sat up, moving from her cross-legged position on top of the cabin to where her feet were on the wet, soapy deck. "I haven't heard that."

"He doesn't want to worry you unnecessarily. Since his arrival we've discovered that there is another stone, the other half. We are on a quest to find it."

"So, it is about the stone. Where is Sam?"

"Resting."

"Why are you here?"

"To ask if you would be interested in helping."

Paul grinned. "Cool."

35

"Not so cool," Kathryn replied. "I almost lost him before. I won't take that chance again."

"Mom!"

"No. And that's final." Kathryn turned her attention back to Sasi. "I hope that you understand."

Fading away, Sasi smiled. "I do."

Becoming aware of the tiny room, the ventilation fan humming quietly, Sasi stared blankly at the firestone while tapping her fingers gently on the table.

Paul, yes. Kathryn, no. That leaves Melissa. Sam said he knew of someone, but she was in school. Sounds like you, doesn't it? What would it take to get you interested?

And you, Aki, somewhere out there. What have you discovered?

*G*et more cheese.

"No. Cheese is bad for you. It's solid fat."

That's what makes it taste good. Get that yellow kind there.

Aki turned toward the produce section. "No."

Aki?

"You're going to plug up my arteries and I'm gonna die. What will you do then?"

I'll find someone else.

"Why don't you go find them now? Get me out of the middle. Find someone who thinks like you, God forbid."

I'm starting to like you, Aki. I think I'll stay. And since I am, let's go back and get that cheese.

"I'm getting lettuce and spinach and carrots and...,"

You're killing me. Oh! Look! There's salami! And pepperoni and..., lunch meat!

"No."

You know what's coming next, right? Because I don't want you to be surprised and embarrassed when you make a scene here in the store.

Aki left with two bags of groceries, Missy's in one hand, his in the other and, trying to justify the bad food and extra cost, he was thinking that this was a good thing because now at least he had equal weight on both sides so he wouldn't have to switch hands walking home.

Taking a short cut across a dirt lot, three men approached from the opposite direction.

Aki, I sense danger.

"Me, too. Should I go back the other way? Get under the streetlight?"

No. Don't turn your back on them. They'll think you're weak.

"I am weak. That's what you keep saying."

That's you. Not me.

"I'm going to get robbed."

If they try anything, you're going to kick butt.

"I don't know how to fight."

I do.

"There are three of them."

Not enough. Too bad for them.

Standing about a foot apart, forming a semicircle, they blocked Aki's path. Aki turned one way, then the other attempting to go around. They stayed in front of him.

"Man. That looks like groceries to me. I'm hungry."

"Me, too. Hey, man. Aren't you going to share with your friends?"

"And give to the poor."

They all laughed.

"I'm poor."

"Me, too. I'm *really* poor."

"And we're all hungry. What's in the bag, dude?"

The man on Aki's left started to reach for the bag. Aki pulled it out of reach.

He can't have it, Aki. That's my cheese!

"Oh, look at the brave little man. You think that's gonna stop us? Give me the fricking bag!"

Aki saw the man on his right start to move behind him. He saw the man in the middle pull a switchblade out of his pocket and snap it open. He saw the man on his left throw a punch.

It all was being seen in slow motion. Aki felt like he had all the time in the world to duck the punch, let the man's arm go by and throw him into the path of his friend's knife. A quick kick to the groin of the attacker on his right stopped him and, as he was going down, a kick to his face finished it.

The one with the knife attacked, slicing air as Aki twisted this way or that. He could see where it was coming and where it was going to go, everything so slow.

Aki caught the man's forearm when he lunged and spun him around. Roaring like a lion, the sound came from somewhere deep inside and utterly surprised Aki, who felt an inner strength surge from his body, threw the man ten feet before he ever touched the ground.

And then, heart pounding, acting as if nothing had

happened, Aki picked up his spilled groceries, carefully placed them back into the bags and continued on.

"Missy, you almost got me killed."

What? We almost killed them. Let's go back and finish it.

"There are laws against killing people."

They were going to kill us.

"Not us, me. They were going to kill me."

So, you should be thanking me.

"I wouldn't even have had to go to the store tonight if you didn't eat so much."

Right. Blame your weakness on me. I'm good for you.

"You're the worst thing that ever happened."

Walk a little faster. I want to try that cheese.

Melissa spotted Paul across the patio at their usual lunch spot, one of the tables on north side of the lab building, usually in the shade by noon. She pulled her backpack over her shoulder and made her way to the table. "Mind if I join you?"

"Hey, Melissa. What's up?"

"Gotta study for a test, so don't bug me. OK?"

"Fine. I wasn't supposed to say anything anyway."

"About what?"

"You can't ask. You already told me not to bug you. So, I'm not."

"But, not telling me is bugging me. Not supposed to say what?"

"Quit bugging me about it. Works both ways. I have to present my lab test results today so I need some quiet time here, too."

"Paul, if you don't tell me, I'm going to hit you."

"Bad logic, appeal to force. Denied."

"I'll scream."

"No, you won't. That'll get us both in trouble. You won't be able to take your test and I'll miss...,"

"OK. I won't give you these two brownies that I baked this morning, still kind of warm."

Grinning, Paul held out his hand. "What's a secret if I can't share?"

Melissa handed him the brownies. "Boy, you *are* easy."

"I wanted to tell you anyway."

"Who told you not to say?"

"Mom."

"What were you not supposed to say?"

"I'm not supposed to tell you about the weird dream I had last night."

"About what?"

"All I remember is that Sasi was in it."

"Who's that?"

"The one who paid for Sam's ticket to Lampung."

"Why would you dream about her?"

"No idea. But when I told Mom about it, her jaw hit the deck."

"What's the big deal? Why shouldn't you to tell me?"

"Last night, Mom dreamed about her, too."

"Kind of odd, I guess."

"The weird part is, when I saw the picture of her and Sam, Sasi looked familiar."

"She's on the other side of the world, right? Has she ever been here?"

"Not that I know of."

"It's about the stone, isn't it?"

Paul shrugged. "That's my guess."

"Sam still coming back on Sunday?"

"No. Cancelled his flight. Says he'll reschedule."

"Your mom's freaking out?"

"Oh, yeah. But I can't tell you any of this."

"That's good, cause I didn't hear anything. Now quit buggin' me."

Sasi placed the bowl of fruit, a plate of rolls, butter and jam on the table, opened the shutters to the balcony off of her living room, noted the weather, cloudy and calm, and then returned to the kitchen for coffee and eggs.

Sam was out on the balcony, deep breathing, when she returned. "So, you are alive. You slept all night."

"I must've been exhausted."

"I've prepared a few things, if you're hungry."

Sam seated himself at the table. "You are too kind."

"Coffee?"

"I'd die for a cup."

Sam reached for a roll while Sasi filled their cups.

"Cream and sugar's right there."

"Black's fine. Thanks."

They ate in silence for the first few minutes, Sam ravenous, Sasi eating lightly and amused by Sam's appetite. When he finally slowed down...,

"Well, Sam, any bright ideas during the night?"

"I think we should go straight for the other half."

"How so?"

"We do what Kashif told us, use this stone to find the other one."

"How would you go about doing that?"

"We use the stone like we did with Kathryn, visit the dreams of the owner. What was his name?"

"Aki. But, the difference is we know who Kathryn is and where she lives. We can focus on her. The hunt for Aki could go on forever and we'd never find him."

"How about the other guy, the diver?"

"He's dead."

"You said that the future is already out there, all of the possibilities. Wouldn't the past be the same?"

Sasi smiled. "Pretty good, Sam. I do have Dimyati's old address and I think I kept his picture from a newspaper clip on the story. We can focus on that. If we're lucky, we can reach him when he's with Aki."

"If the stone had something to do with Dimyati's death, what happens to his spirit?"

"Good question."

"Can you acquire a spirit?"

"Another good question. Keep them in mind. Maybe not acquire. More like control."

There was another side to Missy. At first Aki thought it was just one of her mood swings, but he soon noticed that her catlike personality sometimes gave way to another gentler side that had a desire for knowledge.

When this happened, Missy's voice was softer, inquisitive. "Where is this place? How can we get there?"

When Aki tried to explain that these places were far away, she wanted to know how far. Trying to explain that Earth was a very big place meant nothing.

How big, Aki? Can we walk there?

"No. It's on the other side of the ocean."

Is that where I came from?

"No. That's a different ocean."

Can you swim?

"Not across an ocean. We'd have to fly or take a boat.

You can fly? Let me see.

"I can't fly. But I can buy a ticket onto a plane that can fly and it can take me there."

What does it feel like to fly?

"You feel free. You're not stuck to the ground anymore. And when you land, you're at someplace new."

So, we can fly where I want to go?

"We can fly wherever. But I can tell you right now, we are not going to hunt. Understood?"

I am a lion. I must hunt.

"I believe that you think that. I feel your spirit. But, you're just inside my head, that's all. *We* are not going to get in a fight with anything, especially another lion, any more than *we* are going to hunt gazelle, rabbits, whatever it is that you're wanting to kill. I can't help you. I don't like killing things and even if I did, you're not going to get me to eat anything raw except fruit and vegetables."

How about the fire?

"Fire? What fire?"

Where it rains fire from the sky.

"Oh..., a volcano?"

44

Yes.

"They're all over the place. Which one?"

Aki waited for Missy's reply. Usually their conversation was spontaneous and continuous, but the next few minutes were quiet. "Missy?"

I don't remember the beginning.

"That's a start. Go with it."

Do you remember?

"Of course, not. Nobody remembers being born."

How bout your death? Do you remember that?

"What kind of question is that? No. It hasn't happened yet."

I remember how I died. My flesh melted. My eyes were on fire.

"You were burned alive? Where?"

How would I know?

"And yet, you wound up in the water. Dimyati found you near Lampung. Does that mean anything to you?"

No.

"Any idea how long you were under water before Dimyati found you?"

No.

"Forget about when. Where?" Aki brought up Google Earth. "We're looking down at the Earth from a very high place. All of this is water and all of this is land."

It's not so big.

"That's because we're looking at it from far away. Things get bigger when you get closer. You know that."

Where are they?

"Who?"

The ones like me.

"Missy, there is nothing like you. You're a rock. A stone with a personality. There is nothing like you in this whole wide world."

45

Sitting under the dim light in the cellar, Sasi unwrapped the leather cover and placed the stone on the table. They passed Dimyati's faded picture between them and discussed the circumstances leading up to his death.

"Sam. Do you think that Dimyati killed himself?"

"What? Commit suicide?"

"Yes."

"Didn't you say the police thought it was murder?"

"Dimyati didn't have the stone long enough to know anything. He was a sitting duck."

"How so?"

"I'm very timid about approaching the stone. Sometimes it feels like I'm about to lose control. Always be prepared to back out quickly. I hope he didn't try to hold it or study it too carefully.

"What happens then?"

"It starts with a tingling sensation in the hand that's holding the stone and, if you're brave enough, or stupid enough, I'm not sure which, to keep holding it, the tingling travels up your arm. I put it down when that happens."

"So, you don't know what happens."

"No, I don't."

"What are we going to do?"

"Concentrate on Dimyati, hopefully on those last few moments before his death. Maybe we can catch a glimpse of Aki and...,"

Sam waited, watching Sasi's furrowed brow. "Go on."

"If Dimyati threw himself off of the cliff, it was his spirit that made him do it. It's free to turn into something else."

"Such as?"

"Oddly, I can't imagine. Or, maybe I don't want to."

Aki stared at the stone down by his feet and, leaving it where it fell, cautiously made his way to the edge of the cliff and looked down.

Below, Dimyati was splattered across the rocks, one leg turned horribly sideways, twisted and bent backward, his head turned the wrong way, facing upward, staring back.

It took a few minutes for Aki to absorb what had just happened. Dimyati, obviously distraught, was more anxious to be rid of the stone than getting paid for it. Realizing that, Aki thought he might talk the man down to a more reasonable price.

But, in a sudden, unexpected move, Dimyati threw the stone to the ground and, screaming and holding his head like it was going to explode, ran to the edge of the cliff and jumped.

There was nothing to do. Dumbfounded, it was a full minute before Aki realized what had just happened. Going to the edge and looking down, he had no doubts that the man was dead. Most likely he would wash out with the tide.

Call the police? Certainly that would be the right thing to do. But, what would they conclude?

It was not going to go well. He was the only other person around and it was known that he had come to look at and possibly buy the stone. When Dimyati suggested this place less traveled, it was Aki that was concerned. Possibly just a robbery attempt?

No. Can't call the police. They'll throw me in jail. What'll I get? Twenty years? Hanging? Nope. Not calling the police.

And I know when to disappear.

Aki hurried back to the stone and, using his shoe, pushed it into his backpack, zipped it closed, threw it over his shoulder and, making sure that no one else was around, briskly headed back into the city.

Minutes after Aki departed, a dim, silver mist floated up over the ledge, snaking along the edges until it found the place where Dimyati had made the leap and then followed the path back to where he had been standing. It hovered over the area for several seconds before it started to drift away, like smoke caught in a breeze, thinly following Aki's footsteps.

As the image faded, seeing Sam's astonished look, Sasi smiled while she reached for her tea. "Well..., we never got to see Dimyati alive, but we did see what happened. Aki has the stone. It does exist."

"I did not get a good look at Aki."

"You won't. We never will. Everything is a blur, slightly out of focus. What you'll see is the person's spirit. And even that changes from one time to another, one place to another."

"What was that mist?"

"My guess? Somebody's spirit."

"Essence of life?"

"Isn't that the same thing?"

"How come we can't see it in our daily lives?"

"Some people claim that they can. I am not one of them. In a dream state, who knows? Other than what we've been seeing, have you noticed the background?"

"No. Can't say as I have."

"Remind yourself to take note next time. The background is always moving. If you are in an area of light, you'll see forms, translucent mostly, blurry things that envelope your area of focus. If you're in a dark place, the background will be dim, not the kind of light that your eyes see, but you will notice forms in motion. With practice, you can slow these things down enough to see what's there."

"And..., what is there?"

"At first I thought it was a veil, some kind of curtain between different worlds. I thought I could go through and see what's on the other side. What I discovered is that the veil is comprised of compartments, each is its own world and that there are an infinite number of them. You'll never get to the other side."

48

"What happens to Dimyati's spirit? It's not part of this world anymore."

Sasi shrugged. "I think it depends. If the stone caused his death, then I would wonder if it somehow got control."

"We don't know anything yet, do we?"

"No, Sam. We don't."

Wanting to get away and think things through, Sam told Sasi that he was going out for a morning jog. She was not enthusiastic about that, saying that this was a dangerous neighborhood and that, besides gang members, there were sometimes packs of dogs roaming around.

Sam thanked her for the warnings but still headed out. He had spotted a track about a mile away on the day that he had arrived and it was to there that he headed, moving along at a slow pace, taking in the neighborhood along the way.

It was mostly downhill from Sasi's place to the main road. Sam paced himself carefully, throttling back when the road went down and pushing it a bit on the inclines.

It was a four hundred meter track. There were a few others in varying stages of stretching out, doing wind sprints or what he was going to do, run laps along the outside perimeter.

Sam was planning on ten laps, enough to work out the cobwebs and mindless enough that he could think about how to proceed with Sasi and the stone. His best ideas came while jogging. He never did it for speed or any kind of contest. No. Jogging was a time to go inside and let the mind roam.

So, he didn't notice the two new runners on the track, arriving shortly after Sam's first lap. Nor did he notice the other athletes as they quickly brought their exercises to a conclusion. Before long, other than a few stragglers lingering near the exits, sitting on the benches, changing shoes, quenching their thirst and toweling off, the track was empty.

What did get Sam's attention was that one of the runners was jogging clockwise around the track while the other was running in the same direction as he. Senses tingling, Sam realized that the three of them were going to intersect in about two hundred yards.

He slowed his pace to let the runner behind pass, but

he slowed his pace as well. Seeing that, Sam speeded up, running at about half speed and ready to take it into a sprint. The runner behind did the same.

When all three runners were about to intersect, Sam faked a fall to his right, leaving his left leg outstretched while heading to the ground. Sam went into a forward roll as the runner behind him tripped over Sam's outstretched leg and fell to the ground. Sam came up facing the other runner, who attacked, lunging with a knife.

Sam twisted sideways and guided the arm by. He placed his foot behind the attacker and slammed the heel of his right hand up into the man's jaw. He went down like a sack of potatoes.

The other attacker scrambled to his feet, saw that Sam had the knife and raised his hands. He started toward his accomplice, groaning at their feet, but Sam waved him back.

Taking out his cell, Sam snapped a shot of both men, reached into the downed man's pocket, found his wallet, laid it out on the ground and snapped a picture of his ID. The other attacker ran off.

Sam helped the man to his feet and over to a bench. Seeing that he was going to be all right, he found the nearest exit and took a different route home.

Melissa was confused when she got Sam's text. He had attached a picture of some guy's ID and pictures of two men, one of whom apparently was the owner of the ID. He wanted to know anything about them that she could find. They were obviously residents in Lampung, at least if the ID information was correct.

Sam also insisted that she do all of her homework and studying first. This was to be treated more like a hobby. And don't tell Kathryn.

That second request was odd. The four of them had always been a group, a team. They shared their everyday experiences, funny stories, helped each other get through one kind of a crisis or another and, most importantly, information.

So, her first thought was whether or not she could share this request with Paul. Pretty much, they shared everything.

It took her hours to hack into police records in Lampung, certainly a lot more interesting than doing her homework.

The man's name was Danu. He was a member of a gang and it was through police file images of members of that gang that she found out the name of the other man, Takat.

Danu and Takat had minor criminal records, petty theft, car theft, disturbing the peace and fighting, nothing that ever landed them in jail for very long. But as a result of these infractions, neither was very employable.

When Melissa delivered this information to Sam, he asked another question. Who was the leader of the gang? It didn't take Melissa long to find that out. His name was Hamza.

Sam was reluctant to say much more other than that. He and Sasi were exploring old family ties and attempting to figure out where everyone was living today. And, no. Hamza, Danu and Takat were not part of the family. Sam claimed that he met Damu and Takat at the track while working out and he was wondering what their records were like.

Melissa bought none of this and was getting a bit tired of all of the secrecy. Obviously Sam was onto something and they were not being included. OK.

Kathryn, according to Paul, didn't even like the idea of Sam going to Lampung in the first place, wanted nothing to do with Sasi, and certainly wanted nothing further to do with the stone.

Paul was a different story. Give him a chance to have another adventure, especially one with the stone, and he would jump at it with his next breath.

Everything seemed out of whack.

"Missy, what happened to Dimyati?"

He is dead.

"What happened to him?"

You were there. You saw what happened.

"But, why did he jump?"

He could not accept me.

"So, he killed himself?"

Yes.

"What drove him to jump? That's what I'm asking."

I cannot be separated from the stone and he refused to touch it again. He cannot give it away.

"What did you do to make him jump?"

I told him to pick up and hold the stone.

"A voice in his head, like with me?"

Yes.

"And when he didn't, then what?"

I repeated myself.

"Over and over?"

Yes.

"You drove him crazy."

I cannot be separated from the stone. The only way I can return is through the person holding the stone again.

"And if that can't happen you kill off the host?"

Yes. Releasing their spirit allows me to return.

"If you kill me, what happens to my spirit?"

That's up to you.

"But, I'm dead."

Your body died. You are free.

"You made Dimyati jump."

It was his decision. We were not compatible, not like us, Aki.

"So, if the time comes, you'll kill me if it looks like the stone and I are going to be separated? That could happen at any second of my life. I'm going to die of stress."

You could die at any time anyway. Why worry about it? For now, you've got my strength, my reactions and my

54

advice. *I'm going to protect you because you're my best chance for finding what I'm looking for.*

"And this is, what?"

You know, fire.

"Volcanoes, right?"

Yes.

"OK. Dimyati found you, the stone, near Krakatoa, which erupted in eighteen eighty-three, one of the loudest sounds ever. Do you remember a big bang, something like what we've heard watching live eruptions?"

No.

"Says here that the explosion was so loud that anyone in the area would have lost their hearing. Probably blew out their eardrums."

Can we see it?

"What's left of it? Sure. Does this place have a special meaning for you?"

Let's just look.

Aki typed in the search. "Here it is, Anak Krakatau. That means, "child of Krakatoa."

What does that mean?

"Apparently Krakatoa was destroyed. This must be a new one taking its place.

How do you know this?

"That's what it says."

All of those marks and scratches mean something?

"Right. I've been wondering. How is it that you speak English?"

I do not speak. I communicate. Language does not matter.

"It says that the mountain is active and growing at about twenty feet per year."

Is it raining fire?

"It says it does erupt from time to time. Not continuous, though.

There's no place to run when that happens.

"How do you know?"

Because I can remember it. Aki, I want to use your dream time for my own search.

"What do you mean, dream time?"

While you're sleeping, I want to explore through your dream world...,

"No. My dreams are mine. You already drive me crazy all day long."

Only for a night or two.

"No. Leave me alone. You don't even know what you're looking for."

Aki. For once, you can see how I operate.

"I've seen how you operate."

No. You've seen how you operate with me alongside. You're much improved.

"That depends on who you ask."

What else can you find out about Krakatoa? Who was there?

"That would be impossible to know."

"Who survived?"

"Probably just as hard to know. They didn't keep good records back then."

We're on a hunt, Aki. What else can we know about this place?

Kathryn felt like something was going on behind her back, an odd feeling because she and Paul had always been honest and forthcoming about everything. Maybe it was just that finals were coming up and he was busy with his studies.

She wrote it off to that, but at the same time she also noticed that he and Melissa were spending a lot more time texting and, just the day before when she entered Paul's room while he was on the phone, he mumbled something inaudible before speaking in his normal tone. A little thing, but Kathryn caught it.

"Who are you talking to?"

"Melissa."

"Oh. Tell her I said, Hi."

"Mom says, Hi."

"What's she up to these days?"

"Finals, same as me."

"But, you don't have any of the same classes, do you?"

"No."

"Oh." Kathryn wanted to hang around for a second or two longer, just to get the gist of the conversation. But apparently it was confidential. The room was quiet.

"Mom, did you want to talk with her?"

"No. That's OK." Kathryn turned and headed back to the galley.

"Did you want something?"

"Later." She closed Paul's door on her way out. Sometimes a boat seems so small.

Well, whatever it is, I'm not included. Used to be we never had any secrets between us. Teenagers, such an awkward stage. I'll be glad when they're grown up.

No, I won't. Because then he'll get a job, move out and I'll never see him..., except on holidays. And I'll be older, living alone and how am I going to take care of this boat all by myself? Think he'll come around and help then? Hmm. It sucks getting old.

57

Paul waited until Kathryn had closed the door. Speaking in hushed tones, "He met them at the track?"

"That's what he said."

"Why would he want to check their records?"

"Don't know. Doesn't it seem odd that he took pictures of them? And how did he get hold of this guy's ID?"

"Something else happened. Maybe they tried to rob him."

"Bad mistake, trying to rob Sam."

"Wonder if it's got something to do with the stone."

"That's what I'm thinking."

"Melissa, if it is about the stone, where are you on this?"

"What do you mean?"

"If Sam needs our help, are you willing?"

"Oh, that. I don't know. I'm willing to help getting information and stuff, but I know I don't want to go through something like we did before."

"Why not?"

"Paul, you died. We all could have been killed."

"But, none of us did die."

"And what kind of magic was it that saved us? Come on, Paul. At some point, you have to let that go."

"What if Sam's in trouble?"

"We're just going to have to wait and see. Meanwhile, I have to get back to my studies."

"Right. Me, too. See ya."

"Hey!"

"What?"

"Don't say anything to your mom."

"Right."

"Here's something, Missy. In September of eighteen eighty-three, a shipyard in Jakarta reported that a sailing ship, Nerissa, bound for Teluk Betung, arrived in port where they unloaded passengers and cargo, stocked up on water and emergency supplies and returned to what used to be Teluk Betung."

This is near where Dimyati found the stone?

"Same place. Crossing the ocean, there had been a mutiny. Several crew members were tried and hung in Jakarta. Two others were acquitted and one escaped. The ship was carrying a cargo of wild animals, spices, an odd group of passengers..., and there were rumors abound of some kind of magical stone."

Aki. This is it. This is what I've been hoping for.

"Don't believe everything I read. They used the word, rumor. That means, nobody knew for sure."

Where are these people?

"They're all dead."

What happened to the stone?

"You're kidding, right? How would I ever find out about something like that?"

Keep searching.

"How? Let's see, I'll type in Indonesia, eighteen eighty-three, magical stone. Nope. There's nothing more to know."

Where did the ship come from?

"It says Mogadishu, in Africa."

Keep searching.

"It's impossible to know! This happened over a hundred years ago."

Are they talking about me? The stone that I'm trapped in?

"I've never heard you talk like that. You used the word, trapped. Why?"

Why wouldn't I? If the situation was reversed, how would you feel? Your only escape is through someone

59

else's consciousness.

"I hadn't thought about it. What happens if you don't have a host?"

I live in a perpetual dream, no beginning or end, no input. Just..., waiting.

"How'd you get trapped?"

Right. I know that?

Aki stared at the blank screen, thumping his fingers on the desk. "All right, let's do a search in Mogadishu. We know when Nerissa sailed. There might be some kind of record of that. Maybe we can see who the passengers were."

The names came from the billing log of an old boarding house in Mogadishu that had long since burned down. The list of guests was saved because the bookkeeper had taken the book home that night to work on billing. Years later, after he died, the book was sent to a museum and it was there, on-line, that Aki found what they were looking for.

"Sameer and family, party of seven. Sameer and his wife, two sons and their wives and one granddaughter, stayed four days and three nights while waiting for Nerissa to be stocked and prepared for sail to Teluk Betung in September of eighteen eighty-three. They paid in gold."

"There it is, Missy."

Who else stayed there?

"There's a geologist listed, Geoffrey Bard. That's someone who studies rocks. If he sailed on Nerissa, it could've been him who had the stone."

Any others?

"Someone named..., Bardolf, I think. Paid in silver."

Any more?

"Not that I can see. Everyone else either stayed later or left earlier. Here's something. I just found Sameer and family again, two months later. They stayed for one night."

They left from there and came back. This is where they lived?

"Checking..., oh! The family was murdered and their

60

place was burned to the ground. Two survivors, someone named Kashif and his niece, Mahin."

What happened to them?

"Don't know."

Does it say why they were murdered?

"Geez, Missy. You should be a detective..., whenever you find a body."

I've got one.

"No, you don't. You don't pay rent and I'd love to evict you, except I don't know how. But, if I can help you find someone or something, anything that makes you want to leave, I'm with you. In that regard, we're partners."

You know you like having a friend around.

"One that I can see. I want you out there where I can keep an eye on you."

And you like your new abilities.

"What? Bathing less, lazy. I've got a beard!"

Knowing no one can kick your butt. Having some confidence, finally. I see the changes in you, Aki. You're getting some muscle. Face it. You're better off.

"I'm getting fatter and stressing my heart. Here's something. Bardolf..., wasn't that a name we came across earlier? A month after Sameer and family returned home, Bardolf stayed at the lodge for one night."

Before or after the murder?

"Checking..., before."

What happened to him?

"Doesn't say."

If she had children, where are they today?

"Who? The girl?"

Yes. What happened to the ones that survived?

Sasi drizzled olive oil over the vegetables, sprinkled in her concoction of spices, squeezed lemon juice over the top and mixed it up with her hands. "Sam? Can you please turn off the rice and remove the pan from the burner?"

"Sure. Where do you want it?"

"Just off the heat. Slide it to the side."

"What are we having?"

Sasi folded the foil over the vegetables, making a sturdy, leak-proof boat. "Vegetables and pepes ikan, steamed fish in banana leaves. It won't be too long."

"You are so kind. What can I do?"

"Rinse lettuce. It's in the fridge. We'll be making Asinan, salad with a spicy, sour dressing."

Sam retrieved the lettuce, went to the sink and began pulling off the leaves. "We haven't heard anything from Kathryn. What's next?"

"We have to find Aki."

"Ideas?"

Sasi headed for the back door and, leaving it open, went to the charcoal pit and placed the vegetables on the grill. She nudged them over the highest heat, paused long enough to stir the coals and headed back into the kitchen. "I think we need to follow Aki after he kicked the stone into his backpack, see where he goes."

Sam held his hand over the lettuce as he tipped the plate sideways, shaking the water out. "We can do that?"

"We can try."

"Him? Or, the mist?"

"Mist, I would guess. We'll know soon enough if it's following Aki."

"Can it detect us?"

"No idea."

"What if it's dangerous?"

"You mean like, if it notices us?"

"Right."

"Remember where you came from. That's your escape.

Your defense is whatever you can imagine. Those are a lot of good questions, Sam. Glad you're on it. As I've been saying, you control your own path, where you go and what you do. Don't think something is impossible or not as it should be. Everything is possible."

She motioned for him to follow. "Right now, all I can say is..., it's going to be impossible to keep the vegetables from overcooking if I don't get the fish on the grill. Care to step outside?"

Aki abruptly turned toward his favorite chair, an overstuffed thing in front of his large screen TV, sat down and hung onto the arms, fingernails digging into the cloth. "Missy, you're driving me crazy! Quit pacing!"

We're onto something. We can't get this close and then lose the scent.

"There is no scent. We're at the end of the trail."

What happened to the stone?

"Like I said. There's nothing more to know."

It can't just stop at Mogadishu. There's more to this. You said you can fly. Let's go.

"We're not flying to Mogadishu. All of this information that we have, all of it, ended over a hundred years ago. Nobody is going to know or remember anything."

Aki, if I gave up on the hunt the way you give up, I would starve.

"First off, you don't hunt. You make me feel like I need to hunt and that drives me crazy. Secondly, you won't starve because I keep eating…, also thanks to you."

We're on the verge of discovery. We're going in for the kill.

"Don't know what you're talking about. No kill, nothing more to know. Get over it."

The girl had no children?

"Mahin? No idea."

And the other survivor, he died?

"Kashif? Yes. Everybody's dead, Missy."

Before he knew it, Aki was on his feet again, pacing through his small apartment, stroking his beard. He was in the kitchen when he realized what had happened.

"Missy, leave me alone!"

Since we're here, how about some cheese and ham?

"No. We just ate."

Cheese, ham, you can have some of those horrible crackers, if you want. And…, what's in this bottle?"

"Wine."

How does it taste?

"Worse than coffee, worse than tea. You wouldn't like it."

If it's that bad, why did you buy it?

"It's for guests."

You don't have guests.

"Not since you came around. I can't be in public with you badgering me all the time."

If you don't like it, why would you serve it to your guests?

"Because, because, because. Give me a break!"

I want to try wine.

"I don't drink alcohol."

But, you've got this bottle here.

"I'm not going to sit around watching movies, eating snacks and drinking wine. I will *not* turn into that."

You never drank?

"Of course, I did. It doesn't agree with me."

What happened?

"I got sick."

How does it feel?

"To be sick? Terrible."

Before that.

"It felt good. I was enjoying the feeling."

What kind of feeling?

"Relaxed, happy. Didn't really care about anything, until I got sick."

This is what you need, Aki. I insist. You need to relax.

"You're the one that's making me jittery."

I've never had that feeling, relaxed, calm. Drink it for me, will you?

"Get away from me. I'm not getting drunk just so you can have the experience."

Aki? You know what's coming next, right?

"We have an agreement, respectful of each other. Me getting drunk for your pleasure is not respectful."

And you're preventing me from exploring.

"Normally I'd say that's your problem."

Does it happen all at once? You take one drink..., and

then you're relaxed and happy?

"No. It's not like that. The more you drink the better you feel..., until you get sick. My stomach churns just thinking about it."

So, one sip wouldn't hurt.

"No. That bottle's for special occasions."

What's more special than this?

"No."

How does it taste with cheese? That's what I want to know.

"Missy, stop it."

You need to take a drink..., relax.

"Can't you be quiet for one second?"

Really, what's it going to hurt?. Is this bottle that important to you?

"It's that you're making me do something I don't want to do."

I'd do it for you.

"You're already doing it for you! You can't do it for me, too."

You know you want to. You're just being stubborn.

"You're bringing it out in me!"

How about this? For every sip of wine you take, I'll be quiet for one of your miles.

"What? Oh..., you mean twenty minutes, how long it takes for me to walk to the store and back?"

Yes.

"And you're going to stick to your word."

What does that mean?

"You're going to do what you say you're going to do."

Have I ever lied to you, Aki?

"How would I know?"

I've already said that if I needed to kill you, I would. What reason is there for me to lie about anything?

"OK. What's your angle?"

What?

"Why is this so important to you?"

I want to know what it feels like to relax. I've never had that, Aki. Is that so much to ask?

66

"You make is sound like I'm the bad guy."

You're holding me back.

"OK. I'll take a few sips. You have to be quiet and let me relax as well."

I'll be quiet for one mile, right.

Aki opened a drawer and fumbled through the contents until he found the corkscrew. He cut away the plastic cover and unscrewed the cork. Turning, he opened a cupboard door and, reaching up to the highest shelf, retrieved a wine glass.

Just drink it Aki. You don't need that.

"You have to take your time when you open a bottle of wine. You don't just guzzle it."

That's part of relaxed and happy?

"Very much so."

That's a funny glass.

"It's a wine glass."

Why is it different?

"To let the wine breathe."

Why?

"It's been in a barrel for..., I don't know how long they keep it in a barrel. After that, they put it in these bottles. So, the wine needs to breathe to get its flavor back."

Does it taste like meat or cheese?

"Neither." Aki poured a bit of wine into the glass. "It tastes like grapes."

Let's have some.

"Remember your promise."

What promise?

"You're not going to talk for twenty minutes."

One mile, right.

"Right."

Aki picked up the glass and swirled the wine around, at the same time holding it up to the light.

What are you doing? Just drink it.

"This is an expensive bottle. I want to wring all the pleasure out of it that I can."

What pleasure is there in looking at what you should be drinking?

"I'm checking the color and to see if it has legs."

Legs?

"You swirl it around in the glass. It helps the wine breathe. You get to see the color and you can see if the wine has legs."

I don't see any.

"Not real legs. It's how it drains back down."

Aki, just drink it!

"OK. And then you have to shut up."

We are having cheese with this, right?

"No. You know how much weight I've gained?"

You are looking better.

"That's not what I meant."

Drink. We'll talk about the cheese later.

Aki raised his glass. "Cheers, Missy! Now be quiet."

*T*he mist acted as if it had a mind of its own, drifting forward just above the ground, looking like a faceless, thinly translucent ghost with a purpose, weaving through the different shades of light and dark, separating apart here and finding a way to recombine later on.

Following at some distance, Sasi whispered, "Whatever it is, it's looking for Aki."

"How can you tell?"

"Focus beyond where it's heading, into the wallpaper."

"What?"

"Its path is continuous. Glimpse into the foreground, beyond where it's heading."

"How?"

"Three types of memory. Remember what we talked about? If you think of the future, what are you're going to see when you follow the mist?"

"I have no idea."

"It's out there, Sam. Visualize it."

A flash of light. And for a split-second Sam caught a glimpse of Aki walking near the front of a blurry, fast moving crowd. He was boarding a bus.

The mist moved along the floorboard through hundreds of blurry feet, everyone swaying this way or that as the bus traveled along its route.

"Sasi?"

"Yes, Sam."

"Where..., where are we?"

"Did you see Aki?"

"I think so."

"We're still following."

"How long was I gone?"

Sasi smiled. "Time does not matter in here."

Following the mist down the curb, crossing some street at a dead run, cars screeched to a halt, horns honking with drivers leaning out their windows, cursing the pedestrians crossing against the light.

Inside a blurry, dim room, they lurched forward with a clunk as the car changed direction. A second later, the car behind clunked in protest as did the car after that. Clunk, clunk, clunk.

As the train pulled out of the station, the mist moved along the floor, passing through the passengers slowly, invisible to them as it searched for its target.

"He's on the train, Sam. We're on the train with Aki."

"Looks like it's heading for the next car."

Aki. It's been one mile.

"No. It's been twenty minutes. I haven't moved."

How did you like your quiet?

"Wonderful. I never realized how special quiet time could be."

Are you relaxed and happy?

"Yeah. Actually, right now, I'm more relaxed and happy than I've been in a long time. How does it feel to you?"

If you're relaxed and happy, then so am I.

"You're not so bad if you'd just shut up once in a while."

You like having me around. I can tell.

"No, you can't. There are a lot of things that I don't say."

Your silence says everything. I think we should have another drink. How about you?

"No. I've had enough. I know when to quit."

You've only had one glass. And it wasn't much. Think of how much happier we could be.

"That's why I don't like you hanging around. You're always pushing me."

You're afraid you're going to fail.

"I'm not a failure."

No. But you're never going to be anything either.

"How can you say that? You don't know me."

Where are your friends?

"I like being alone."

Right.

Aki thumped the empty glass with his fingernail, intrigued with the resultant resonating hum. "I *do* like being alone."

I didn't say anything.

"But, you don't believe me."

Right.

"It's none of your business anyway."

Sounds like your happiness is fading. Let's have another

71

drink.

"No. I know when to quit."

You haven't even gotten started. Are you so afraid to let loose? Be bold, for once.

"It's not about boldness."

What, then?

Aki tilted the glass and peered into the bottom. Not even enough to wet the tongue. He filled his glass half way, took a long sip, more like a gulp, set the glass down and folded a slice of ham around a thick sliver of cheese, took a bite and chewed quietly.

Aki?

"I'm drinking. Are you happy?"

Only if you are.

Aki reached for his glass. "That's going to take some more wine."

What is it?

"You don't have to know everything."

It doesn't sound like you're getting happier.

"Then don't keep pestering me about things I don't want to talk about."

If it bothers you that much, you should get it out but..., I'm not asking you to say. Just some advice because we're friends, that's all. I'm thinking of you.

"I'm drinking again so you have to shut up for another mile."

Aki, starting to slur his words, slapped his left cheek to see if he could feel anything. Nope. He took another drink and turned up the volume.

I don't know why you like jazz, Aki. It's boring.

"I'm not ashking you to…, like it." He burped. "Gotta have music when I drin…, k."

I thought you didn't drink.

"When I do."

I've heard better than this.

"When?"

Sometime before you.

"Maybe," Aki swayed in his chair. "That's a clue. What kind?"

Of clue?

"Music." Aki held his hand over one eye and tried to focus with the other, a struggle with either eye. "Didn't I say music?"

No.

"That's what I meant. Music, I mean. You sure?"

The music I liked had singing and it made me want to move with the beat.

"Just in case you're wondering. I don't dance."

I wasn't.

"What?"

Wondering.

"About what?"

If you danced.

Aki giggled, kind of a quiet internal joke. And then he started to laugh. "Who would I dance with? You?"

I've been meaning to ask. Don't you have a girlfriend?

Aki took another long sip and, miscalculating the table top, set the glass down hard. "Oops! Alcohol abuse!"

I think you've had enough.

"No, no, no! A fine bottle of wine? No, Mishy. Once it's opened, it *musht* be drunk!" Aki laughed. "Just like me! I'm drunk. I never thought I'd do that again. Missy, you're

73

bad for me!"

I didn't tell you to drink the whole bottle.

"Last time I did that...," Aki trailed off.

What? When was that?

"I...," Aki slapped his cheek. "It's getting worse. Now I *really* can't feel anything."

You had a girlfriend.

"Oops! Spilled my wine."

Aki?

He laughed. "Mishy. Go get the sponge, will you? I'm too drunk."

You really want me to do that?

"Just like when we took out those three bums. Wham! Bam! Thank you, Ma'am!"

I'll get the sponge. You tell me about your girlfriend.

"Nooo..., I don't think so."

Why not?

"It's..., personal."

Oooh. You had a boyfriend!

"No, no. She..., Missy?" He burped. "We need the sponge."

I get the sponge and you tell me about your girlfriend.

"You can *do* that?"

I'll clean up the mess. You talk about her. Agreed?

"Do your thing, baby!"

Missy was instantly on Aki's feet and striding confidently toward the sink.

"Wait, wait! Go..., *slowly*, Missy! I'm getting sick!"

Should I run over there, just in case?

"Nooo..., don't do that. Just..., walk slowly. Let me get used to this."

This is how you should always move, Aki. Strong, in control.

"Definitely..., I'm not in control."

He watched as Missy rinsed out the sponge, cleaned up the mess and returned to the chair.

Aki giggled. "I feel like I'm on the cleaning channel."

Your girlfriend. What was she like?

Slouching in his chair, Aki closed one eye and rolled his

head side to side. "Where's the camera, Missy? Are we on a commercial break?"

Was she special?

Groaning, Aki pulled himself out of the chair, leaned against the table, closed one eye and aimed for the hallway. "I have to pee."

You can walk and talk at the same time.

"Yeah, Missy. She was...," He bumped into the corner and bounced away, laughing. "Oops! Wrong eye."

What did she look like?

"She was...," Aki felt his way down the hallway, turned the corner into the bathroom, ran into the half open door, causing it to slam into the toilet, bounce back and nail him in the forehead.

"Ow!"

Should I take over?

"No. This is my party."

Where is she?

"Not here, Missy."

Aki?

"Leave me alone."

The mist passed through the weathered steel and glass door like smoke drifting through a screen. Between the two cars, out in the turbulent air, could it maintain its integrity? Or would it swirl into nothingness and make their attempts to follow in vain?

A small distraction, but enough to make Sam question his ability to will himself past the door. His mind whirled with the impossibility of the task.

"Sam? We're going to lose it."

"I know. It's...,"

"You're questioning too much, losing your concentration. The mist. Where is it now? Focus."

No one noticed when the mist entered their space, drifting slowly along the bottom, moving in between the blurry legs of the many passengers, all siting in neat little blurry rows of benches and seats, smudges of color huddled together inside the swaying motion of the car.

Up into the shirt sleeve of a man reading a paper, who experienced a sudden itch somewhere on his chest, across the isle, drifting across the top of the bundle held by an elderly woman who had a sudden urge to pull packages closer as she edged to the end of the seat, crossing the aisle, drifting into the face of the woman holding her purse, looking down at the floor of the coach. She coughed.

"It affects them," Sam whispered.

"Their subconscious must feel it."

"It's searching."

"Shh."

The mist drifted across a little girl's hands and through the marbles she was holding. Suddenly, one of them broke free, rolled off of her lap, across the seat and down to the floor. It hit the hard surface with a pop and rolled across the aisle into someone's black shoe, rolled toward the back of the car behind someone's red heels and then disappeared into the shadows of several blurry feet.

Aki, sitting on the same bench and watching it roll

76

by, beads of perspiration on his forehead, would have returned it to the little girl. But, as the mist engulfed him and his backpack, he was hit with a coughing spell that allowed the marble to meander out of view. He smiled apologetically to his fellow passengers, all of them a blur, and then stared blankly at the floor.

Sam, suddenly remembering that he and Sasi were, at this very moment, sitting at the table in her small dug out room, was struck with the impossibility of such a thing, and it was during that instant that the mist had advanced on him, as if somehow he'd let his defenses down and could now be counted as one of the crowd.

A faint, exploratory finger of the mist drifted into his space, his dream state of mind.

"Don't move," Sasi whispered.

Snuffling, breathing heavily like some kind of animal inspecting its prey, Sam felt a tongue across the back of his neck, a burst of hot air in his ear.

"Sasi?"

From somewhere a clawed paw of some large animal was wanting to turn him over. Sam curled into a fetal position.

"Sasi?"

A rabbit hiding inside the thick branches of the chaparral, two coyotes circled outside, one looking for a way in, the other calling the rest of the pack...,

A frantic dove taking to flight as the hawk swoops in from behind...,

The ventilation fan hummed quietly in the distance, getting louder as Sam became aware of the room, a candle flickering, Sasi across the table, shadows dancing across her face.

She met his gaze. "What happened?"

"It can see us."

"You disappeared. I couldn't find you."

"I was trying to get away.

"It was aggressive?"

"Very much so."

Sasi swirled her tea and watched the leaves resettle. "I

don't understand why it went after you. It knew where the stone was."

"It wasn't aware of me until I broke my concentration."

"We were focusing on it. That made us different from everyone else on the train."

"Whatever else, we now know that we have an awareness of each other."

Aki decided that flossing and brushing in this condition was not safe. He kicked off his shoes while leaving the bathroom, tried to take off his socks going down the hallway in the dark, but quickly failed, getting one sock half off, losing his balance and then stepping on it with his other foot. When he couldn't take the next step, he fell like a top coming to the end of its whirl and spiraled down to the floor.

Aki?

"Go away."

You're going to lie here all night?

"Nope."

Then, get up. Finish it, Aki.

"I'm..., resting."

You're giving up."

"Nope."

Passing out in the hallway? You're better than this.

"I drank the whole bottle."

No. You didn't. There's still some left.

"It feels like the whole bottle.

Is this relaxed and happy?

"Yep. Relaxed. That's what I am."

You didn't say happy.

"One outta two."

What makes you happy?

"Quiet."

Besides that.

"I'm happy lying here."

Aki? You still haven't told me about her.

"She's gone, Missy. Let it go."

Either you get up and go to bed or I'll keep asking about her.

"Youch."

Aki? I'm asking.

"She left with my best friend. Now, leave me alone."

Was that so hard?

"Yeah...,"

You got hurt?

"What do you think?"

You ever see them again?

"Quit asking."

Aki?

"No. Why would I want to?"

You'd take her back?

It felt so good to rest. Aki smiled with the idea of it. The bathroom was just a few feet away from his head and his bedroom was at the other end of his feet. Not important. He closed his eyes.

Aki?

He burped. "He's..., not home right now...,"

Did you ever see them again?

"Who?"

Your girlfriend and your best friend.

"Who's asking?"

It's me, Missy. You need to tell me. I'm your new best friend. Did you ever see them again?

"Nope."

I'm going to help you up, Aki. You with me?

Aki laughed. "Carry me?"

Taking control, Missy helped Aki remove his socks, stand up and walk to his bed where she pulled back the covers, helped him in and waited quietly until he was sound asleep.

Aki?

"Leave me alone."

Are you sleeping?

"Beyond." Aki rolled over in bed, groaning. "Why are you bothering me?"

You were snoring.

"I feel sick."

Don't get sick. I don't want to clean it up.

"Then don't wake me up!" Pulling the covers up, Aki turned away.

That's not going to help.

"What do you want?

I'm hungry.

"No, you're not. Because I'm not."

Ham and eggs?

"Oatmeal." Aki rolled toward the edge of the bed and kicked off the covers. "Even that sounds terrible." He stumbled through the doorway and down the hall, raised the toilet seat and heaved.

At least you made it.

"Shut up."

Now that we're up...,

"*We* are not up. It's me. I'm up." He heaved again into the toilet, dry heaves. "Well, sort of."

Wine does this?

"Drinking does this. And it's your fault."

I just wanted you to be happy.

"No. You wanted to know what it was like to be relaxed and happy. Did that work for you? Because I'm not going through...," another dry heave, "this again."

So, what's the cure?

Aki sighed. "Probably ham and eggs. Something greasy. That's what my stomach wants."

Now we're talking.

"Quit saying *we*. It's me. You're just hanging around. Are you ever going to leave?"

Why would I want to? You're giving me food, shelter, and you're helping me. As soon as we have breakfast, we can get back to that.

Aki stood, wobbly, but steadying himself against the sink, washed his hands, face and rinsed out his mouth. "I think I'll take the day off, go for a walk."

Where are we going?

"Not, we. Me. You can stay here."

I asked where, not who.

"There's a lake close by. I jog around it from time to time."

After breakfast.

"Right." Aki grabbed the bottle of aspirin from the medicine cabinet and made his way to the kitchen. "I'm not going anywhere without aspirin, eating, coffee and a shower."

Not coffee again.

"You owe me. I didn't want to drink. Coffee it is."

Aki. You're going to use real eggs, right?

"This carton has real eggs, just without the yolk."

They don't taste good.

"My, God. Why won't you go away?"

Use one egg at least.

"Deal."

Four slices of ham.

"One."

We'll starve. Three.

"You're going to kill me off early. Two, and that's final."

Deal. You're making the coffee too strong.

"I need to. Thanks to you."

Are you going to melt cheese into the egg?

"No. Onion with salt and pepper, scramble egg into it. No cheese."

It goes so well together.

"We're already getting nitrites and nitrates from the ham, high cholesterol from the egg...,"

All the things we need.

"No. Shut up, will you?"

How about with cheese and salsa?

82

"Deal."

After breakfast, Aki headed out without doing the dishes. Missy was wanting to leap down the steps but Aki was taking his time.

Let's go, Aki. Where's your enthusiasm?

"Catching up. Let's just walk in peace for a while. OK?"

Where are we going?

"To the park."

Have I been there before?

"No."

What's there?

"A lake, ducks. There's a path that goes all the way around. We're going to walk that. It's a good hike."

Ducks?

"We're not going to chase any ducks."

I think I've had duck.

"Not since you've been with me."

Of course, not. You eat boring things.

"I thought we were going to walk in peace."

How far away is it?

"About a mile. It's another mile around the lake so we'll do a three mile hike."

Let's run!

"No. We..., I am not running. I've got a hangover. This is supposed to be an apology to my body for what I did to it last night."

You were relaxed and happy. How is that bad?

"Alcohol poisoning. How about some quiet until we get to the park?"

Deal.

They entered from the east side, walking beneath several Eucalyptus trees, across the parking lot and over to the path circumventing the lake.

I see that there is a refreshment stand over there.

"We won't be stopping. We've got food at home."

We can catch it on the way out.

"We'll discuss it when we get there."

It smells like they have hot dogs.

"And they can keep them. Check out the lake."
Can you swim?
"Of course, I can. What kind of question is that?"
In case you do something stupid.
"So, you can what…, kill me?"
Or save you.
"Which ever one suits you best, right?
Aki, you're so negative.
"Anyway, you can't jump in. It's illegal."
Even if you want to?
"Right."
But…, look at all of those ducks out there.
"I already said we're not chasing ducks."
I guess we can get a hot dog on the way back.
"We're only going three miles. Stop thinking about food."

They approached a woman, about Aki's age, taking photographs of the ducks, sitting on a rock next to the water, feet on the bank while bending down to get a better shot. She looked up and smiled.

"I get better reflections if I'm closer to the water."
Ask her how they taste.
"No. I'm not going to do that."
"Pardon?"
"What kind of camera is that?"
"This?" She sat up and studied the front of the camera. "It's not mine. I borrowed it. That's why I don't know. Here, a Minolta. It uses film.

"Why are you shooting in film?"
"It's for a class."
"Oh." Aki waved and continued on. "Good luck."
"Thanks."
Aki. Don't let her get away.
"I'm out for a walk. I'm not here to pick up on anybody."
Do you think she is pretty?
"Yeah, she is."
Go back, Aki. Introduce yourself.
"No."

You're afraid you're going to fail.
"That's not it."
Then, what?
"I think I've seen her out here before."
So, you already know each other.
"I don't want to get involved. I've got you on my mind."
If I wasn't here, you'd try?
"Maybe."
No, you wouldn't. You're afraid that you're going to get hurt again.
"Doesn't matter what you think. I'm going to jog for a while."
You're running away.
"Shut up."
Did you like her smile?
"Yeah, Missy. I'm still not going back."
She does look familiar.
"If I don't know her, you don't know her."
Before you.
"Maybe when you were with Dimyati?"
Before that.
"Before that was water. You were under the sea. There's no way you could know her."
Maybe...,
"I've seen her around here a few times, before you. Subject closed."

Kathryn felt Spittin' Image list slightly to port. Paul, stepping onto the boat, was back from school. Capn ascended the steps to greet him at the companionway. Setting his backpack down, Paul gave him a good pet and then peered down into the cabin, "Hi, Mom."

Kathryn pulled the salsa out of the fridge and opened a bag of chips. "Hey, Paul. How was school?"

"OK. I've got to do a report on my best day ever. Ten pages. Should I write about Bardolf and Capn and all of that?"

"Don't you dare. Nobody would believe you anyway. Got chips and salsa here."

Paul nudged Capn out of the way and stepped down into the galley. "I could say that my best day ever was writing fiction and this is what I wrote."

"Where's Melissa?"

"She went back to the car to get something. What's this all about?"

"I'll wait until she gets here."

Paul sat next to the bowl and began devouring chips, dipping them heavily into the salsa and spilling it across the table. Kathryn balled up a paper towel and threw it at him.

"Hey! Take it easy. Leave some for everybody else."

"We're having tacos?"

"Right."

"Carne asada?"

"Fish."

"Well, that's pretty good, too. We have guacamole?"

"Yeah. But I'm not getting it out. There won't be any left for tacos. Go wash your hands."

Paul was at the sink when Melissa's head popped into the companionway.

"Hi Kathryn. Permission to come aboard?"

"Hi, Melissa. Come on down. Chips and salsa here. What's left of them. They suffered a Paul attack."

"I'm surprised there's any left."

Paul finished wiping his hands and joined them back at the table. "We're having tacos."

"I know. She texted me."

"You two text each other?"

"On occasion. What's this all about, Kathryn?"

"I haven't seen you in a while and just wanted to invite you over for dinner."

"Don't believe her," said Paul, reaching for another chip. "There's a reason she does everything."

"Not always."

Paul looked over at Melissa with a big grin. "Wait for the other shoe to drop."

"So, how are you and your dad doing?"

"I'm doing great. He's finally dating. That's good. I've got my three cats, you and Paul, my second family."

"That's nice..., that you consider us family.

"Does that mean you consider me a *brother*?"

"I consider you a work in progress."

"I'm always in progress."

"That's not what I meant. You're always needing work."

"I'm already perfect. I just need a little buffing out."

"Chiseling."

Kathryn got up, went to the counter and retrieved a cutting board, a large red tomato, half of an onion and her paring knife. Returning to the table, she sat down and started chopping. "However, in this case there is another reason...,"

Paul laughed. "There's the other shoe."

"As you both know, Sam is in Lampung...,"

Melissa and Paul exchanged glances.

"And I have, let's just call it a mother's intuition, a feeling that something is going on that I'm not a part of and I want it out in the open. Paul, let's start with you. What up, dude?"

"Gee, Mom. Nothing really."

"You had a dream about Sasi and she looked familiar in the picture. You want to add to that?"

"Not much more to say. It was odd that we both dreamed about her on the same night."

"Odd. Is that the word you want to use? Spooky, maybe? Coincidental? Abnormal? Lots of other words, Paul."

"OK. Spooky."

"Melissa. Did he talk to you about it?"

"Um, yeah. He did, actually. But, it wasn't his fault. I made him tell me."

"You suspected something?"

"He can't keep a secret. Don't ever play poker, Paul."

"And what did you think when he told you?"

"I didn't really think too much about it."

Finished with the tomato and onion, Kathryn headed back to the fridge for cabbage. "Anybody want anything to drink?"

"I'll take a beer," said Paul, grinning.

"No, you won't. Melissa?"

"Water, thanks."

"Paul, soda?"

"Sure. Thanks, Mom."

Returning to the table with their drinks and a glass of wine for herself, Kathryn sat down with a sigh. "Sorry to be the heavy here, but I've got to know. Anything else going on?"

Once again, Paul and Melissa exchanged glances. Was it fair to keep Kathryn out of the loop? She had been with them all along, risked her life to help Sam and, yes, even though she was pretty much the cause for all of the things they'd been through, didn't she deserve to be kept informed now?

"OK," said Melissa, at last. "There is more. Sam wanted me to search for information on two men."

"Why?"

"He didn't say."

"When was this?"

"Three days ago."

"What did you find out?"

"They were petty criminals."

"And...?"

"That's about it. He was very cryptic. Paul and I...,"

"Paul?" Kathryn glanced over at her son, who stopped halfway to his mouth with the chip. Salsa dripped onto his pants. "Anything you want to say?"

"Um," he grinned sheepishly. "Hang on. I have to finish this."

"It's not his fault. I asked for him not to tell you."

"Why?"

"We didn't want you to worry," said Paul, wiping his pants.

"I was already worried. You knew that. You think keeping secrets is going to make me feel better?"

"Sorry, Mom."

Kathryn turned her attention to Melissa. "Did Sam ask for you to keep this quiet?"

"Yeah."

"Did he say why?"

"He didn't want you to worry."

Kathryn took a long sip of wine. "Well. That's a fine kettle of fish!"

"Speaking of that. When are we going to eat?"

Melissa threw a chip at Paul. "Be nice!"

"That's as nice as I can get."

Kathryn suddenly stood and headed for the fridge. "You're right. Let's eat. Paul, get the grill going. I'll hand the fish up to you. Melissa, can you shred some cabbage?"

"Sure.

"You guys want soft tacos, or fried?"

"That shouldn't even be a question," said Paul, heading up the steps. "Fried."

Melissa shrugged. "Fried, I guess."

"If you had your choice?"

"Soft."

"Me, too. We'll cook ours first. After we eat, let's have a nice long talk."

Much later, Melissa gathered her things and stored them up on the shelf behind the seat. "I'm glad this is out in the open. Same with Paul."

"I heard that," said Paul, coming back into the room carrying an armful of blankets and a pillow. He handed them to Melissa. "Sam's just trying to keep us out of it, whatever it is. I think we should ask him, what up?"

Melissa spread the blankets out, tossed the pillow at one end, grabbed her laptop and settled into a sitting position on her berth, leaning up against the pillow. "When is he coming back?"

"No word." Kathryn showed the image of Sam and Sasi to Melissa. "She looks familiar?"

"No."

"Good. All of this worrying for nothing. Sam'll probably take care of business over there and...,"

A low pitched moaning sound filled the room, so quiet that Kathryn wasn't even sure she'd heard anything. Everybody hesitated, quietly waiting. Again, a slightly higher pitch this time. Paul ascended the first couple of steps and peered out over the deck. "It's Capn. Out at the bow. I was wondering where he was."

"He's been doing that," said Kathryn. "And it's not even a full moon."

More howling, a few notes higher, but wavering sourly through them.

Paul cringed. "Let's give him a spoonful of oil, smooth him out."

""He'll get his pitch pretty soon," said Kathryn, joining him at the steps. "He just needs to warm up."

"Missy. You won't believe what I've stumbled onto."

That scratching? Looks like two birds got in a fight.

"It's a genealogy chart."

What's it do?

"It tells me the history of families, who was born, who died, who married whom and if they had children, stuff like that."

How did you find it?

"I built it. Little bits of information here and there, put together, add up to something. Mahin had a brother. Their mother was away the night that the family was murdered. She was pregnant and had a son, who lived long enough to have another son and I've traced that lineage to someone called Sameer. Does that sound familiar?

He's alive today?

"As far as I can tell."

Does he live near us?

"Us? Me."

I'm here, too, your guest.

"You stopped being a guest a long time ago."

I'm now your bodyguard, consultant, constant companion and your best friend. I think I'm holding up my end.

Aki sighed. "I'm not going to argue."

Good. Where does he live?

"In America..., maybe."

Let's go.

"Impossible. That's on the other side of the world."

How far away..., in miles.

"Too many to count."

Aki. This is our chance. He might have information about the stone.

"You've got to be kidding. If the magic stone they talked about was a rumor a hundred years ago, today it would just be a fable."

What does that mean?

"A fairy tale..., nothing. It has no substance, not worth

91

the air it takes to say it."

That's a little harsh and negative for someone who claims to be helping me. Maybe you don't want me to leave, after all.

"It gets expensive, flying."

You have a better suggestion?

"I can't just hop around the world looking for your magical stone."

Why not?

"I can't afford it."

Aki, this is your chance to be rid of me. If you were the one trapped in the stone, you know that I'd help, right?

"I doubt that. You really want to go, don't you?"

We've come this far, Aki. How can we stop now?

Sasi stirred the hot coals around in the pit so that the heat was more evenly distributed. Using a brush, she dipped the bristles into a small bowl of sesame oil and spread the oil across the grill in a spat of flames. "So, you're going back to the states?"

Sam held the dish so that Sasi could fork the slices of chicken and skewers of vegetables over the heat. There wasn't enough room for everything at once. Replace what you take. That's how this meals works. Sam put the bowl back on the table. "I have business to attend to, bills to pay. I have to work."

"How about if I give you money?"

"I can't take your money."

"You're helping me with the firestone. I'm paying you."

"No, Sasi. I've already overstayed my allotted time. I've got classes to teach and I can't keep relying on friends and colleagues to do my work."

"Are you giving up?"

"No. But, I have other commitments that have to be resolved. I can come back later and we can pick up where we left off."

"That would be welcome." Sasi, rotated the vegetable skewers. "When are you leaving?"

"Tomorrow morning. My flight leaves at eleven."

Sasi smiled. "Then tonight is a special occasion. Had I known, I'd have baked you a cake."

"Every minute here has been special. No need for a cake."

Using tongs, Sasi turned the chicken strips, now sizzling, edges starting to char, and brushed a marinade over the tops.

Sam leaned into the smoke. "That smells delicious. You'll give me the recipes?"

"Promise you'll come back?"

"You know I can't do that. But, I'll try. What are you going to do next?"

93

"Write down the recipes, I guess. I don't even think of the amounts any more. I just pour stuff in."

"After that."

Sasi laughed. "Cook."

"You know what I mean."

"We've learned so much. Maybe it's good that you're leaving. This will give us both some time to think things through."

"I don't know what to think."

"Grab a plate, Sam. We're ready to eat. Rice is on your left, inside that...,"

"I know. I've been here long enough to know the operation, except for the recipes."

"Number one on my list," said Sasi. She removed the lid from the rice pot, stirred the rice and left the paddle on top. "We know Aki took a train. My thinking, so far, is to see if I can't identify where it was headed."

"By yourself? Isn't that dangerous?"

"It didn't detect me. It went after you. I think I'm safe. I'll keep my distance." Sasi removed one of the vegetable skewers from the grill and, using her chopsticks, slid the vegetables down and onto her plate. "I'll let you know if anything interesting develops."

"What are you going to do if you find him?"

"Number two on my list is to call you if I get into trouble."

Aki, *this is a very busy place. It makes me nervous.*
"Get used to it. It's going to get worse."
How?
"We have to go through Security."
What do they do?
"Check me out, make sure I'm not carrying any weapons, anything dangerous."
"You're not, are you?
"The only thing I can think of is the stone."
If they think it's dangerous, what happens?
"I guess they'd take it."
If they take it and you can't get your hands back on it long enough for me to leave, I have to kill you.
"We'll just cancel our flight, that's all. We'll take our stuff and go home, find another way to travel. Kill me. My God. Don't get so upset."
You don't fully understand...,
"Missy, quit worrying. The stone is in our..., my luggage, not in our..., my carry-on. It's probably already on the plane."
We're separated already?
"And we're going to be that way for several hours."
This makes me very nervous.
"I couldn't carry it on the plane with me. It's considered a blunt object, not allowed."
What are all of those people doing over there?
"Security. We have to go through that line."
This doesn't feel good.
"What happened to the brave lion, walk with confidence, all of that?"
This is not a natural surrounding.
"I agree. But, you wanted to fly. Don't talk now. When I answer, it looks like I'm mumbling. People get suspicious."
You don't have to mumble. I pretty much know what you're thinking. Try it.

"You think you do."

I heard that. You think you do. And you didn't move your mouth. What is that roaring sound?

"A jet taking off."

Why does it make so much noise?

"Shh. I have to look normal."

I think I don't want to fly.

"We have to go now or my luggage and your stone will leave without us. You don't want that, do you?"

Aki?

"Shh."

You're taking off your shoes? Emptying your pockets? Watch, everything. Aki, is this what you have to do to fly?

"Shh."

Do you get all of your stuff back? Oh. I see. It comes out the other end.

"Shh."

Whew! Glad that's over. None of them looked friendly. We could've taken them, though.

"No, we couldn't. Get those thoughts out of your..., my head." Aki walked over to a window and pointed to a jet. "That's what we're going to fly on. See where they're loading the baggage? That's where the stone will be."

We're flying on that?

"Right."

It's not what I imagined.

"Well, you're not what I imagined either, so get over it."

Are those supposed to be wings?

"They are wings."

I don't think they can flap. How does it get off the ground?

"Missy, I can't explain all of this now. They have jet engines that burn fuel and...,"

Burn? There's fire?

"Oh, yeah. Lots of it. But, it's safe and...,"

We're not going.

"Yes, we are. They're boarding right now. Let's go, brave lion. Walk like you mean it. It'll be over soon."

96

Aki, what is all of that whining noise?

"Air conditioning. The plane needs to keep air moving through the cabin so that we don't all suffocate."

I don't like it.

"But, it's necessary."

Why are there so many people?

"It costs a lot of money to get from here to there. The more passengers they have, the more money they get."

There's too many. I feel like I'm in a herd.

"We are in a herd. Get over it."

They're filling every seat!

"They said it was a full flight. At least we have a window."

It's not much of one.

"They have to keep it small because...,"

What's that noise?

"They're starting up the engines."

Sounds like it's getting out of control.

"Missy. You have to calm down. All of this is normal. There are going to be a lot of noises that you've never heard. Relax. Remember that feeling?"

We need some of your wine, Aki.

"They will serve drinks."

Not the whole bottle this time. OK?

"They don't serve bottles. We'll get a weak drink in a small plastic glass."

So, we only have two or three then, Right? I don't want you getting out of control.

"It's you I'm worried about."

More noise. What is that?

"They're starting up another engine. Relax. There's four of them.

I hear another one. Oh! And another!

"Had I known that you were going to be so nervous, I'd have had a couple of drinks before we got onto the plane."

We're moving!

"They're taxiing down the runway."

I can run faster than this.

"You say that now. Wait a minute and then you'll see how fast this plane can go.

How will it ever get off the ground?

"OK, Missy. I want you to be prepared for this. It's going to get very noisy and it's going to feel like we're going to crash. This is normal. Pretty soon we'll be up in...,"

What's that roaring?

"We're taking off. Look out the window."

Aki. I want off the plane.

"No. Relax. Look out the window. We're gaining speed."

Right. I can't run that fast.

"You can't run at all. It's me you're talking about and yes, I cannot run this fast."

We're in the air! We're flying!

"We just finished takeoff, that's all."

How much higher do we have to go?

"You know how far it is for us to walk to the grocery store and back?"

Yes.

"One mile, right?"

That high?

"Higher than that. More like if we walked to the store and back six times. That's about how high we'll be flying."

Seems like all you need is just to get over the tops of things.

"The people on the ground wouldn't like that. You think it's noisy in here. It's much worse outside.

We need that drink.

"We finally have something we agree on. And I'm going to make it a double. One for you and one for me."

Sitting behind the wheel, Kathryn reached down and pulled the latch that opened the trunk, watching in her rear view mirror as Sam put his baggage inside. He closed the lid, reappeared on the passenger side of her car and got in. Before buckling his seat belt, he leaned over and gave her a hug.

"You didn't have to pick me up. I could've gotten a taxi."

Kathryn checked her side mirror and, seeing that it was safe, pulled away from the curb. "Are you kidding? You've got a lot of explaining to do. I jumped at the chance."

"Explaining?"

"I had a long talk with Melissa and Paul the other night. Seems everybody's keeping secrets."

"What kinds of secrets?"

Kathryn glanced over at Sam. "The ones surrounding you."

"I didn't know there were any, except when I was coming back."

"You had Melissa do some investigating for you?"

"Oh, that. A couple of bums tried to jump me. I wanted to know who they were."

"So, you asked Melissa. Really? Why not the police?"

"I didn't want to create a big scene. She can get results discreetly."

"And?"

"She did. They were just a couple of petty thieves."

"No more to it than that?"

"As far as I know."

"What about Sasi?"

"What about her?"

"Come on, Sam. Something really weird is going on and all of us are curious. You're going to have to fess up."

"I'm dying for Mexican. How about we stop at that little hole-in-the-wall and pick up some lunch? I'm buying."

"You don't have to buy."

"I'm flush. Sasi wouldn't let me pay for anything. Where are Melissa and Paul?"

"Back at the boat, waiting for you."

"I'll give them a call and see what they want."

"Give Paul one choice. Otherwise he'll break you."

"Anything exciting happen while I was gone?"

"Not really. Mostly it was all about you. Capn's acting a little weird. That bothers me."

"How so?"

"Keeps going up to the bow of the boat and howling."

"That again, huh? He seems to have a sixth sense."

"What does that mean?"

"If you're really curious to know everything, it'll be a long story. Why don't we wait until we get back to the boat, so I only have to tell it once."

"She has the firestone?"

"Yes."

"What have you learned?"

"Later."

"Right. What do you mean, Capn must have a sixth sense?"

Sam laughed. "Later."

"Is it bad?"

"I can't say that. I can't say it's good, either."

"You're being very cryptic."

"What can I say without telling it twice?"

"You rat."

"How about this? If I tell you something that only one other person in this world knows, will you not ask anything more about it until we get to the boat?"

"You are a rat."

"Agreed?"

Kathryn nodded. "OK."

"There are two firestones."

Turning onto Harbor Drive, Kathryn frowned. "You are a very mean person."

100

Sam opened the fridge door and grabbed another beer. "Anybody else want anything while I'm here?"

"I'll take one," said Paul.

Kathryn gathered up the empty containers and began stuffing them into a paper bag. "One, what?"

"Beer."

"No, he won't. You've had enough soda, too."

"Wine?"

"You're too young. Water."

"I even died once. I should be allowed. I'm celebrating life!"

"Maybe that's where he got his brain damage," said Melissa, smiling.

"Not funny."

"Anyway." Sam closed the fridge door. "I'm going to sit. You all can hash it out." He popped the cap on his beer and, after taking a long sip, looked over at Paul with a big grin. "Ah, that's refreshing."

"Not amused."

Kathryn set the bag on the companionway steps. "Paul, since you're not doing anything, how about taking this out to the trash?"

"I get no respect."

Kathryn poured herself a cup of tea and joined Sam and Melissa at the table. Paul got up, stretching as he did, and then rubbed his belly. "That was excellent. Thanks, Sam."

"You're welcome. It feels good to be back in San Diego. I can eat a lot of different foods and Sasi was a great cook. But if I had to choose one kind of food for the rest of my life, Mexican."

Everybody nodded in agreement. Kathryn pulled her cup a bit closer and blew off the steam. "What are you going to do now that you know there are two firestones?"

"Sasi wants to track down Aki. She'll let me know if she finds something."

Melissa got up, went to the sink, rinsed out the sponge and came back to wipe down the table. "He's the one with the other firestone, right?"

"As far as we know."

"Do they both have the same kind of power?"

"That's a question I'd like to have answered."

"The question I have," said Kathryn. "Why were they trying to bring the two together in the first place?"

"According to Kashif, each is only half of a dream, therefore broken. Join them."

Paul, carrying the trash up the steps, stopped. "What happens then? Is there an explosion, or what?"

"Good question."

Kathryn sipped her tea. "What's it feel like to be in two places at once?"

"You're not really in two places at once. You are at the focus of your attention, visiting with Kashif or sitting with Sasi near the stone, amazing"

"I'm ready," said Paul.

Kathryn gave him a sharp look. "No, you're not. Thank you, Melissa. You noticed that the biggest mess was by Paul?"

"Noticed." She rinsed out the sponge and dried her hands. "What if she finds Aki? Are you going to try to connect?"

"I don't know."

"You're probably going to need help, huh, Sam?"

"Paul, stay out of it."

Sam held up his beer, saluting Paul. "Thanks, buddy. But I won't be needing help. It's a family thing now. Sasi and I can work it through."

"When are you going back?"

"I've got a million things here I've got to catch up on first."

"Any chance she might come here?"

"I doubt it. We don't think the firestone could get through security."

"Mail it?"

"We've already been through that. The stone glows. It

has energy and I'm pretty sure some kind of detector would pick that up. We pretty much concluded that the firestone has to stay where it is, locally anyway."

"So, both firestones are still in Indonesia?"

"We think so, unless Aki, or whoever owns it, has some kind of private transportation."

By now, Paul had forgotten about the trash. He was sitting on the steps. "What all does the firestone do?"

"Sasi and I talked with Kashif and Mahin. It was as real as all of us sitting here."

"You're saying," said Melissa, studying her hands and noting that her nails needed work, "that a whole other world exists out there?"

"Not just one. An infinite number of them. Once you focus, that's your reality."

"How did you get into our dreams?" Kathryn asked.

"That was Sasi's idea. I didn't know what kind of effect it would have."

"She has no right to intrude into my dreams."

"I agree."

"If it's so powerful," Paul asked. "Why do you want to lose it? If it can do all of that, I'd say keep it."

Sam sipped his beer and studied the three of them. "If the firestone is in your life, it's all consuming. Nothing else matters. My entire time there with Sasi was all about the stone."

"Exactly my point," said Paul, hands open as if he was holding it. "It's the ultimate video game, a true alternate reality!"

Kathryn shook her head, disapproving. She looked over at Sam. "What's the worst that can happen?"

Sam, thinking of the mist back on the train. Was that real? If he and Sasi talked to Kashif and Mahin and agreed that the encounter was real, then looking at it from the other side was just as real. "I think we don't know."

Aki pulled back the curtains and checked out the view from his second-floor hotel window. He did not have a view of the ocean, which was what he was expecting, but he did overlook the pool below.

A young girl, probably around ten, wearing a pink two-piece bathing suit, was standing at the end of the diving board, afraid to make the jump. Three older girls, waiting for her to clear the board, coaxed her on.

A party of ten or fifteen were gathered in the shade on the other side of the pool, apparently having some kind of casual meeting along with brunch. And in the shallow end of the pool, two mothers in the water with their babies.

Aki, there are a lot of women in this place. This is a great opportunity to...,

"I'm not here to chase women. We're going to track down this Sameer guy and find out if he knows anything. As soon as we do that, we're out of here."

I don't want to fly again.

"Well, you're going to have to. Unless you want to stay here."

It seems like a nice place.

"Forget it, Missy. We're not staying."

I really don't want to fly again.

"Tell you what. I'll hold the stone so you can go home. I'll leave you on a bus stop somewhere until some fool comes along and picks you up."

I am disappointed. I thought you liked me more than that. You would do that, leave me here?

"In a heartbeat."

You would miss me. You would go home and think of all of our good times. Your apartment would be too quiet.

"At least I'd get my diet back. I need to work off this extra weight."

That's muscle. And you're better off for it. Face it, Aki. I'm good for you. You just won't admit it.

"You're a mixed bag, Missy. Nice discussion. But right

104

now, Sameer is our focus."

Just a reminder. We haven't eaten in a long time.

"I'm aware of that. It doesn't hurt to go hungry once in a while."

I think there are many good things to eat here.

"How would you know?"

I can smell them.

"If I can't smell them. You can't smell them."

I take note of food, much more than you.

"They say Mexican is pretty good."

Let's go.

"First, Sameer. I'm not sure how to approach him."

Approach him?

"We can't just come out and start asking about the firestone. He'll know we're up to something. And then we won't learn anything."

How do you know this?

"It's how humans are. We protect what we have and we get suspicious if we think someone is trying to get it."

Selfish.

"Says the pot, calling the kettle black."

What does that mean?

"You killed Dimyati to get what you wanted. That's selfish."

I killed Dimyati to get what I needed. That's different.

"At least I haven't killed anyone."

But you beat up three thieves.

"I didn't do that. It was you. And it was because they were going to take your cheese. So, you are more selfish than humans, whatever you are."

Right. Blame it on me.

"OK. You need to be quiet so I can find Sameer. We can go eat after that."

Deal.

Kathryn pulled into the driveway and followed the pavement to the other end of the complex. There were several small businesses located here, just off of the main drag, a small print shop, a dance studio, radiator repair, a couple of consulting or sales enterprises and, at the far end, Sam's studio.

He had rented a double wide office, sectioned off part of it for his living quarters and used the rest, most of which was covered with tatami mats for his classes. Rice paper covered the inside storefront window while a curtain covered the door.

Pulling up, Kathryn set the brake, kept her car idling. "Front door delivery."

"Ah, it's good to be home. Thank's for the ride, Kathryn."

"No problem. Thanks for lunch. What are your plans?"

"Short term, I've got a class tomorrow morning and a seminar in the afternoon. Long term? No idea. I'll let you know if I hear anything from Sasi."

"Appreciated. It's good to have you back."

Sam leaned over and gave her a hug. "It's nice to come home to you guys. We're family, of sorts."

"I don't know what we are."

Sam smiled, kissed her on the cheek and opened the door. "Whatever it is, it's good. Don't you think?"

Kathryn smiled, surprised by the kiss. "Wouldn't have it any other way."

"Pop the trunk, will you?"

She watched as Sam grabbed his suitcases and closed the lid. She had always been attracted to the man but there always seemed to be something to keep them from moving the relationship forward. Ain't that something? A kiss.

She watched Sam pause at the front door while he found his keys and opened up. After they waved goodbye, she continued around the corner, drove along the back side of the building and headed back to the main road.

Sam set his luggage down next to the row of chairs along the front wall and, thinking that a hot shower would be absolutely fantastic, turned to lock up.

His car was parked straight across from the door and, while insuring that it hadn't been vandalized in his absence, noticed another car pull up and park two spaces down.

Getting out of the car, a man pulled a piece of paper from his pocket, surveyed its contents and then scanned the building for addresses. Seeing a match, Suite 1G, he headed for Sam's front door.

Before getting out of the car, Aki looked in his rear view mirror to insure there was no food in his beard, turned off the radio and checked his notes.

I'll say it again, Aki. Carne asada burritos are great, except for the green stuff.

"That's called guacamole. It's made from avocado."

They can skip that part.

"That's the best part. I liked the salsa, too."

I noticed that a lot of the foods were covered with cheese. We'll have to try everything on the menu. I love this place, Aki. We have to stay.

"We're not going to be here long. We'll know soon enough if Sameer knows anything."

You said approach him. How are you going to do that?

"I'm going by a different name."

Oh? Why?

"Because my name is associated with Dimyati's death. I left the scene even though it was not a crime. Since there are no witnesses other than me, everyone will think it was murder. So..., while we're here, I'll be known as Argo."

Argo. That's the best you could do?

"What's wrong with Argo?"

It's very close to Aki.

"I don't want to stray too far away. I want something I can remember."

What are you going to say?

"Don't know. I'll wing it. I just have to make sure that I set up a second meeting before leaving."

What's your excuse for seeing him?

"He teaches martial arts. I'll sign up for some kind of class."

Martial arts?

"Self-defense, how to fight."

You already know that..., as long as I'm with you. Attackers have to come through me first.

"You talk as if you have a body."

I do. And I'm protecting it.

"It? I'm an "it" now?"

You've always been an it. Inside the stone, you're just a thought, a memory. But out here, Aki. It's us!

"Nice save. But I don't believe you."

I'll say it again. I'll never lie to you. I have no reason.

"But you'll kill me if need be."

Yes.

"OK, Missy. I'm going in. This trip works for both of us. You get info about the stone. I get info about how to protect myself without you."

You seem so eager.

Aki rolled his eyes. "Well?"

I do appreciate you making the effort. And now you're going to get beat up. Thanks, Aki.

"I'm not going to get beat up. He's going to show me how to fight, not fight me."

You learn what works best when you fight.

"It's not about fighting. It's about having confidence. So, maybe this is good.

That's what I've been saying all along.

"You weren't so brave at the airport."

That's different.

Aki opened his door and stepped out into the heat of a hot, sunny afternoon, read the address he'd written down and found it on the building.

"OK, Missy. You're going to have to be quiet. No mess-ups here."

You go..., Argo!

Sam did not bother to turn on the lights over the mats. This time of day, late afternoon sun hitting the rice paper illuminated the entire room in a clean white light. Waiting at the doorway until Aki arrived, he pulled back the curtain and motioned for him to enter.

Stepping inside, Aki held out his hand. "Hi. I'm Argo."

Shaking his hand, Sam studied the man. His handshake was gentle and his face, although smiling, appeared strained. "I'm Sam. May I help you?"

"You teach martial arts?"

"Of sorts, yes. Are you interested in something like that?"

"Yes."

"Were you looking for private lessons? Or a class?"

"What's the difference?"

"If you sign up for classes, you can attend any class that I teach. I teach five one hour classes a week. It's cheaper and you'll be working out with anywhere from ten to twenty other students, more or less."

"And private?"

Does he look familiar to you, Aki?

"You and I work out together, one on one. Or I could pair you up with another student and you two can split the cost. Either way, if you take private lessons, you can attend any of my other classes."

"What kind of self-defense do you teach?"

"Usually, people come in, watch a few lessons and then decide if they want to join. You can sit right there in one of those chairs and watch. I don't teach any particular style. I draw from every art."

"Tournaments?"

"No. You'll get none of that here."

"Colored belts?"

"No. I demonstrate the techniques and help you learn them. I suggest that you watch a class and then make up your mind."

110

"When is the next one?"

"Tomorrow morning at seven."

"Then..., I'll be here. Thanks."

Aki shook his hand and turned to go, but bumped into Sam's luggage. Sam caught his arm before he fell.

"Sorry. I should've warned you about those suitcases."

"They were there when I came in. I should remember that." Straightening out Sam's luggage he noticed the tag. "Oh. Just getting in? I should've called. Don't know why I thought you'd be open."

"What inspired you to choose here, if I may ask?"

"I just picked your name out of the listings."

"Just luck, huh? OK. Maybe I'll see you tomorrow morning. My web site lists the times of my regular classes, any upcoming seminars and lists the fees for private, semi-private and regular classes. It also gives you a basic idea of what my philosophy is concerning martial arts."

"Thanks."

Sam let Aki out, locked the door behind him, picked up his luggage and headed for his bedroom. Something about the man was familiar but he couldn't put his finger on it, not so much his face. What was it?

Nice going, Argo. You tripped in front of your teacher. That'll make a good impression.

Aki fumbled for the keys in his pocket while he crossed the lot to his car. "It turned out good. Did you see the tags on his suitcase?"

You know I can't read.

"One of them said, Indonesia. He might've been on the same plane as us."

Maybe that's why he looked familiar.

"If I didn't notice him, you didn't notice him."

Not true, Aki. They may be your eyes but we see different things. You hardly noticed anyone else's food today but I studied everything that passed by.

"Looking for cheese, right?"

Not just cheese. I could quit hunting if we had food like that.

"You don't hunt and if we ate food like that all the time, I'd get fat. The thing is, he might've been on the same plane. And if he was, he was somewhere close to where Dimyati found you."

You should've asked where in Indonesia.

"I showed up without an appointment and he was kind enough to talk. I didn't want to intrude any more."

You're going to have to be more aggressive, Aki. Ask lots of questions.

"I'll be doing that tomorrow.

Are you going to take private lessons?

"I don't know. If there are a lot of other people around, it'll be hard to ask questions. Maybe I should've just come right out and asked if he knew anything about a firestone."

That's what I would've done.

"Right, like you're so wise."

How are you going to know if you don't ask questions?

"If the firestone was a rumor back in eighteen eighty-three, and if it survived, it's probably top secret to anyone who owns it now. Like am I going to talk about the stone to a stranger? They'll put me in a funny farm."

He's not a stranger. He's the guy we're looking for. You mention firestone and we'd be invited for tea.

"Right. Like you know."

There is a room in the back where he cooks.

"Right. You know this, too. Just be quiet for a while. I need to think."

He asked why you chose him. What did you say, picked his name from..., what?

"It doesn't matter. If you're going to talk, get back on track. Why was he in Indonesia?"

Aki, I'm getting hungry.

"No, we're not. We're going back to the hotel and do some research. Don't you want to know if he was on that flight?"

When I say that he looks familiar, it's not his face so much as his spirit that I recognize.

"Oh, great. Past lives?"

More like, our paths have already crossed.

"Since you've been with me?"

Aki, there's a whole lot more going on that you don't know anything about.

"Such as?"

All you see is this, these things that we do. Inside the stone, it's not like that. It's about awareness, where you are when you're not here. In some previous world, I've crossed paths with Sameer.

"That's significant. How would I explain that to him?"

You don't have to. I need some of your dream time to explore.

"We've had this conversation a thousand times. No. I will never give permission for you to control my dreams."

Aki?

"No."

There were thirteen students in Sam's class the following morning. Aki took a seat in one of the several chairs along the wall and watched with interest as Sam guided them through fifteen minutes of stretching and another ten doing forward and backward rolls.

Can you do those things, Aki?

"Of course. Call me Argo."

I watched you fall in the hallway. You have no concept on how to land softly.

"I was drunk."

Splat. That's what it sounded like..., Argo.

"Don't talk to me, Missy. I can't answer you in here."

You don't have to answer.

Sam picked a young athletic looking man, college student, Aki was guessing, for help demonstrating a defense against someone attacking with a knife. The motion for this demonstration was a forward jab at Sam's midsection with a wooden knife. Sam had him attack several times at regular speed and then slowed the whole process down and explained about the dynamics of that kind of move and how to work with it.

He then instructed everyone to pick a partner and practice between themselves, taking turns being the attacker or defender and then for the next ten or fifteen minutes he moved from team to team, answered questions and helped them figure out why it wasn't working as he had shown.

He's pretty good, Aki. You might even learn how to stand up straight with this guy teaching you.

"My posture is fine."

Right. Look at yourself when you're not thinking about it. You have slumped shoulders and your stomach hangs out. You look like a victim waiting for a place to be assaulted.

"I'm not talking to you right now."

Right. Change the subject. Are you going to take classes or get private lessons?

114

"Private lessons are too expensive. These classes are fine but I don't see any opportunity to have a private conversation."

Why don't you just come right out and ask if he knows anything about a firestone? If he has, he's going to want to know what you know. Forget all of this other stuff.

"It's good to know what he knows."

Sam clapped his hands and motioned for everyone to sit. He chose a middle aged woman with curly blonde hair and big smile, had her stand in front of him and then, in slow motion, jabbed the knife toward her abdomen. She guided his hand by OK, but rushed the defensive move. Sam stopped and explained about waiting for the force to play out naturally. Rushing it only gives the attacker a chance to recover.

"Try working with your partners at different speeds. Go slowly at first. Get it right. And then start speeding it up."

And so, for the next hour they practiced the technique, changed partners and tried again. At the end of the hour, Aki was impressed. Everybody's techniques looked a whole lot better than when they started.

He's pretty good, Argo. You're going to learn a few things. I already know what he's saying.

"Like you know everything."

I know how to fight.

Sam came over and shook Aki's hand. "Well, what did you think?"

"Impressive. Where do I go to buy the uniform?"

"It's called a Gi. I've think I've got one your size in the back, if you're interested. I sell them at cost."

"Fine."

"Are you interested in the group class?"

"Either private or semi-private. I don't have a partner, though."

"Just so happens that I know someone who is looking for one."

"Are they already taking your classes?"

"On and off over the last couple of years. She knows the

basics and can help you with that."

"She?"

"Is that OK?"

"Fine. When do we start?"

"Give me some times that you're available, your contact info and I'll see what works for her."

"I can start anytime."

"You already said you're not in danger..., right?"

"Right. Just anxious to get started."

"Perfect." Sam turned and started back across the mats. "I'll be right back with your Gi."

Argo, you're going to be practicing with a girl!

"So..., what?"

How are you going to learn from a girl? They don't know how to fight.

"Are you kidding me? They can be vicious."

Well, at least you'll meet a girl. I'm going to enjoy watching this.

"You stay out of it. I'm doing this for you. Don't forget that."

Who says I can't have fun along the way?

Sam returned with the Gi and handed it to Aki. "I'll contact Zoe today and let you know when."

"Zoe?"

"Right. Your new partner."

Aki, you look like a zebra without the stripes.

"Don't make fun of me. This is for you."

Does it embarrass you to be seen like that?

"Everybody else was wearing Gi's."

Yes, but they were inside the building. Most of them changed back to regular clothes before leaving.

"Did they? I was talking to Sam and didn't really notice."

That's why you need me, Aki. I see things you don't.

"Food is all you ever notice."

If I were you, and I am, I would change clothes over there. You don't want to be seen like this.

"Why not? Everybody dresses for what they're going to go do.

Like I said, a zebra without the stripes. In the wild, I would attack.

"Make you a deal. You go back to the wild and I won't dress like this."

I don't know why you're so anxious to lose me.

"You're sure there's a place to change over there?"

Yes. Second door on the left. They have a shower, too.

"How come I didn't notice all of that?"

Like I said..., Argo. I've got your best interests in mind.

"OK. I'm changing. I don't want to be late for my first lesson."

Zoe arrived after Aki. She and Sam were discussing using batteries rather than compressed air for something. Aki, coming out of the dressing room, was interested in the subject, but they fell silent when they saw him. They met out on the mats. She held out her hand and smiled.

"Hi. I'm Zoe. I hear that you're my new partner?"

Zoe was not a tall woman, just over five feet and appeared to be about thirty. She was rather plain looking, a few freckles, straight, short cut brown hair, no make-up or jewelry, but she did have some kind of dragon tattoo circumventing her neck, most of which Aki could not see because of the high-necked shirt beneath her Gi. She had a firm handshake.

"I'm Argo. Nice to meet you."

"Have you had any other training before?"

"No. First time."

Sam motioned for them to sit and got them started stretching. Zoe already knew these stretches and easily went into them. Aki, almost as stiff as a board, struggled.

Aki, you've got to do better than that! You look like you can't bend.

"I can't."

"You have to ease into it," said Zoe. "Don't try to do too much at first or you'll hurt yourself."

"How did you get so limber?"

"I've been doing this for years."

OK, Aki. One for her. None for you.

"Sam said that you've already taken some lessons?"

"A few. He's shown me the basics."

She's going to kick your butt, Aki. I can't wait.

"What made you decide to take lessons?"

"I own a small manufacturing firm and some of our products pertain to home security. So, I thought I'd explore the self defense part of it. How about you?"

"I just thought I'd try it. I'm curious what Sam is going to teach. I watched his class yesterday."

"You won't be doing that for a while, I don't think. Will he, Sam?"

"First things first," said Sam, standing. "You have to learn how to fall."

Doing forward rolls, Zoe sounded like a quick breeze over the mats. Swoosh. Aki was more like, thumpity, thump, thump. Doing tight rolls, she could get six forward rolls into the space of the mats while Aki could only get three. She could nearly fly through the air and clear most of the mat in one roll, land softly and come up standing. Swoosh! Sam did not recommend that Aki try that yet. For that, Aki was grateful.

Aki, you're making a bad showing. You want me to take

over?

"No."

You sure? I can make you look better.

"No."

Backward rolls were even harder. The concept of falling backward, to Aki, was to avoid hitting his tailbone or head and let everything else fend for themselves. That's what doctors, chiropractors and acupuncturists are for.

Zoe rolled backward to her left and to her right and hardly make a sound. Aki was a slow-motion collapse to the mat sounding like someone had just dropped several heavy books. Sam immediately set about correcting that. Before long, Aki was starting to get the idea that falling over backward was really not a fall at all. Rather a controlled roll going in the opposite direction.

Well, Aki. I'd say that you're a complete failure. Two for her. None for you. How does that feel? Oh, wait. I already know. I'd say we have to go have a carne asada burrito to drown our sorrows. What do you think?

"No."

"You keep saying no," said Zoe. "You can't expect to get everything right the first time."

"I thought I'd do better."

"Don't expect too much at first. These things take practice."

"I know what I'll be working on tonight."

Wine and cheese, Aki. I'm with you!

Wanting to know a bit more about Indonesia, Melissa logged into one of the English newspapers in Lampung. She was reading through the travel section, hoping to get information about parks near Krakatoa, when she stumbled upon a short blurb about someone, Danu something or other who was wanted for violating his parole. He looked familiar and the name sounded familiar enough that, going back to her correspondence with Sam, she realized that this was the same person.

This is something Sam would want to know. What was the other guy's name? Hmm. Here it is, Takat. What can I dig up on him?

Searching for more information about Takat, Melissa discovered a missing persons report about a professor at a local college. Melissa did not know Sasi's last name, but the picture shown was similar to the one that Kathryn had on her laptop of her and Sam. Seeing that, she placed a call to Sam.

"Melissa! What's up?"

"Just thought you should know, Sam. I think your cousin in Lampung has been reported as missing."

"What? Are you sure?"

"I was checking police reports and came across the alert."

"I'll try to contact her. Does it say who reported her missing?"

"Someone named Joko?"

"Her brother. Uh, oh."

"What are you going to do?"

"First, confirm. Anything else?"

"She failed to show for a class that she was scheduled to teach. Probably not related, but Danu, one of your attackers...,"

"I remember him."

"He's wanted for violating his parole. But it doesn't say why."

"Do you remember who the other one was?"

"Takat."

"Right. Anything about him?"

"Haven't got that far yet. Thought I'd better tell you about Sasi first."

"Thanks, Melissa."

"I'll keep snooping around. If I find anything, I'll let you know."

"I'll try to contact Joko. I should've gotten his info before I left. Sasi mentioned one of her old students, Hamza. Check him out if you can. Does it mention the name of the gang?"

"Hang on, going back to Danu. Here it is, Bulan Biru."

"Any idea what that means?"

"Checking. I've got a translator on my laptop. Hmm."

"What?"

"It translates to blue moon."

"Like Kathryn says, the coincidences keep piling up. Thanks, Melissa. I'll let you know what I find. You'll do the same?"

"Of course. Are you going to let Kathryn and Paul know?"

"I shouldn't. But I said that I would. No more secrets, right?"

"That was the agreement."

Argo, we have a new favorite, cheese enchiladas!

"Saw that coming. It's not *our* favorite."

I know. You keep eating all of that green stuff.

"I have to counter you."

You're always working against me.

"Because you'll take over if I let you."

Aki, you're so pessimistic. You need to learn to go with the flow.

"If I go with your flow, I would be fat and lazy. Now..., keep quiet. I need to stretch."

Why do you need quiet to stretch?

"I just need quiet. Don't you ever shut up?"

You're going to miss me when I'm gone.

"They wrote a song about that."

I like stretching. I've done that a lot in the past.

"You never mentioned it until Sam brought it up."

In past lives.

"Back when you were a lion?"

Back when I was whatever I was. I just remember the stretching.

"Funny how you remember some things but not the others."

Some things are common no matter what you are.

"Says the spirit of the firestone to the human."

So, you liked this morning's breakfast better than the cheese enchiladas?

"Huevos rancheros? That was good. But it's egg and I can't eat too many of those. Tomorrow, it's oatmeal."

You can't eat too many eggs.

"Not up for discussion. I'll decide how many eggs I eat.

So..., now that we've eaten, what do you think of Zoe?

"Don't know enough yet."

She smelled good.

"OK. She did smell good."

She knows how to move.

"She does. Rolled over those mats like a breath of air."

Unlike you. You should be practicing how to roll. Anybody can stretch.

"You're a nagger. That's what you are. Nag. Nag. Nag."

That's right. You can't roll. Take it out on me. I'm trying to help you look good for her.

"You're reading too much into this. She's my training partner. That's all."

She sure showed you up. When's your class?

"In about an hour. That's why I need to stretch."

So, you can look much improved?"

"So, I can be much improved."

I thought so. You do like her.

"I want to appear competent."

Too late for that. You still remember how to roll?

"I've got the bruises to show me the way. Just follow the pain."

And you haven't even started the techniques yet.

"It'll be interesting to see what Sam shows us today.

Are you going to ask about the firestone?

"At the appropriate time."

I wonder if Zoe drinks wine.

"She's my training partner. That's all. Quit trying to hook us up."

I'm looking out for you, Aki.

After the lesson Sam invited Aki and Zoe to join him for tea. They seated themselves on the cushions around the table while Sam set about heating the water and scooping tea leaves into the teapot. Waiting for the water to boil, he joined them at the table.

"Argo, you did much better today. How do you feel?"

"I didn't know I had so many moving parts."

Zoe smiled. "You'll be reminded tonight."

There was something about Zoe that Aki was trying to figure out. When practicing pushing hands, she effortlessly guided the force of his attempt to push her off balance so well that Aki lost his. Yet, going the other way, her touch was so light that he often never even felt the nudge that took him off balance.

When that happened, she smiled and even though their eyes met during those times, he never felt that her smile was mocking him or that it was for him. More like she had some secret agenda that she was pursuing.

"You're right. I'll have to soak in a hot tub."

And wine, Aki. Don't forget the wine. Maybe she'd like to join us?

"Your forward rolls were much better than last time. You'll have all the rough spots worked out pretty soon."

"I still have a hard time with the back rolls."

Another one of those smiles. "At least you're not crashing down."

Yes, he was. I can attest to that. You should hear him from this side.

Sam put the tea on the table and retrieved a pink box from the top shelf next to the stove. Opening it, he removed three pieces of Danish, placed them on a plate and cut them into thirds. "Cheese Danish, here. The one with almonds is called a Bighorn, I think. It's filled with some kind sweet almond paste and the other is lemon filled. Dig in."

Aki, try the cheese Danish!

Zoe reached for a piece of the lemon filled. "What's the occasion?"

"This is an apology of sorts.. I'm not going to be able to teach for the next week. I have to be somewhere."

Aki scooped up a piece of the cheese Danish. "Didn't you just get back?"

Take a bite, Aki. Quit the small talk.

Zoe looked puzzled. "How would you know that?"

"I tripped over his luggage at the front door."

Zoe nodded, as if that was completely believable. "So, Sam. Where are you going?"

"I've got to make another run to Indonesia."

Aki! He was on that plane!

Sam poured a bit of tea into his cup, was satisfied that it was strong enough, and filled all of their cups. Aki watched the steam evaporate over the rim.

"What part of Indonesia?"

"Lampung."

"Oh. I'm familiar with the area. On business?"

"No. Personal reasons."

Aki wanted very much to ask, where in Lampung, the purpose of the visit and about a thousand other things. But he was the new guy and didn't want to appear to be too nosey. Everybody would clam up.

Zoe attempted a sip of tea, blowing the steam off as she did. "So, no classes for the next week. Well, Argo." There's that smile again. "That'll give you a chance to heal."

Aki. Take another cheese Danish. They won't notice.

"Actually," Sam hesitated, studying Zoe. "You already have a key. If you'd like to keep working out with Argo, you're welcome to use the do-jo."

Zoe has a key? Aki...,

"I could do that. I was going to ask you if Jill and I could practice here. She has a tournament coming up and wants to do a little extra training."

Aki reached for a lemon filled. "A tournament in what?"

No, no, no, Aki. Go for the cheese!

"Judo."

"Oh. So, if we practice, she'll be here, too?"

"Yes, more or less. Sometimes she's early. Sometimes late. She's not so exact with time, but very good in Judo."

"How will that affect our training?"

"I'll just keep working with you on your rolls and start showing you some basic techniques, stuff Sam taught me."

"And Jill?"

"She can show us a few things about Judo. You'll learn a new way to fall, too."

"How? Front rolls and back rolls, right? What else is there?"

Zoe smiled. "This one's called a break-fall."

Jill had a Mohawk. Aki couldn't tell at first whether the sides of her head were shaved or braided into some kind of tribal design leading up to the rest of her hair. She kicked off her sandals and bowed at the edge of the mat, a slight lowering of her head, before coming over to greet them.

As she approached, Aki saw that the braided hair was actually a black tattoo that started just above her ears, a sharply pointed design that wrapped around to join at the nape of her neck, looking something like a stylized nape of a dragon. She had a slim build, about six feet tall, and with her thick black Mohawk, white Gi with black belt, she was, to both Aki and Missy, a sight to behold.

That's a girl, right, Aki?

She gave Zoe a hug and then reached out to shake Aki's hand. "Hi. I'm Jill."

She had a firm handshake. "I'm Argo. Nice to meet you."

"Zoe says you're learning quickly."

Aki laughed. "She's an optimist. I feel the pain."

That kind of broke the ice. Aki went back to his stretching while Zoe and Jill worked out on the mats.

Watching them, lesson number one, stay on balance. Lose that even a little bit and there's the opening. It wasn't long before Jill, with a slight nudge into Zoe's space, suddenly threw Zoe over her shoulder. She landed flat on her back, slapping the mat with her free hand at the same time.

Ouch!. Aki, that looks dangerous.

"It's a sport, Missy. Don't talk to me."

You're going to get your butt kicked. I can see it coming.

"They're going to show me how to fall."

I don't think you get much chance to practice. You're on your feet and then you're on your back. There's not much time in between.

"Don't talk to me."

127

The mat area was about thirty feet deep by fifty feet wide. Aki practiced his rolls along one edge of the short side while Jill and Zoe practiced in the middle.

Aki. You smoothie, you. Now you're going to be working out with two women in an otherwise deserted room. I didn't think you had it in you.

"You're a pervert. What you're missing is that Zoe has a key. If he trusts her with a key, their relationship goes a lot deeper than what we know."

After a short break, Jill showed Aki how to hold her Gi and then proceeded to show him some of the different moves she might employ for his take down. Zoe showed him how to fall and how to use his arm to cushion the impact.

Holding Jill's Gi, Aki worked on keeping his balance as she tested it, a nudge here, a tease push or pull there. It happened so fast that Aki wasn't even sure that he resisted. With a tiny step into his space, Jill thrust her hip toward him and threw him over her shoulder. Aki was flat on his back.

Aki, she nailed you!

Jill held out her hand to help him up. "Are you OK?"

"I think so. Did I break my fall?"

She smiled. "Yeah. You did. Does it feel like it?"

"Ask me later."

"Try again?"

Zoe was laughing. "I'm sorry."

Jill smiled. "Why are you laughing?"

"Should've seen your face, Argo. I know I shouldn't laugh."

"What did I look like?"

Zoe placed her hands on an imaginary opponent's Gi and moved her feet accordingly with a set jaw and serious frown and then threw her hands up, wide-eyed, mouth open, and then laughing. "Sorry. It's very rude of me."

"The thing is, I did a break-fall. It happens so fast."

They spent another hour practicing techniques, Jill teaching about Judo, Zoe what she had learned from Sam. Lesson concluded, Aki tried to pay.

Zoe shook her head. "No. We're partners. We're supposed to practice together."

"Do I pay Sam?"

"Of course, not. He's letting us use the do-jo. We'll keep an eye on it for him."

Jill shook Aki's hand, gave Zoe a hug. "You'll let me know if you're going to do this again?"

"Sure. See you tonight."

Aki went to change clothes while Zoe checked all the locks. They met at the front entrance, turned out the lights and locked the door. They shook hands. Zoe smiled. "Tomorrow, same time?"

"Sure. Can I have your number in case I'm so sore I can't make it?"

She handed him a business card. "The number's on here." She waved goodbye, went to her car and drove away.

Aki, you are a smoothie. Got her number, practiced with two fine looking, dangerous women and got us another date. Let's go celebrate.

"It's not a date, Missy. That's my partner."

Call it what you will.

"And she's got a key to Sam's do-jo. Hmm."

Let's go ponder that over carne asada. What do they drink in these parts?

Joko, a balding, thin man appearing to be about fifty, smiled and reached out to shake Sam's hand as he got into the car. It smelled like he'd been drinking. Sam clicked his seat belt into place as Joko eased out into traffic, pulling away from Tanjungkarang Railway Station.

"It's about thirty minutes to the house. How was your trip?"

"Long."

"Do you need to eat? Or can you wait until we get home?"

"I'm good."

Joko had a habit of constantly readjusting his glasses, thick, coke bottle lenses, up onto his nose, over the hump where it appeared that it must have been broken sometime in the past, possibly at the same time he lost a front tooth.

"Any news on Sasi?"

"Nothing since we've talked. The police came to the house, looked around, confirmed that she was gone, filled out some reports and created lots of paperwork."

"No ransom notes? Phone calls asking for money?"

"Not yet."

"Where was she kidnapped?"

"They're not even calling it a kidnapping. She's just missing."

"Was there a break-in at the house?"

"No. The front door was unlocked, no signs of a forced entry or struggle. I didn't get home until two days after she was reported missing."

"Fingerprints?"

"They found mine, but I live there. The rest they can't identify. If they know you're in town, they'll take you in for questioning."

"I have an alibi. I was on the other side of the world."

"And I was out of town. But that doesn't mean anything. If she turns up dead, they'll be looking at me."

130

"Why?"

"For one, the house is mine. I guess that means that I have a motive."

"Do you?"

Joko laughed, a hoarse kind of laugh that comes from too much drinking and smoking. "I'm hardly ever there. Other than a few nights a month, I'm always gone. My business, you know? To me, the house is more of a liability than an asset."

"Does anyone know when she went missing?"

"After she failed to show up for a seminar."

"You've contacted her friends, business associates?"

"Everybody that I can think of."

"She mentioned someone named Hamza when I was here. Do you know him?"

"He used to hang around a few years back, one of Sasi's students. They were pretty close for a while, until she figured out that he was trouble. I'm surprised that she even mentioned his name to you."

"He knows about the firestone."

"Oh, that? Yeah. He might be interested in something like that. But, he hasn't been around for years."

"He also knew that she had a short time to live."

"That's what she tells everybody. Keeps 'em at a distance."

"Is it true? Does she have cancer?"

"Your guess is as good as mine. Did she tell you that the doctors give her six months, but she thinks she has six years?"

"Exactly."

"Well, she's been saying that for years."

Joko pulled a pack of cigarettes from his shirt pocket, tapped it so that a few were exposed and offered one to Sam, who refused. Lighting one, he blew the smoke out the window on his side. "Sorry. Bad habit. I'll keep the smoke over here, best I can. How long can you stay?"

"I'm giving myself a week. Don't know what we can do in that time. Where is the firestone? That must be part of all this."

131

"Oh. I see where you're going. You think Hamza is involved?"

"Who else knows about it?"

"No one that I know of. I was surprised when she contacted you."

"What do you know about the stone?"

"Piss on that thing. It's been nothing but trouble. She's spent her whole life studying it and what's it got her? She should have been a scientist."

"No doubt. So..., where is the firestone?"

"She used to keep it somewhere in that little cubbyhole beneath the floorboards in the closet. After you left, she was concerned that your visit would make people suspicious. I suspect that she moved it to a new hiding place."

"You don't know either?"

"No." Joko took another long drag off of his cigarette and blew the smoke out the window. "If I did, I'd throw it away."

"That's what I said when I first heard about it."

"And? How do you feel about it now?"

"I don't know."

Hi Kathryn,

Staying at Sasi's house with her brother, Joko. No news on Sasi. I'll keep in touch. Miss you guys already.
S

Sam cleaned up, said good-night to Joko and went into Sasi's room. Last visit he'd slept in Joko's bed, an odd feeling, switching rooms.

The whole ambience of the place had changed. Joko did not cook, smoked like a chimney, kept a bottle by his chair in front of the TV, which he turned down only when Sam wanted to talk, and never turned it off. He watched game shows, reality TV, the news. During Sam's stay here with Sasi, he didn't even know that they had a TV.

Sam was starting to think that this was going to be a wasted trip. Joko didn't seem to be too concerned about Sasi and with him thinking that the police were doing all they could, was not very enthusiastic to do any more. He'd already contacted all of her known friends and acquaintances and concluded that he was at a dead end. Nothing more to do but wait.

Sam folded back the covers, sat on the edge of the bed and pulled off his socks, wondering what kind of plan he could put into action tomorrow.

Search the house, find the firestone, starting with the cubby hole. Even that doesn't make sense. If she left on her own and wasn't planning on coming back, she would have taken it with her. And she would have locked the front door.

She had to have been kidnapped. And if she was, the stone was part of the deal..., unless she had a chance to hide it. Maybe she buried it in the ashes of the fire pit. She probably knows Joko won't cook out there. Maybe in the teapot. He probably won't make any of that either.

Gotta rent a car. Looks like he won't be cooking. I'll have

133

to pick up some groceries. I wonder if he knows where the grocery store is.

Thirty-two hours from San Diego to Lampung. It had been a long day. Sam drifted off quickly. Sometime around three...,

"Hello, Sam."

Hearing her voice, Sam was seeing Sasi, sitting across from him in the flickering candlelight down inside the cubbyhole. She was there, blurry and fluid, like watching her reflection in a pool of water.

"We've been looking for you."

"Follow me."

Aki, out on the cliffs, kicking the stone into his backpack, crossing busy streets at a run, boarding a train, an endless ride to somewhere, doors open, a bus, ascending two flights of stairs..., home.

"This is where he lives, Sam."

Opening his eyes, Sam studied Sasi's bedroom, dimly lit by a steady yellow light coming from beneath the door. There were voices in other parts of the house.

Sam got up, dressed quickly and quietly opened the door. Stepping out into the tiny hallway, he peeked out into the living room. Joko was snoring on the couch.

Sam turned off the TV, moved Joko's half-drunk bottle of beer out of the way so he wouldn't step on it, checked the locks on the doors and went back to his room.

Sasi's alive, I think. And she's found where Aki lives. That doesn't help me. Where are you now, Sasi?

Hmm. I still have to search the house tomorrow.

Normally, Sasi kept the firestone in the wall of the cubbyhole. Although the floor was dirt, the sides were made of concrete block, one of which Sasi claimed was removable.

Inspecting the mortar lines of the block, Sam finally thought he knew which one. Sasi kept a small tool next to the table, down in the dirt at the base, something that resembled a darning needle except for the fact that the tip was curved.

She always treated it like it was just unwanted trash, good for nothing, but it always seemed to be around whenever they were exploring with the stone. Studying the tip, Sam noticed that the curve of the tip was small enough yet strong enough to enter into a tiny hole beneath one of the blocks. No way a finger, screwdriver, anything could remove the block without taking the weight off of the bottom first. Putting the tool in place, Sam pulled the block out.

As expected, the firestone was gone. Sam carefully replaced the block, got down on his hands and knees and checked beneath the table, under the chairs and finally, working his way up, the rest of the wall. He pulled the grill away from the fan and checked inside.

OK. Nothing here. I'm pretty sure of that.

Sam climbed out of the cubbyhole, closed it up, and pulled the rug back over the trap door. Next came the kitchen, the fire pit, her room. About two hours later, Joko was up, eating peanuts, sipping on a beer, smoking and catching up to Sam, who was now inspecting the outside of the house.

"You're not going to find anything."

"You're so sure?"

"She's very careful. Everything has a reason."

"What do you mean?"

"She left the front door unlocked, didn't teach the seminar and disappeared. She wanted to create a mystery."

135

"She's certainly done that. Any idea why?"

"My opinion? She wanted you back here."

"Well, now that I am here, she needs to show up. Otherwise, what's the point?"

"Maybe you're right about Hamza."

"Any idea where he lives? Works?"

"Sometimes he comes into this bar where I go, down by the water."

"Name of the place?"

"I'm going for lunch after this beer. You can join me, if you want. After that, we can stop by the place."

"Sure. Thanks."

While Joko went to get cleaned up, Sam sent off a couple of quick e-mails.

Hi Melissa,

If you get time, I need home addresses, work places and, if you can, images of Hamza, Danu and Takat. I'll buy you lunch when I get back. I owe you big time.

Thanks, Sam

Hi Zoe,

Did you practice with Argo? If Jill showed up, how did he do with break falls? What did he think of her? Also wondering how the testing went with the battery version. Better? Update, please.

Thanks, Sam

Sam decided that he needed his own transportation. He got Joko to drop him off at a car rental place and to help him through the process. After that, he followed Joko over to The Alibi, a dilapidated building that looked like it had once been used to process the comings and goings of fishing boats before the dock fell into disrepair.

The inside was not much better. Looking at the cleanliness of the glasses, Sam ordered bottled beer and paid for the first round. They sat up at the bar.

Joko seemed to know everybody and engaged in a lot of bantering with some cigar smoking guy sitting at a table with an overweight woman who appeared to be in her mid-fifties, lots of makeup, bright red lipstick, partially unbuttoned blouse and a skirt way too short for what she had to show. Sam smiled at the jokes, nursed his beer and kept his eye on the door.

Sometime around five, Joko did a quick tug on Sam's shirt and, with his eyes, motioned for Sam to take note of the two new arrivals.

"Hamza in front," he whispered. "Don't know the other guy."

Hamza looked to be about six feet, stocky, sporting a beard a couple of days old and curly black hair, He wore two gold chains and had a diamond earring in his left ear. His accomplice was a bit taller, maybe two or three inches, shaved face and head. He wore no jewelry. Silently, Sam named him Bozo.

They said their hellos to various customers, finally got up to the bar and ordered two beers. Waiting for their beer, Hamza looked over and noticed Joko.

"Hey, loser. How come you're not out looking for your sister?"

Joko did not reply. Instead, he held up his beer and smiled his missing tooth smile as if to greet them hello.

"Not talking?" Hamza approached the two of them, sat next to Joko while his friend stood behind all three. Sam turned on his bar stool to face him. Hamza put his arm around Joko's shoulder.

"I'm talking to you, loser. It's not polite to not answer."

Joko shrugged. "I don't know where she is."

"You don't know nothing, fruitcake.

Joko nodded respectfully. "You're right."

"Of course I am. You're just a drunk, a waste of good air."

"Back off," said Sam, quietly. "He's not bothering you."

"Oh?" Hamza pushed Joko forward toward the bar so that he could get a better view of Sam. "A hero? Are you the loser's hero?"

"I'm his friend. When he's with me, you treat him with respect."

"It's OK," said Joko. "I don't mind."

"But I do," said Sam. "If there are any losers in this bar, it's the man sitting on the other side of you."

Hamza was off his stool in a flash. Bozo tried to grab Sam, who slipped under his arm, spun him around and landed three hard blows to his kidney. Going down, he tripped up Hamza, who fell forward into Sam's kick to the face. It was all over in about three seconds.

Hamza stood, mouth and nose bleeding. He threw another punch at Sam, who brushed it by, moving to the outside of the blow, spun him around until the fingernails on his left hand found the right side of Hamza's nose and his right hand did the same on the left side of Hamza's neck. He pulled each in the opposite direction.

"Your choice," said Sam softly. "Which one do you want to lose?"

Hamza dropped his arms, blood soaking his clean, white shirt. Bozo was still on the floor, groaning. Sam held him there with his foot.

"My turn to ask some questions," said Sam. "Let's start with Sasi. Know anything about her?"

"I'm a dead man," Joko whispered, staring blankly at the bar. "Soon as you leave."

138

Hey Sam,

Practiced with Argo a couple of times. He's learning fast and seems anxious to keep going. Jill enjoys practicing with him because he's heavy and strong enough to resist. Still, she throws him around like a paper doll.

As far as the testing goes, battery powered, more efficient and lively and it's easier to change out when they're dead. But if they get wet, they foam up and are useless. Maybe a waterproof housing? That complicates things. Ideas?

The do-jo's fine. We're enjoying having it to ourselves. How's it going over there? Any idea when you're coming back?

Zoe

Hi Sam,

Got some dirt on Hamza. He's a suspect in a murder investigation, attached. Someone looking like him was caught on video the night a guard was killed at a storage facility. He's got an alibi. Several witnesses, his friends mostly, said they were with him at a nightclub that night.

How's it going over there? All of us are curious. Any word on Sasi? Kathryn says, be careful. We all miss you.

Melissa

Sam read the info on Hamza. Melissa had included the address of the storage facility. Good for her. He brought up Google Earth and input the address.

Bird's eye view, he determined where the murder had taken place, got the overhead layout and noted the location of the entrances and exits, coded gates.

The owner of The Alibi had called the police. When they arrived, Hamza refused to press charges. There was no damage to the place other than a stool being knocked over and a couple of spilled drinks, although the police had a

139

lot of questions for Sam. He showed them his papers and Joko reluctantly admitted that Sam was staying with him. There was a look in Hamza's eyes when he was leaving that said that their paths would cross again, soon.

Hi Zoe,

Go with the battery powered, eliminate the stars and convert to pellets. It's lighter weight and easier to waterproof. How's that?
Thanks, Sam

Hi Melissa,

You're the best. I don't know how you do it. Just don't get into trouble. I owe. I owe.
Doing fine. No word on Sasi but making progress. Give everyone a hug for me.

Sam

Fred rented the space three units south of Sam's dojo and used it for his machine shop. His was not a big business, but the income was substantial enough that he and his family, wife and two kids, could rent a three bedroom house in a not too bad area of town.

They couldn't afford any real luxury items like a new car but they did have a big screen TV, mountain bikes for the kids and, just recently, a second car.

The second car was a blessing because it freed him up from having to drop the kids off to school in the morning and having to take time off from work in the afternoon to pick them up.

Cass, his wife, decided that just plain old housekeeping was boring and, now that they had two cars, she could take some classes at the local community college and eventually get a job, add to their income and hopefully put away enough money so that they could buy a house. Renting, she claimed, had no future.

Why give the money to someone else when they could buy a place and deduct the interest payments from their income? A no-brainer.

Fred bought into all of that. It only made sense to have two incomes. Wouldn't it be great to have a house with a garage, tool shed, all of the amenities that come with owning your own home?

Cass was taking classes in finance and one of them was at night. The first few classes, she had been home by eight. Lately, she wasn't getting home until nine. When Fred asked about that, she said that some of the class had stayed late to work on a project. Nine became the new norm. Last night she came home after ten.

Fred was a quiet man. He didn't say what was on his mind most of the time. But, looking up the credentials of her instructor, he saw his picture and just couldn't help what he was feeling.

Cass was cold to his affection last night, as she had

been lately and he was not too happy the next morning. He left without breakfast or saying good-bye. Inside, a storm was brewing.

His latest project was on a ultra-light frame for an electric car, the kind of work Fred loved. New designs, ideas, take it to the extreme. But, on this morning, everything was out of whack.

Got home after ten. Doesn't want to talk about it? What else am I supposed to think?

Inside his shop, Fred wandered around the prototype feeling like a volcano was about to erupt.

She has to talk about it! If I'm this angry, we have to talk!

Fred headed for his front door. He had parked his car in front of his unit and hurried around to the driver's side. He flung the car door open just as Aki was driving by. Aki slammed on his brakes and, without even thinking about it, honked his horn.

Fred was not pleased and signaled as much with his hand. He started toward the driver's side door, but when he'd cleared the front of Aki's car, Aki waved, smiled apologetically and headed for a parking space closer to Sam's do-jo.

For Fred, that was not good enough.

Everything I've worked for. Everything we've worked for, our kids, our dreams. Where are they now?

What's she doing out there so late at night? Our marriage is falling apart. I can feel it.

I'm suffering and this guy's happy as a lark? I don't think so. Let's go see how good his martial arts are.

Fred went back into his shop, found a nice heavy iron bar, about three feet long, and walked over to Sam's do-jo to have a word with Aki.

Aki, I think that man was very angry. Did you feel that?

"Yes. He's got some issues. Let's get inside."

He glared at us all the way over here. Does he think that's your fault?

"I don't know. He opened the door right in front of me. Who does that? You're always supposed to wait until the car goes by."

I saw him go back into the shop.

"We both saw him in the rear view mirror. Let's get inside."

Zoe was already there going through her stretch routine on the mats. Aki waved, sat on one of the chairs to remove his shoes, bowed before crossing the mats and then headed for the dressing room.

By the time he'd changed, Jill arrived. He could hear them greeting each other and, anxious to be a part of that, opened the door and headed toward them while still tying his belt. He joined them on the mat and started to stretch.

Fred came through the front door, threw back the curtain, did not bother to remove his shoes or to bow or to partake in any kind of conversation. He only had eyes for one man in the room.

Aki, danger!

"I get it."

Zoe looked up. "May we help you?"

Fred did not answer. Walking briskly, he approached Aki threatening him with the bar. "You want to honk at me? I've been here ten years. You come in and think you own the place?"

"It was a reaction. I didn't mean to...,"

"That's right. Nobody ever means to . But they do and I'm sick of it!"

He swung the bar like a baseball bat. Aki kept backing away. Another swing at his knees. Aki jumped away.

Sorry, Aki. This is my fight now.

In slow motion, Aki saw the bar coming down. It was going to hit directly above his left eye. He moved ever so slightly to Fred's side, felt the whoosh of the bar going by and, using his left hand to take control of Fred's elbow and his right hand to put forward pressure on the back of Fred's neck, continued the motion so that it looked like a windmill leading Fred head first over the tips of his toes to where he landed flat on his back. Aki crooked Fred's arm behind him and took the bar away.

Don't stop now, Aki. Hit him with it!

"I'm very sorry if I startled you. It was a reaction, not out of malice."

Aki waited, holding Fred in this neutralized position until he regained his composure. Finally, when Fred stopped struggling, he helped him up.

After he had gone, Zoe went to the front door and locked it. Coming back into the room, she studied Aki.

"Argo, are you hiding something from us?"

"What do you mean?"

"Those weren't the moves of a beginner."

"It happened so fast, I...,"

"Exactly my point. It takes years to learn how to move like that."

Jill nodded. "I agree. What are you hiding, Argo?"

Zoe pointed toward the back of the do-jo. "Let's go have some tea and talk about it."

"It was nothing..., really."

Aki. You're having tea with two fine looking women. You're taking it to the next level! This will be interesting.

"No. It won't."

Zoe motioned for Aki to join her. "What?"

"Nothing. I mumble a lot."

Jill nodded. "Yes, you do. It's like you're talking to someone else all the time."

144

Two hours later, Zoe gathered up their cups and headed for the sink. "So..., how come you didn't just come right out and ask Sam about the firestone?"

"I had to know if he was the one we were searching for."

"We? Who is this other person?"

"Missy, the one I'm always talking to."

"You're saying," Jill used a napkin to wipe up a spill on the table, "you have a split personality?"

"No. We coexist."

"Sounds like a split personality to me. That's the definition."

"I keep asking her to leave."

"And she doesn't..., why?"

"Like I said, she's using me to help in her search for the firestone. I have access to information that she wouldn't have if she was back in the stone."

Zoe turned and studied Aki. "Where is this stone?"

"In my backpack, in the dressing room."

"Do you take it everywhere?"

"Of course."

"Why?"

Aki sighed. "It's a long story. The stone is like her home if she's not cohabiting someone's body. If I die, she needs quick access to go back to the stone."

"And then what?"

"She waits for the next victim."

Aki? You're not a victim. You invited me in."

Jill stood, readjusted her Gi and turned to go. "Well, all of this is crazy. I'd love to hear more, but I have to go to work." Looking over at Zoe, "Let me know how it turns out."

"Sure."

And then, looking at Aki. "When we're practicing, which one of you am I practicing with?"

"Me."

"Which me is that? Argo or Missy?"

"Argo."

"If I was competing with Missy, what would happen?"

"I don't know. When she takes over, everything is in slow motion. I have all the time in the world to react."

"That's some power that you have. I would like to practice with her sometime. What are your plans?"

"Don't know. I keep asking her to leave. She's on a quest."

With a shrug and a wave goodbye, Jill left. Zoe followed her to the front door, locked it after she was gone and returned to the tea room.

"Let me see the stone, Argo."

When Aki returned, he placed it on the table. "Doesn't look like much, does it?"

Zoe nodded. "Doesn't look unusual at all. If I hadn't seen what you did out there on the mats, I'd drop this partnership and say you were crazy."

"I wasn't like this before. I lived alone and was happy."

How can you say that? You're better off with me.

"You understand that I'm going to have to let Sam know."

"Of course. Why is he in Indonesia?"

"Visiting a relative."

"My first time in the do-jo, I tripped over his luggage. I noticed that one of the tags was from a flight from Indonesia. I think he just came from there. Has Sam ever talked to you about a firestone?"

This time it was Zoe that sighed. "OK, Argo. You've been honest with me, I think. It's a long story and it'll take time to tell. Let's go get some lunch."

Joko set his two suitcases down by the front door and then turned to shake Sam's hand.

"There's a pretty gal up the coast that's been wanting to get married. I'm going to take her up on that. And I'm going to take on her last name. I put you in charge, Sam. It's here in writing. If they don't find Sasi, sell the place. I know how to contact you. I'll check in from time to time."

"Joko, you don't have to go. We're going to resolve...,"

"No, *we* are not. I'm a dead man in this town. I'm hoping to get out alive. Good luck. Tell Sasi hello for me if you find her. I cannot say it's been a pleasure."

"Not even another day?"

"No. Curse that stone."

Joko opened the door, handed Sam the keys, picked up his bags and was gone. Closing the door, Sam stood there for a moment, listening to the quiet of the place.

This was Sasi's home, not his. It must've bothered her greatly when he came to stay. With him gone, with the TV turned off, balcony doors open, messes cleaned up, the place felt like Sasi's again.

Sam went into the kitchen, found the rice right where she'd left it and filled the pan with water. Watching her, he'd learned how to make it, how high to turn the heat and about how long it was going to take, twenty minutes.

That done, he cleaned out Joko's room, changed the sheets and brought his suitcases in. Suspecting trouble, he'd also packed a few precautions.

Two of them, spiffy looking coffee cups with a San Diego logo, were actually motion detectors in all three hundred and sixty degrees, except for the handle. When triggered, a signal was sent to Sam's location, silent to the intruder.

The two teacups and teapot were actually motion detectors that, when triggered, delivered a loud siren on and off at fast intervals and a strobe light that kicked on for half a second and then stayed off for several seconds, the idea being to blind the intruder with light and then let them stand in the dark for a few seconds before being hit with it again.

Taking these items out into the living room, he set the teapot and two cups down on the table next to the balcony. Get everything into position now. Set the alarms later. One coffee cup went on the kitchen counter next to the sink, close to the back door, the other at the other end of the house on the floor next to the couch, about where Joko put his empty beer bottles.

Sam checked the rice, saw that it had a few more minutes to go. He'd seen a roll of duct tape that Sasi kept in a cupboard by the back door, retrieved it and placed it on the kitchen counter before returning to his luggage.

In the reinforced edges of the suitcases, Zoe had designed a nifty way to package knives. The material was springy and, folded into a straight line, fit into the compartment like it was manufactured that way.

Removing it from the compartment allowed the blade to widen, the handle to expand and, while not very useful for cutting, they were excellent for throwing. Sam removed all six.

Also packaged into the reinforced lining, a plastic straw and, carefully stuffed inside, ten tiny darts, tranquilizer tipped.

Figuring that if an attack was going to come, it would come in the middle of the night, Sam ate, locked all of the doors, set the alarms and went to bed early.

Thinking back about how they had gained access, Sasi figured that Danu and Takat had scaled the steep bluff outside her living room balcony and entered her flat through the open balcony doors, something she thought was nearly impossible. That idea was confirmed because, leaving with them, she noted that the front door had never been unlocked.

They found her down in the cubbyhole with the stone on the table. Fortunately, she had not yet attempted to use it so, to them, it only appeared to have a slight yellowish glow. Taking it and her, they departed quickly out the front door.

Blindfolded in the car, Sasi estimated travel time to be about forty-five minutes, about thirty in traffic, the rest on more open road and ending into some kind of gated area. Coming to a stop, she heard the car's window being powered down, the sound of pushed buttons, seven of them, and metal wheels grinding slowly across a metal track.

Her living space was approximately ten feet square and contained a cot that was visible when the door was first opened. She quickly moved that to the other side of the room. There was no outlet near the bed's new location so she left the bedside lamp and table where they were. A small table and two chairs were located directly across the room from the entrance along with a supply of water, cups and tea.

Their routine was easy enough to figure out. Takat would return in approximately two hours to collect the dirty dishes and allow her out for a short walk and bathroom break. They had installed a buzzer if she needed to use the facilities off schedule. She was allowed an hour every morning for breakfast and a shower.

At night Hamza came to visit, sometime around eight. He was trying to be sociable, wanting to persuade her that he was not as bad as his reputation, hoping to gain her confidence.

Sasi didn't feel like she was in danger, but knew that Hamza had little patience for endeavors that did not provide quick results. She could already hear the frustration in his voice when she claimed that the stone had lost its power.

"I don't believe you, Sasi."

"I am sorry to hear that."

"You said that it was stolen."

"Because I didn't trust how you were going to use it."

"So..., I cannot believe you now that it's lost its power."

"It has."

"And yet they found you down in the cellar with it on your table."

"Trying to figure out why it wouldn't work."

"I don't believe you."

"Give me time. I should know something soon."

The other thing Sasi was most worried about was that Hamza would tire of this method of persuasion and just take possession of the stone.

If that happened, it would only be a matter of time before he discovered the face inside. Would he continue to hold it?

Of course, he would. Hamza was like that. If something caught his interest, he would possess it. But, Sasi was wondering, which side would take possession of the other?

After dinner, Takat came to collect the dishes.

"Where is Hamza?"

"He won't be coming tonight."

"I see. Is he, all right?"

Takat left without answering. Hearing the lock click, Sasi removed her shawl and stuffed it along the bottom edge of the door. Unwittingly, they had made her task easier, no windows to cover. She pulled out the stone and placed it on the table.

The alarm went off sometime after three. Sam was up as soon as he heard the soft, intermittent beep, triggered from the motion detector in the kitchen, entering through the back door.

Sam put on the glasses that Zoe had designed, polarized, one hundred percent UV protection and infrared capability which allowed him to see like a cat at night.

Quietly opening the bedroom door and stepping into the hallway, Sam slipped a dart into the straw and waited. The first person coming into the living room set off the alarm. Between ear-piercing blasts of horn and a brilliant flash of light, the intruder took a dart in the neck, slapping the sharp pain as if he'd been bitten by a spider.

Behind him, another man with a gun pushed by the first, spotted Sam in the hallway and fired twice. One bullet shattered the wooden door frame while the other whizzed by Sam's ear. The light blinked off.

Crouching low, Sam crossed the living room, cupped the shooter's gun hand between his two hands and, pointing the gun up and away, spun beneath the man's arm, crooked it backwards and forced him down to the floor. Two kicks took him out, one to the groin and one to the head.

A third person turned to flee, but Sam grabbed him by the hair, pulled him over the other two and, with a foot sweep, landed him flat on his back. Sam grabbed the man's wrist, crooked his elbow and pulled it across the man's chest, forcing him over onto his stomach where he pinned his arm against his back.

Kitchen lights on. Duct tape for everyone, wrists and ankles. Sam went to shut down the alarms.

Back in the kitchen, one was sleeping, one cursing and one quietly lying face down on the floor. Sam retrieved the gun, a Glock 17, and tucked it into his belt before turning the third person over onto their back, a woman.

"Name?"

She didn't say anything, instead choosing to study Sam, who sat her up. With a slight nod of her head and a sideways glance toward her partner, she indicated that she preferred to talk out of hearing range. Sam scooped everyone's weapons, taped the first two intruders together, took her into the living room and turned on the TV.

"Name?"

"Nadya."

"Who sent you?"

"You already know this."

"I want to hear it from you."

"Hamza.

"Where is he now?"

"Is that who you're after?"

Sam sat back and studied her. Nadya appeared to be in her early thirties, had short, shoulder length black hair and was about five feet four inches tall, medium build, no make-up or jewelry. Beautiful in an odd way, her spirit burning inside. Maybe it was her eyes.

"You suggest someone else?"

"Aren't you looking for Sasi?"

"OK. You tell me. I've just arrived."

"I know where she is, about an hour from here. I can show you."

"And why would you do that?"

"Because I want to help her."

"Why?"

"I've been to her seminars. I've talked with her. She's a brilliant woman."

"And yet you work for Hamza."

"I also work for the government."

"You can prove that?"

"I don't carry ID."

"Why this hit squad?"

"Payback. Hamza wants you, dead or alive. He'd prefer alive so he could do it himself."

"So, you were coming here to capture me?"

"Kill Joko, capture you."

"Your government allows you to kill an innocent man?

152

Joko's harmless."

"I'm here to help prevent it."

"Apparently Hamza trusts you very much. Why?"

"We used to be lovers. Now, we're friends."

"You say it's an hour from here?"

"Yes."

"I'm going to remove the tape. Don't mess with me. Understand?"

"Yes."

"How did you get here?"

"Car."

"Is there room for four?"

"Yes."

"We load the one who's sleeping into the trunk. You can drive?"

"Yes."

"I'll ride behind you. Your partner will...,"

"He's not my partner."

"He'll ride shotgun. Where is this place?"

"Like I said, about an hour away."

"Not how long. Is it the storage facility?"

"I suppose that you could call it that."

"Where the guard was murdered?"

"You know so much for just arriving."

"Is it?"

"Yes. Takat is the new guard."

"We've already met. He'll remember me."

It was four A.M. before everyone was loaded into the car. A light mist filled the air and the clouds, moving slowly, choked out what was left of the moon's light. Nadya found the controls for the windshield wipers and turned them on. A screeching sound echoed through the car.

Sam frowned. "There's no rubber on the passenger side."

Nadya squinted through the distorted view. "Driver's side isn't much better."

Aki. We are closer than ever to the other firestone.

"No, we're not. It's on the other side of the world. It's cost us all of this money just to find out that it's where we just came from."

But, now we know that we've got the right man.

"But, we don't know where he is, how he's involved, or who he's involved with. Zoe was very cautious with her information."

She did admit to another firestone.

"No. She admitted to Sam going to investigate the disappearance of a relative who knew something about a firestone. Not the same thing, Missy. Don't jump to conclusions."

I didn't like the place that Zoe picked for lunch.

"Because they didn't have any cheese?"

That, and raw fish. What's with that?

"It's called sushi. We've had it before."

Too much rice. Not enough meat. Next time we go for lunch, let's get her a carne asada burrito.

"We're after the firestone, not food."

I didn't notice you leaving any food behind.

"Off subject. Zoe is going to contact Sam. We have to wait for her call."

How is this going to help us?

"We're probably going to have to fly back home. We've got to meet up over there."

Leave this place? Aki...,

"We're after the firestone. Not carne asada burritos."

What about your lessons? You've got two women on the hook.

"No, I don't. I'm lucky they even talk to me."

They liked your moves taking that guy out.

"Those were your moves. They're in awe of you, but think I'm crazy. I'll get nowhere with that."

Maybe we should get a bottle of wine and some cheese and think this through.

154

"We are thinking it through. We're waiting for Zoe to get back to me."

So, we have some spare time.

"No. I'm going to arrange for a flight back to Indonesia. We need to be able to go on a moment's notice."

We're going to fly again?

"Of course. How else are we going to get home?"

You know how I feel about flying.

"And you know how I feel about cohabitation."

Let's just wait for him to come back.

"Missy, I'm beginning to think that you would rather stay here than find the other firestone."

This is a nice place.

"No. We are going to become two separate things as soon as I can figure it out."

An idea. I go back into the stone. You're free. Give it to Zoe and point out the face inside. I'll do the rest.

"She'll have you eating lots of vegetables, rice and sushi. It'll be a continuous battle. You won't like it."

Not like with you. We're pretty good together, aren't we?

"Memorable. That's how I describe it."

You're so negative. We could be so much more.

"Or, less. Right now, we're waiting for Zoe. Oh, here it is."

Hi Argo,

I've attached Sam's contact info in Lampung. He wants to meet with you as soon as possible. I enjoyed our sessions together. Maybe, some other time we can resume our partnership.

Good luck,

Zoe

Keeping the stone on the table, Sasi gently turned the firestone in a clockwise direction, studying how the dim light from the lamp reflected through the translucent surface. What appeared as a ribbon of light at one angle, appeared as a brightly lit pin just a slight turn away. When that happened, if she turned it just right, a burst of light appeared somewhere on the other side of the stone.

There were so many things to see. It was easy to get lost, to feel like floating in the clouds, going away somewhere, coming out of the other side and discovering a whole new place and time.

But the most powerful thing of all was the face. Holding it hundreds of times, there was some kind of energy that wanted to come out, tempting her hands and arms with a tingling sensation, energy flowing upward, wanting to merge with hers.

Sasi always put the stone down when it came to that. She would not let it get out of control. Know your limits and stop before you get to them.

She poured herself a bit more tea and turned the stone so that she could not see the face. It works both ways. Staring at it always comes with the feeling that it is doing the same.

After all these years, what has this hesitation gotten me? What actually happens if I don't put the stone down?

Aki, what happened to you? Did you share the same fate as Dimyati? Or, have you moved on? Where are you now?

Maybe it's better to let Hamza have the stone, point out the face and watch what happens. He won't wait much longer anyway.

As always, the question was and still is, why did Dimyati take his own life? With a wife, two children and apparently happy, he had everything to lose.

Sasi turned the stone again so that she could view the face. The corners of the mouth were neither turned up

156

nor down, mood of the firestone, neutral. The long, curved line representing the ridge of the nose leading up to and ending somewhere between the eyes, that line seemed blurry compared to other times. The eyes, normally looking into the distance, tonight seemed to be concentrating on her. Once again, Sasi turned the firestone away.

Is it trying to say something? Is it trying to tell me to let go, get over my fears and take the leap? That's the problem. I don't want to take a leap, not like Dimyati.

Sasi stood, pushed her chair back to the table and paced the room. There were too many unanswered questions.

I know I've been reported missing. They must be looking.

Joko was coming to stay. Did he? He's the only one that could notify Sam. Did he?

Sam. Would you drop what you're doing and come back?

Hamza's going to push. Do I take a chance with the firestone? Or do I let him?

Which is worse?

Why am I thinking this way? I've seen so much, been with people I'd never have a chance to meet, seen through the centuries, all of it through the stone.

I've been afraid all of these years and it has given me insight, knowledge and yes, even fear. Do I want Hamza to have a chance at this before me?

Sasi turned and headed for the table. She pulled out the chair, made herself comfortable, took one last sip of tea and picked up the stone.

OK. You've been waiting patiently. Let's meet.

Nadya dimmed the lights and turned off the wipers before pulling up to the gate, lowering the window and inputting the code. Out beneath a rusted metal box a motor came to life, whirring noisily in the night, pulling the chain through the gears.

"I'm hoping he's sleeping. Maybe we can sneak by."

Hatta squirmed in the seat next to her. "I have to pee. Untie me."

"You'll have to wait," said Sam. "If you can't, go ahead. You're the one that's going to be sitting in it."

"Actually," said Nadya, watching the gate grind open. "Unless you're planning on him coming back with us, that's where one of us will be sitting."

Hatta glared at Nadya. "I knew it. I even warned Hamza about you."

Allowing the car to move ahead at idle, Nadya steered past the main office and headed toward the back of the lot, driving alongside a long storage building past two of three other rows perpendicular to this one. She turned into the drive between row two and three and stopped midway to the other end.

Getting out, she went to the door, shined a light from her key chain onto the lock and shook her head. "Lock's been changed."

"You sure this is the right place?"

Nadya backed away from the building and counted the doors. "Yes. It was the middle one. Wait. I'm going to check the doors on either side."

"Check all of them."

Pushing his knees together to hold it back, Hatta smiled. "Things never go right, do they?"

"At least I'm not sitting where you are."

"Yet."

Nadya climbed back into the driver's seat. "I checked all of them. We're going to have to go back to the office."

"You're sure she's in there?"

"Last I looked. I never went in. But I saw her in there with Hamza, night before last."

"If I knock on the door, can she hear me?"

"Once you go in, there are three separate storage spaces. She's in the middle one. What good would that do anyway? You still can't get in."

Nadya put the car in gear and idled along the blacktop between the buildings with just her parking lights on. They stopped just short of the office.

Hatta squirmed in his seat. "Are we all getting out? Cause I *really* have to pee."

Sam put duct tape across Hatta's mouth, across the beard and ear to ear. "Sorry. That's really going to hurt when it's pulled away." And then he pulled Hatta's head back against the headrest and wrapped duct tape around that. You're just gonna have to hold it, partner. We'll be right back."

Nadya quietly opened the door and started to get out. Sam stopped her, putting his hand on her shoulder. "Where is Takat?"

"He has a room behind the office. Usually he sleeps on a cot against the wall."

"Which wall?"

"The one behind the door."

"Alarms?"

"If he set it, there's one that goes to an alarm company. But I don't know the code to cancel it. They'll call to see if it's legit."

Sam tapped Hatta on the shoulder. "Well, my friend. If you can make yourself useful, I'll let you pee. You know the code?"

He couldn't get much of a nod in, but it was distinguishable. Sam unwound the tape holding his head to the headrest, left the one over his mouth and cut the tape wound around his ankles and hands. "This could go very well for you. Or, very badly. You choose. Understand?"

Holding it, Hatta got out, hurried a few feet away from the car, pulled it out and let go with a great sigh of relief, his pool of urine following a crack in the blacktop and gathering around the short tufts of grass poking through. He waited another several seconds, knowing that there was more, and when that was done, tucked everything back in, zipped up his pants and turned back to join them.

The lights were off in the office. Nadya used a key to open the door and shined her pen light around the room. A light began to blink on the alarm panel. Sam escorted Hatta to the panel.

"Do your thing."

Hatta stared at the glowing screen, pressed the disarm button and waited, hoping that the action would be enough. It was not. The system wanted a coded input and although he knew what it was, he always got confused when it came time to push the buttons. The code required both letters and numbers and to go from one keyboard to the other required pushing a button that made the switch. The system allowed three attempts.

Sweating, Hatta input the code, whispering to himself.

"One, three, B, F, D." The alarm blinked out, much to Hatta's relief. Seconds later, it blinked back on.

"Try again," Sam whispered. He glanced over at Nadya who had gone to the key cabinet, opened it and was shining her light at the keys. Hatta failed two more times. The phone rang.

Door creaking open, Takat stumbled into the room, cursed when he stubbed his toe on the desk chair answering the phone. "What? No. I don't know why. No. Don't send nobody. I'll check it out."

He hung up and, mumbling to himself, went to the wall switch, turned on the lights and spotted Nadya at the key cabinet. "What are you...,"

Sam pointed the gun. "Hands up."

It took Takat a few seconds to take it all in. They were supposed to go kill Joko and Sam, not bring them back and certainly not to give him the gun and her access to the keys.

Nadya pointed to the key cabinet. "Which one for

Sasi?"

"Nadya? Hamza will skin you alive."

"First he has to catch me."

Sam motioned for Nadya to join him, nudged Hatta toward Takat and motioned for the two of them to stand by the key cabinet. "The key. We can get it the easy way or the hard way. You choose."

"*M*ust I state a name?"

"You must."

"What difference does it make?"

"It assures me that I am in control."

"You've already lost that. Put the stone back down on the table, if you can."

Yes, Sasi had allowed the energy to enter her fingertips, felt the tingling sensation traveling up her arms, a glowing feeling, like being wrapped up a warm, cozy blanket.

Willing her hands to put the stone down brought a feeling of dread, blanket removed, no protection, out in the cold.

She reminded herself that this had nothing to do with comfort. This was all about control. That was a challenge. But, lowering her hands, willing them to let go, gave her instant remorse.

If I set it down, he'll be gone. I may never know what powers lie within. He? I've already determined that this power is masculine?

I don't want to put it down. I've spent my whole life waiting for this moment. And now I'm going to let it go?

But, it was a challenge and Sasi had already determined that she was going to stay in control. She forced her hands down to the table, but they did not release the stone. Trying more forcefully, a sharp pain shot up through her elbows and landed somewhere behind her eyes. A more determined attempt was met with a slightly harsher response.

Sasi recomposed herself, sitting up straight, slowly inhaling while cupping the stone gently between her hands.

I can't compete. Not on his terms. This cannot be an action against him.

There is a time when the stone was on the table. There is a time when I picked it up. There is a time when I was challenged to put it down. There is a time when I placed it on the table and that is where I want to be.

Opening her eyes, Sasi noted, with satisfaction, that she was free of the stone, that it was placed in the middle of the leather cloth that normally contained it, but she had no memory of placing it there.

Did I alter the future? Is that what this stone can do? Or, did I put it there and just don't remember?

She added a bit of tea to her cup, sipped contemplatively as she rotated the piece, watching the dancing light.

OK. I know how to stop you. Kashif, did you get this far? My guess is that you did. Otherwise, how could you have sent Sam and his companions back to a world of his choosing?

Sasi picked up the stone again, cupped it gently and embraced the tingling sensation. She felt like she was inside a cocoon, warm, safe.

"May I come in?"

"Your name?

"Rools. Yours?"

"Sasi."

"May I come in?"

"You will leave at my request?"

"I cannot promise that."

"May I ask, why?"

"I have to protect myself as well. What you do affects me. We'll both be looking out for us."

"I cannot allow that."

"Then..., I choose to leave."

The warm, fuzzy feeling dissipated and the room, dimly lit, seemed eerily quiet. Opening her eyes, Sasi placed the stone, barely glowing, back on the table.

OK. Kashif? What did you do? Was it a mutual relationship, each respecting the other's needs? What did you have to give up?

If I can alter the future, wouldn't that be something? But, is it worth everything?

Picking up the stone, she waited for the tingling sensation. But the firestone remained cool.

163

There was no insulation between the drywall walls of the storage units and the ceiling was not much more than some kind of chain link top with a tarp covering the upper side. Whatever was between that and the roof couldn't have been too much because the scent of a light rain easily permeated Sasi's room.

Sitting in the dark, listening to the drops hitting the corrugated metal roof, Sasi became aware of muffled noises, shuffling footsteps, whispers inside the building. The outside door hinge always creaked when opened or closed and now, whoever had opened it was in the hallway.

Sasi quickly wrapped the leather bag around the firestone, placed it back in the box and put it beneath her pillow, knowing at the same time that her actions weren't going to help anything. Everyone knew that it was here in the room.

She hurried across the room, retrieved her shawl from the bottom of the door, turned on the lamp and then sat at the table waiting with folded hands to see who would come through the door.

She was not surprised to see Hatta and Takat, but very surprised to see Nadya and Sam standing behind them. All four entered the room. Using the gun to point, Sam motioned for the two men to sit at the table and gave the duct tape to Nadya, who began taping them to the chairs, ankles to the legs, arms to the backs.

Sasi retrieved the firestone and joined Sam, who was standing guard near the door, keeping an eye on the hallway. "I was wondering if you might show."

"You know I wouldn't let you down."

Nadya finished taping the men to the chairs and put tape over Takat's mouth. That finished the duct tape roll.

They turned out the light and locked both doors on their way out. Standing outside, Sasi paused for a glance up at the black sky, enjoying the rain hitting her face while breathing in fresh air. "You don't know how much you miss this until you don't have it."

Sam put his hand on her shoulder, patted it and nudged her ahead. "True. But we have to hurry."

They walked back to the front office taking a different path, this time staying on the other side of the units. When they got to the car, they could hear thumping and banging as the car shook from some turbulence inside. Nadya opened the trunk. The man was awake.

"What do you want to do with him?"

"Let's take him into the office. We'll tie him up in Takat's bed."

Nadya laughed. "That'll make Hamza happy. I can see his face already."

They pulled him out, stood him up and helped him hop up the three steps to the front door. Inside, after making him lie down in bed, they wrapped extension cords around him and the bed frame and tied the knots below the mattress.

"Good enough," said Sam, assessing their work. "Let's get out of here."

It was almost six when they finally drove through the exit. Sam, riding in the back seat, put his hand on Nadya's shoulder.

"Stop here for a minute."

"What's wrong?"

"I want to make some adjustments to the gate."

"Oh?"

Sam slipped through the opening before the gate closed, found an old two by four, a rock and, using the rock as the fulcrum, lifted the gate off of the rail track. He then used the rock to destroy the buttons on the panel and, just for good measure, wedged the two by four in between the supporting column and bars of the gate. Slanted at an angle, it also became the ladder to help Sam get out.

Getting back into the car, "That should slow them down."

Nadya smiled. "You really know how to make friends."

165

Aki collected his luggage from the carousel and headed for the exit. "That wasn't so bad, was it, Missy?"

If I never fly again, it will be too soon.

"Isn't it amazing? We can go from one side of the planet to the other in just hours."

What's amazing is that we survived the food.

"It wasn't very good."

Certainly nothing close to a carne asada burrito.

"Or cheese enchiladas."

I miss San Diego already. If I ever fly again, it will only be to go there.

"I'm the one doing the flying. You just tag along."

We're in this together. Are you going to stop and pick up some groceries on the way home?

"I have to. Whatever's in the fridge is probably a science project by now."

What?

"Stuff turns moldy."

I don't know what that means.

The green stuff that gets on food that's been sitting around too long. Like, if you leave bread out, it'll get mold on it."

What happens then?

"I throw it away."

Does that happen to cheese?

"Not with you around. It doesn't have a chance to get old."

So, I'm understanding that we have to eat everything quickly so that it doesn't get moldy.

"Yes. Buy small amounts, stuff that you can consume in the next few days and go shopping more often."

That's what I've been saying all along. Eat more. Get more.

"You're missing the point. Buy fresh. Eat fresh. I'm talking vegetables."

At least meat doesn't do that.

"Of course, it does. All things go bad after a while, especially if we don't refrigerate it."

Wine?

"Some wines get better, the older they get. Red wines, mostly."

So, we could buy several bottles of that. We just have to buy cheese more often.

"What's with you? You're more interested in food than you are in finding the firestone."

And drink. Let's not forget that.

"It's Sam that we should be concentrating on, not food."

Aki..., Argo, whatever you want to call yourself. Some things are inevitable. They are beyond you, out of your reach. You cannot affect them so you might as well not worry about them.

"How can you say that? With my research, I've brought us this far. We re going to find the other stone and come face to face with it. That is my goal. After that, it's up to you, Missy. I've done everything that I can."

You have been a great help. And I have to admit that I've come to like you. I just hope that I don't have to kill you after all you've done.

"What's going to happen?"

Whatever it is, it'll be beyond your control.

"No one can know the future?"

Slightly incorrect. You cannot know which future.

Somehow, everyone always winds up in the kitchen. Sasi cracked open all of the remaining eggs, five of them, into a bowl and beat them with a fork until they were well mixed. Chopped onions sizzled in the pan. "Where is Joko?"

Sam was slicing bread from the loaf. "He left yesterday for parts unknown. We had a little confrontation with Hamza the night before."

"He never did like confrontation. Is he coming back?"

"From the sound of it, no."

"What happened with Hamza?"

"He slipped on a banana peel and broke his nose."

"How does that affect Joko?"

"I guess you could say I was the banana peel and Joko was sitting with me."

"I see. That's why Hamza didn't show last night. I was wondering."

Nadya filled the teapot with water, placed it on the burner and began the search for the tea.

"Over there," said Sasi, pointing to a tin on the counter. "Put in three level scoops."

Sasi wasn't sure yet about Nadya. She watched her out of the corner of her eye and kept her silence. This was a new piece of the puzzle and, somehow or other, she had managed to get Sam's trust in an unrealistically short time. And now, right here in the kitchen, Sasi felt like the snake was in the mouse's den. She watched Nadya put the leaves into the water.

"You worked for Hamza?"

"Yes."

"What made you change sides?"

"I've heard your lectures. What he was doing was wrong."

"He's always been doing wrong."

"Kidnapping you went beyond."

"My lectures weren't that good. What else?"

"Yes, they were. I like how you cut through all of the religious baggage, cultural misconceptions and human acceptance of things that are not true. I admire your vision and I can't tolerate someone messing with it."

Sam put the sliced bread in the toaster, looked over at the eggs, still in the bowl, and decided to wait. "You said you worked for the government."

"That's not true. I had to say that to gain your confidence."

"What are you going to do now? Hamza will be looking for you."

Sasi stirred the onions, decided that they were cooked enough, stirred the eggs one more time and added them to the pan. "What are either of us going to do? Sam, as soon as you're gone, we're victims."

"We need to get the police involved. You need to press charges and he needs to go to jail."

"That will jeopardize the firestone. As soon as the police hear about it, they'll confiscate it."

"That might be a good thing, Sasi."

"I can't believe you said that. You know more than anyone what this stone is capable of."

Nadya went to the cupboards looking for cups. "I keep hearing about this thing. Hamza talked about it from time to time. What does it do?"

"It's a long story," said Sam. "Hopefully, it's all coming to an end. That reminds me." Sam pushed the toast down and left the room. He was back in the kitchen before the toast popped up. "No messages yet."

Sasi retrieved three plates from the cupboard and dished out the egg while Sam buttered toast and Nadya poured tea. They retreated with their breakfasts to the tiny table by the balcony and opened the double doors.

Sasi sat by the window, keeping an eye on the road. "No messages from whom?"

"We've found Aki."

"Where?"

"Hopefully, coming back here. He was in San Diego."

"Does he have the stone?"

169

"More than that."

"What does that mean?"

"According to Zoe...,"

"Who's Zoe?"

"An accomplice in San Diego. Apparently, Aki has made some sort of truce with the force, unlike Dimyati."

"How do you know this?"

"Unwittingly, I set up Zoe and Aki to be partners in training. He was calling himself Argo at the time so I didn't make the connection. She witnessed him defending himself against an attacker with an iron bar. Aki was a beginner, less than that. Yet Zoe said he handled himself masterfully. She got suspicious and got him to fess up."

Sasi sipped her tea. "So, it is true. The spirit controls the body."

"And the stone controls Aki?"

"OK," said Nadya. "I am completely confused. How many stones are there?"

"Two."

"Aki has one and you have one, right?"

"Right."

"Where did they come from?"

Sasi studied Nadya. "It's very complicated, dear. We'll get you caught up later." She turned her attention back to Sam who had finished his eggs in about three bites and was working on the toast. "How did Aki get the stone through customs?"

Mouth full, Sam shook his head. "No idea."

"Maybe," Sasi absentmindedly forked a small bit of egg and forgot to put it in her mouth. "If the spirit is transferred into a human, the stone looks normal."

"Doesn't glow?"

"Right."

"Can I see this stone so that I can at least know what you two are talking about?"

Sam looked over at Sasi. "It's up to her."

Sasi spent a bit of time sipping tea. She didn't want to reveal her secret hiding place beneath the floor so she had hidden the stone in the back of the lowest dresser

170

drawer in her bedroom, not satisfactory, but the best she could do under the circumstances. If Nadya knew that the firestone was in such easy reach, well, that was not satisfactory either.

"I don't think so. Let's wait a bit and see what develops." She looked over at Sam. "Are you waiting for Aki to contact you?"

"I was told that he was on his way."

"So..., it comes down to who gets here first, Hamza or Aki. My goodness, Sam. You really know how to throw a party."

Relieved to be home, Aki let out a big sigh as he put the key into the lock of his apartment and heard it click open. "OK, Missy. Home at last."

Are we going to eat before we meet Sam?

"We're going to shower first, then eat, then get a little rest, then meet up with Sam."

We could eat first, then shower.

"Food tastes better if I'm not all grubby."

How can that make a difference?

"We've been in public transportation for most of the day. I can't help but think that I'm covered in germs. I don't want them falling off into my food."

Thanks for buying cheese. Maybe we should try a little taste before we shower.

"We don't shower. I shower. You're getting too comfortable with thinking that we're a couple."

Not true. If my vote counted a shower would never happen. Lions don't shower.

"You're not a lion."

But I do need to eat.

"No. You don't. You just enjoy the pleasures of life and don't bother with the consequences. That's because you know that you'll be leaving and I'll be stuck with the mess."

If you live.

"Stop bringing that up. We're in the same town as the other firestone. It's across town. We know where it is and who's got it. We're almost there. It's all going to be over soon."

I'm going to miss you, Aki. You've been the best.

"You're going to miss cheese and carne asada burritos. I'm just the guy in the middle."

You're more than that. We're best friends. We've confided in each other.

"I will admit that we could stay friends. You just need to get your own body."

172

If I was female. How would that work out?

"I couldn't handle it."

Oh? So, you do like boys.

"Not like what you're implying. You keep thinking that you're going to become something, usually a human. What if it turns out that you transform into a dog?"

I'll never be a dog. If I can't be a human, I'll be a lion.

"You'd be happy hunting things, ripping them apart and eating them raw?

What do they make carne asada from?

"Beef. It comes from cows."

If I was a lion, I could take down a cow.

"That doesn't mean it's going to taste like carne asada. Anyway. you don't know how to cook."

I can learn.

"Lions are afraid of fire and if you're a lion you won't have hands. How are you going to cook? This conversation is ridiculous."

Aki, you are so negative. The good part is that I won't have to eat all of that green stuff that comes with it.

"I'm tired of this conversation. I'm going to take a shower.

173

"Sam," said Sasi, looking beyond his shoulder. "I just saw two cars go by, cars that I don't normally see coming up this road. Both of them had at least four passengers inside."

"Hamza?"

"Of course."

"Well, they're going to have to come through either the front or back door, maybe both. I don't see them coming up that wall outside your balcony."

"What's your plan?"

Sam studied Nadya, wondering if he'd made a tactical mistake. Yes, she had taken them to Hamza's storage facility and helped him free Sasi. But, was all of that just a ruse to bring them all together? Could she be trusted with a gun? The one thing that would get her back into Hamza's good graces would be to shoot both him and Sasi.

So..., what? Give her the darts and blow gun? Have her protect the entrance to the back door? No. Just as bad. Worse, actually. If she shot him, certainly Hamza would have a fine time taking revenge when he woke up. No. Nadya cannot have a weapon.

Protect her? Yes. He would do that. Without her, he'd still be looking for Sasi. She'd already proven herself to be valuable, extremely valuable. She would be protected but not trusted. Ironic.

"Sasi, do you know how to use a gun?"

"No. I've never held one."

"I do," said Nadya.

"I'm sure that you do. No offense, Nadya. But, as much as you've helped already, I'm not comfortable with you having a gun."

"My life is in danger, same as yours. Worse, maybe, if he catches me alive."

"If you shot the two of us," said Sasi. "You'd probably be forgiven. I'm with Sam."

"So..., how do I protect myself?"

Without answering, Sam got up, retrieved the motion detector coffee cup in the living room and placed it outside the front door near the gate. The one in the kitchen he set outside near the fire ring that Sasi used for cooking. Coming back into the house, he used his cell phone to turn them on. Both Sasi and Nadya looked on with interest.

"Motion detectors," said Sam, sitting beside Nadya. "We have an early warning system." He handed Sasi the gun and showed her how to turn the safety on and off. "Point and shoot. Pretty simple. There's not much kick to it but do expect it. It will shoot as fast as you can pull the trigger. Aim for the chest."

"Maybe we should call the police."

"I think it's too late for that. If those two cars represent Hamza, it's all going to happen in the next ten or fifteen minutes."

"How will you protect yourself?"

"I've got an idea...,"

"Wait," said Nadya. "No offense. But I'm uncomfortable with Sasi having the only gun. Can I say something?"

Sam nodded. "Please do."

"Why don't we group together in the middle? In the hallway. You keep the gun. We'd have access to either bedroom if needed. If they come in the front and back doors at the same time, they'd be shooting at each other. All we have to do is start the fight."

"A wise woman," said Sasi. "I wouldn't trust me with a gun either."

"Good idea." Sam set up the teapot and cups in the living room, same as before. "This won't work as good in the daytime but the noise will startle them."

Sasi looked doubtful. "A teapot? Really, Sam?"

"If you've got earplugs, wear them."

"What's it going to do, whistle?"

"It emits a loud blast and a strobe. The strobe won't do much in the daytime, though."

Nadya nodded. "Noise works. I almost jumped out of my

shoes last night when it went off."

"Because you weren't expecting it. If Hatta is with them today, he might've already mentioned it."

"Still, it's a shock when it goes off."

Sasi's inclination was to head for the hallway, stand there and wait. Instead, she headed back to the table next to the balcony, sat down and sipped what was left of her tea. "This is making me very nervous. I never thought it would end like this."

Sam joined her at the table. "It hasn't ended yet. We don't even know if that was them."

"Did Aki say how long before he got here?"

"I just got a text from him. He was going to shower, get something to eat and then come over."

"Is he aware of our situation?"

"Not yet."

"Maybe you should let him know."

"We could try to meet him somewhere else."

"We shouldn't have come back here. Too obvious."

"I'll warn Aki. We don't want him to arrive in the middle of a gun fight."

"Wouldn't that be something? Everybody arriving at the same time."

Nadya headed for the hallway. "Excuse me. I have to use the rest room."

Watching her movements when they first entered the house, Nadya noticed that Sasi was carrying the firestone when she went into her bedroom, but did not have it when she came back out.

Heading for the bathroom, she paused at Sasi's bedroom door and studied the layout. There was a night stand with a lamp next to her bed and some kind of cabinet below, a closet with a sliding door and, across the room, a dresser with four drawers. The window next to the dresser was closed and locked.

The box was not in plain sight. Logical. If it was that valuable, who in their right mind would leave it out?

On her way out of the bathroom, Nadya paused at Joko's bedroom and noted the layout, a single bed, dresser, closet, a window above the bed at the long end of the room, locked.

It's not that she wanted the stone, but she did want to see it. Hadn't she risked her life to help Sam rescue Sasi? Didn't that prove that she was trustworthy enough to at least see the stone?

Listening to Sam's and Sasi's conversation, this Aki person had some kind of super power, whatever that meant. And didn't Sam say that he defended himself from an attacker with an iron bar? And Sasi implied that he made a truce with the force. Is that what she said?

If these things were true, why wasn't Sasi interested in using the stone now when danger is so near?

Turning, she joined them back in the living room and sat next to Sam. There was a bit of tea left in the pot which she offered up. Both refused.

Pouring the tea into her own cup, she asked a simple question. "If this stone is so powerful, why aren't you using it now?"

There was a long silence at the table, each pondering the question. Finally, Sam looked over at Sasi.

"We haven't had time to talk. What have you discovered

about the firestone since I've been gone?"

It seemed so long ago already, her encounter with Rools. Was that just last night? Sasi wanted very much to talk about it but was hesitant with Nadya sitting there at the table.

Looking over at Nadya, Sasi wondered if Nadya had actually attended any of her seminars. Was her face familiar? There were always a few that sat back in the shadows, late to arrive, first to leave, unwilling to be noticed. She turned her attention back to Sam.

"His name is Rools."

"Whose?"

"In the firestone."

"You've met him?"

"It's more of an encounter than a meeting."

"What did you discover?"

"He wants control, absolute control. I was unwilling to give it. He tested me immediately, as soon as we had an awareness of each other."

"How so?"

"He challenged me to put the stone back down on the table."

"Apparently you did."

"With great effort. It's nearly impossible to overpower him. He wedges himself into your consciousness."

"How?"

"Remember how I talked about the three types of memory?

"The past, present and future?"

"Yes. I had to remember putting the stone down, even though I never had. That was the only way out."

"Remembering the future."

"Yes. But..., I don't remember ever putting the stone down, physically. So, did I change the future? Or have a senior moment?"

"Why didn't you try again?"

"I could not coax Rools back out. And then you arrived. I haven't had a chance since to deal with it."

Nadya cleared her throat. "Why not now?"

178

"How many reasons do you want? There's a good chance that two carloads of armed men are ready to invade my house. There's you, an unknown. Aki on his way sometime soon with the other half and me. I don't want to give control of my life, especially now."

"Yet," said Sam. "Zoe said it helped Aki."

"And how long have he and the stone been together? Have they gotten used to each other? Is there a compatibility issue like with Dimyati? Or, it could be good. Maybe they've learned how to work with each other. I don't know. I'm not willing to take that chance until I have a few quieter moments with the stone."

"Missy, I just got a text from Sam saying that we might be going into a very dangerous situation."

How so?

"He said that the owner of the stone, someone named Sasi, had been kidnapped and...,"

Kidnapped? What does that mean?

"She was taken from her home, or wherever she was, and held prisoner against her will."

Kind of like what I've done to you?

"Yes, like that. Except you didn't take me anywhere. You're holding me prisoner in my own house."

I'm looking after you, Aki. You're very valuable to me.

"I'm still a prisoner. You're using me for your own gain. I have no control."

That's not true. I let you decide what to eat most of the time. And I let you decide what we're going to do.

"Right. Going to San Diego. That's what I wanted to do, fly half way around the world at great expense. It's been on the top of my list for as long as I can remember. And that's the problem. As long as everything's to your benefit, you go along with it.

Tell me that you did not enjoy carne asada burritos.

"OK. They were good. A nice memory. I'll never have another one."

Did I not save your life twice?

"I wouldn't have been in those situations if not for helping you."

Right. Blame your weaknesses on me. Tell me you didn't enjoy working out with Zoe and Jill.

"OK. I did. If I had the chance to do it again, I would. But that's over now. And we're getting off subject. Sam says we're heading into danger. What do you think?"

What do I think about what?

"Shall we not go there until it's safe?"

That's the old Aki talking. You're Argo now, right?

"That was just a guise. I'm the same old Aki."

No. You're not. That's the problem with you. You keep living in the past. You don't know how to use your new skills.

"What new skills? Two lessons of martial arts? That's not a skill."

You've got some bulk. You're stronger, faster, more coordinated. You're smooth with the ladies.

"That's not going to help anything. I've gained weight. I'm not as flexible as I used to be and I'm not sure about my stamina anymore. I'm probably cruising for a heart attack from all of the bad food. If I'm in a dangerous situation, I might have one."

I won't let that happen.

"It's not a matter of choice. Arteries get plugged up from eating high fat food and your heart can't pump blood through them anymore."

What's an artery?

"You're messing with me. Should we go over there, or not?"

Aki, after all we've been though, I think there's no choice but to go, no matter what.

"No matter how dangerous it is?"

Right. I'm not the one dying.

Peering out past the front room curtain, Sam saw four men heading for the front door. Hatta and Takat were among them. The front and back doors were kicked open at the same time.

Sam shot the first person coming through the back door and fired two rounds at the first one coming through the front before ducking into the hallway.

A hail of bullets whizzed by, hitting the door frame, splintering the wood and ricocheting away. Moaning, someone fell in the living room, a clumping thud amongst the many curses. Similar sounds came from the kitchen.

"Don't shoot!" Everybody was yelling. "It's us! Don't shoot! Holy crap!"

In the chaos, shooting from inside the doorway, Sam hit someone in the kitchen with a dart. He reloaded quickly and, not seeing any more action in that direction, moved to the other side of the door. He put another dart into the back of someone rounding the couch. Feeling the sting, the man turned, spotted Sam and fired.

The bullet hit Sam in the leg, cutting through the cloth and ripping through his thigh just below his hip. Seeing that he had been spotted, he attempted a swift backward roll but the man was too fast. Blood began to soak through his jeans.

Seeing Sam bleeding, watching from the other side of the doorway, Sasi gasped, putting her hand to her mouth to stop her scream. She started toward him but Sam waved her back, pointing at the same time for her to go into Joko's room.

Approaching from behind the living room couch, following the man with the tranquilizer dart in his back, Sam spotted Takat and shot him, the bullet hitting him in the ribs. He heard a sound of footsteps from the other side of the wall, coming from the direction of the kitchen, and shot twice through the wall. Whoever it was, crumpled to the floor. Minutes later, someone in the kitchen fell, sounding like he'd grabbed the oven door on the way down. A minute later, the man hit by the dart in the living room collapsed to the floor. An eerie quiet settled over the house.

Gun in hand, Sam did a leaping, forward roll from the hallway over to the sofa and came up into a crouching position, surveying the room. Hatta, shattered gun hand, transferred his weapon to his other side but was shot before he could take aim. Sam turned toward the kitchen, someone moaning, shuffling sounds.

"You in the kitchen, come out with your hands up, no sudden moves and I'll let you live. Do it..., now!"

The back screen door creaked open and slammed shut. Someone ran past the bedroom windows, heading for the street. Sam made his way into the kitchen. Two men were down.

Pain was starting to settle in around Sam's hip. He grabbed a dish towel, folded it into a square and pressed it against the wound, hoping to slow the bleeding. Grimacing, he fell into a chair.

Sasi ventured out, gasping at the men sprawled out everywhere, splattered blood, her house full of holes. She found Sam in the kitchen, gun sitting on the table as he squirmed in the chair.

"You all right?"

Sam nodded with a tight smile.

She retrieved two more dish towels from a drawer and tied them around his leg holding the other towel in place.

"I've got to call an ambulance. Looks like we'll need a few."

"Where's Nadya?"

When the shooting started, Nadya headed for Sasi's bedroom. That wasn't her preferred location or what she wanted to do. She would rather have had a gun, crossbow, knife, anything with which to defend herself.

After Sam fired the first two shots, he ducked back into the hallway and wound up between her and Sasi, splitting them and forcing them to opposite sides of the door. Seeing Sam signal for Sasi to head into Joko's room, she went into Sasi's.

She hadn't been looking for the firestone. The truth of the matter was that she was hoping for something like a baseball bat, something that she could use to whack the first person coming through the door. Not finding anything useful in the closet, she headed for Sasi's dresser and began to rifle through the contents, hoping for a knife or something that she could use to stab.

The box just found its way into her hands. Hearing gunshots and fighting, she really wasn't thinking clearly. Unwrapping the cloth and holding the firestone, wondering what to do with it, thinking that possibly she could throw it at her attackers if they entered the room, she noticed a tingling sensation in her hands.

Was that a voice? In the middle of all of the turmoil, was someone talking clearly? Asking her name? Compared to the violence in the house, this voice was more like an island in the storm.

"Nadya," she answered, glancing around the room. "Who is this?"

Rools. May I come in?

Nadya answered with a short nod, wondering at the same time how Rools was going to make that happen. In an instant, he was sitting beside her on some sort of couch inside her head.

Thank you.

Nadya forgot about everything else. She whirled around, looking for someone, dismayed to find no one.

184

I'm not out there. I'm in here, with you.

"Go away!"

No. Not until I choose to leave.

Remembering the stone, Nadya tried to throw it down, but she could not let go. Her hands were stuck together, both clenching the stone. The harder she tried to rid herself of it, the tighter her grasp.

Nadya, for your own good, relax. There are more important things going on. I hear gunshots.

"Who are you? *Where* are you?"

Rools. You are in danger. Where is your weapon?

"I..., I don't have one. Where are you?"

Inside your head.

"Go away!"

Set the stone down. I will allow that. Take off your shoes, grab that glass on the dresser and see what's happening on the other side of the door. Take the pillow with you.

"I will not!"

I'm doing this for you.

"No!"

The pain started behind her eyes, feeling like they were being pulled inward, stretching out of shape. A high pitched whistle wailed loudly between her ears. Nadya collapsed onto the bed

Set the stone down.

That she agreed with. She put it on the night stand and held her hands over her ears, to no avail.

Grab the pillow. Pick up the glass.

Getting the pillow was easy. Nadya wrapped it around her head hoping to make the sound go away. The pain began to subside after the pillow so she reached for the glass.

I'm your partner, Nadya. I'm looking out for you. Go over to the door, open it quietly and investigate.

Peering through the crack of the opened door, Nadya saw no one. Cringing at the sound of a creaking hinge, she left Sasi's room, tip-toed over to the doorway leading into the rest of the house.

Three men were sprawled out on the living room floor,

185

two of them shot, lying in pools of blood, the other looking more like he was asleep.

There were voices coming from the kitchen. Sam and Sasi? Nadya started in that direction.

Stop!

The voice was so commanding that Nadya froze in place. Takat, crawling on his hands and knees, leaving a trail of blood, crawled out from behind the sofa, heading toward the kitchen, stopped when he caught a glimpse of Sasi, her back turned toward him as she attended to Sam's wound. He raised his gun.

Nadya, throw the glass where it will shatter. Throw the pillow at him and duck out of sight. Do it, now!

The glass shattered next to Takat, who jumped at the sudden noise. He whirled around to shoot his attacker but was hit with the pillow. From the kitchen, two shots rang out. Takat fell to the floor.

Something was wrong with Nadya and Sasi was trying to put her finger on it. Before the battle she seemed to be reasonably composed, even coming up with the plan that likely saved all three of them from assassination.

But now she was mumbling. If Sasi didn't know better, she was thinking that the woman had suffered a setback from shock, gunshots, bullets flying everywhere, everything getting ripped apart.

Was it shock? Really? Nadya had a pretty good grip on what to do before this shooting. She'd been with Hamza. She would know about violence. "Nadya? You OK?"

"Uh, yeah, fine."

"You need a shot of something? Whiskey? I've got some of Joko's stuff still here, unless he took it."

Nadya sat down at the table opposite Sam. "I..., I'm fine."

Nadya. Seems like I came in at the end of something. Who are these people?

"Sam..., and Sasi."

Both of them turned their attention to Nadya, speaking at the same time. "What?"

"Uh, nothing. I'm just..., having a moment."

Sasi went to the cupboard, retrieved a glass, filled it with water and handed it to Nadya. "You need something stronger?"

"Yeah. I'll take a shot of that whiskey."

"Me, too," said Sam. "I could use a little something to soften the moment."

Sasi retrieved three small glasses from the cupboard, grabbed the bottle of whiskey, relieved to find that Joko had left it behind, poured some for everyone and left the bottle on the table.

"Joko must've been very anxious to leave if he left this behind. This is an expensive bottle."

"To Joko," said Sam, raising his glass.

Sasi nodded. "To you, Sam. For keeping us alive."

187

They clinked glasses. Sam finished his in one gulp. Sasi sipped hers, frowning with the sting of alcohol going down. Nadya watched the two of them and then sipped hers.

Nadya, what was that?

"Whiskey."

This is not good for you.

"Shh."

Sasi set her glass down, filled another with water and took several sips, wanting to smooth her throat. "What about whiskey?"

Nadya seemed surprised by the question. "What?"

"You said something about whiskey and then shushed yourself. Are you OK?"

"I'm fine. Just a little shook up."

Sam stood. "Sasi, could you get me the cord I saw in your cupboard? That, or something a little stronger. I want to tie these two up before they wake up."

"Right. And then I'm going to call for police, ambulance, house repair. You're bleeding pretty bad, Sam."

"I'm OK. Let's start with this guy here in the kitchen."

Nadya set her whiskey down and started to stand. Sasi tapped her shoulder gently. "That's OK. We got this. You rest."

Aki, what was that sound?

"When I was getting out of the car?"

When we were getting out of the car. Bang! Bang! Something like that.

"It sounded like gunshots."

The front door is open.

"I see that."

You never leave your front door open.

"That's because I never know who's going to come through."

You never have visitors. You could leave your door open and it wouldn't make any difference.

"You're saying that I have no friends?"

Yes, except for Zoe. I think she likes you.

"Really? You think so?"

No. Not like that. I think Zoe and Jill have a thing for each other, if you ask me.

"I'm not asking. I'd rather think that she likes me. We're off subject. You *always* do that. What about this door?"

Approaching their prey, a lion would stay out of sight until they are close.

"Sam is not prey and you're not a lion. But I agree with you."

Aki slipped through the gate quickly and approached the house along the edge of the walkway, keeping an eye on the front door. Coming up to the entrance and peering inside, he spotted bodies sprawled out across the living room floor.

Yuck, Aki. Blood!

"You talk about taking down a cow. This shouldn't bother you."

Cows are tasty. Not so sure about humans.

"Do I go in?"

You have the firestone handy?

"Of course."

Then, I would say, yes.

189

"You really don't care if I live or die, do you?"

We're very close to the end. You'll probably be rid of me within the next mile, or two.

"Twenty to forty minutes?"

You count your way. I'll count mine.

"At least Sam's not one of these guys. If the firestone is here, what are you going to do?"

Lions never plan ahead. We have to see what happens.

"You're not a lion."

How can I predict what I'm going to do until I see what's going on?

"Good point. I'm going in."

Are you going to knock first?

"Undecided. If Sam's dead, the person that killed him might answer the door."

Agreed. I'd say go in. Don't step in the blood.

"It's very messy. I hear voices."

Are you going to sneak up on them?

"Don't know. Don't want to get shot."

The stone's in your pocket, right?

"You're more worried about that than you are me."

As it should be.

"After all I've done for you."

Your heart's pounding.

"Of course, it's pounding."

You're the one who mentioned heart attacks.

"I'm fully aware of that. Shut up."

Be calm.

"Shh."

It's just that you have been good. If I walk away from this happy, I want you to walk away happy, too.

"A nice sentiment. Thank you. Now shut up."

What's with all the dead people?

"Like, I should know?"

Aki stepped over the first body and walked around the second. "Hello? Anybody here?"

That was brave, Aki. I didn't think you had it in you.

"Get ready to duck."

Staying on the floor and twisting around to the side of the doorway, Sam grabbed his gun, released the safety and watched the approaching shadow on the living room wall. "Stop! Or, I'll shoot."

"It's me, Argo. Is that you, Sam?"

"You alone?"

"Right. Just me."

Just me? Aki, I'm here, too.

"Shh."

This is my moment. You have to admit that I'm here.

"Not yet."

Sam peered out from behind the doorway. "Who are you talking to?"

"I'm very nervous, Sam. I'm talking to myself. Am I allowed in?"

Sam motioned for him to enter. "Yeah. You're allowed. Very bold of you to come in here."

"I debated."

"Watch out for broken glass."

Aki stepped around Takat, crunched through the glass and entered the kitchen. There, he spotted three more bodies and Sasi, standing over one of them with a roll of cord. Nadya was at the table with a drink.

"Looks like I missed something."

"Party's not over," said Sasi, reaching out to shake his hand. "I'm Sasi."

"That's Nadya over there," said Sam. "I'd stand, but I want to tie this guy up. Cord please, Sasi."

She handed him the cord, scissors and then headed off to call the police. She decided to call from her bedroom where the kitchen conversation would not interfere.

But, entering her room, she spotted the dresser's spilled contents, stuff scattered on the floor and the firestone sitting on top of her night stand.

Oh - My - God!

She picked up the firestone, noted its coloring, that

191

it felt cold and waited for a tingling sensation. Nothing. Forgetting to make any calls, she hurried back into the kitchen and helped Sam finish tying the man up.

"That was quick. Did you call?"

"Not yet. The man in the other room moved so I'll help you out there first."

"I'll get him. Go make the call."

"You're hurt," Sasi said, rather sternly. "I'll help *you* and then call."

The tone wasn't right, not from Sasi. Seeing her motion with her eyes toward the living room, he finished up and stood. Aki spotted the blood-soaked towels.

"Sam! What...,"

"It's nothing. Sit down. We'll be right back."

"Should I sweep up the glass?"

"No. Don't touch anything. Wait for the police."

Going out into the living room, out of their hearing range, Sasi whispered, "Nadya had her hands on the firestone. I think she's possessed. Thought she was acting strange."

Nadya, did I not help you save a person's life?
"So?"
You might've been the next one killed.
"So..., what?"
That should tell you that I'm looking out for you.
"I don't know who you are, but...,"
Rools. I keep telling you.
"You need to go away."
And I've already said, no.
In a sudden move, Nadya grabbed the glass and gulped a large quantity of whiskey.
I'm looking out for you, Nadya. Why don't you trust me?
"Go away."
No more of that stuff. It hurts our throat.
"My throat."
I feel what you feel.
"No, you don't. Never."
Push the glass away.
"No."
The pain began behind her eyes. Nadya blinked several times, attempting to keep the room in focus. She wanted to wipe her sudden tears away but kept her hands on the glass.
Let go of it.
"No."
Nadya?
"No."
"I will not give in. I will not. I will *not!*"
Inside her head, sirens, high pitched, wailing, a low volume pain.
Nadya?
She gritted her teeth, closed her eyes and tightened her grip on the glass. "No."
Louder, tickling the highest pitch she could possibly hear, louder, becoming unbearable. Letting go of the glass, she sat quietly at the table in a stunned and now

somewhat drunken silence.

I do this for you, Nadya.

Aki sat down beside her, nodding hello as he took the adjacent chair, wanting to keep an eye on the living room doorway. She looked up with a short smile. "Hi."

She pushed her whiskey glass away, put it next to Sam's empty glass. A few seconds later, she pulled it back in her direction. The glass wound up somewhere in-between.

Aki watched with interest. "Can't decide?"

He waited for her reply, but when there was none, turned the bottle so that the label was facing him. "Whiskey?"

"I'd drink rubbing alcohol if I thought it would help."

"What happened?"

Nadya looked at him like he was insane. "Um, looks like a shoot-out to me."

"Who are these people?"

"They work for Hamza, did anyway."

Nadya abruptly reached for her drink, took another swig and, exhaling, set the glass down hard. "Yes, I will."

"You will..., what?"

"I didn't say anything."

"You said, "I will." But you didn't say what."

"Did I? I was wondering if I was going to finish this."

Aki was thinking it sounded a lot like his conversations with Missy. "This is forty percent alcohol. You should eat something with that so you don't destroy your stomach."

Good move, Aki. See if there's any cheese in the fridge.

"No."

This time it was Nadya that was confused. "No..., what?"

"I was just thinking that I should see if there's something for you to eat."

"Why?"

"So you don't screw up your stomach."

"There are dead people lying around. You think I'm worried about my stomach?"

"Probably not. That's why I said, no."

"You always talk to yourself?"

"A lot more than I used to."

194

You're not talking to yourself, Aki. You're talking to me!

"Six people are dead," said Nadya. "Anybody still breathing is probably talking to themselves."

"How'd you get involved?"

"Hamza kidnapped Sasi. I didn't agree with that."

"Who do you work for?"

"It was Hamza. Nobody, now."

"Is he," Aki waved toward the bodies, "one of these?"

"No."

"His flunkies?"

"Right."

Aki tilted the bottle into the light so he could read the label. "How is that whiskey?"

Now you're talking, Aki! Don't forget the cheese.

"I can't taste it. I should be calling the police. They told me just to sit here. I feel useless."

"Me, too. Why did they kidnap Sasi?"

"Something about a firestone."

Aki! This is it! The firestone is here, in this house!

"Firestone?"

"That's what I'm told. I haven't seen it yet."

That's not true, Nadya. You will not be telling lies. I won't allow it. Tell him about us.

"How do you know Sam?"

"I met up with him in San Diego and..,"

"San Diego?"

Nadya? Tell him about us.

"California..., America."

Land of cheese enchiladas and carne asada burritos! Tell her about that, Aki. We can all move there. This place is depressing.

"OK?"

"I was starting to take lessons from him but he was suddenly called back here."

"Lessons?"

"Martial arts."

"So, you followed him to Lampung?"

"Not exactly. I'm from here. I just came back."

"OK, wait. Why are you here now? In this house. Did he

195

ask you to be here?"

"Yes."

"Today?"

"Right."

"At this time?"

"He said as soon as possible and gave me this address."

"How are you connected? Wait. That didn't sound right." Nadya laughed at her joke, a slightly drunken perspective, and then abruptly grabbed her glass and slammed the last bit of whiskey. "Who are you?"

"Argo."

You might as well stop using that name, Aki. It serves no purpose anymore.

"Are you the police?"

"No."

"Good, cause you didn't look like one."

"What do they look like?"

"Smug."

"I'm not that."

"I feel like I know you from somewhere."

"I was thinking the same thing."

"Do you live around here?"

"No, up the coast."

"Where'd you go to school?"

"Hawaii."

"Oh, not that. Hobbies?"

"Nothing, really. I'm into healthy living, eat well, exercise...,"

Way to wow them, Aki. Healthy living. Really? No wonder you don't have any girlfriends.

"And you, hobbies?"

"Photography. But I don't think that's going to make me much money. I've gotta find a job. What kind of work do you do?"

Aki! She was the one at the lake, taking pictures of ducks. Remember?

"I make my money in stocks, mostly. Are you in danger from..., what's his name? Hamza?"

"Maybe. But he's going to jail. I just have to avoid him until they catch him. Sam better give me my gun back."

Aki was beginning to feel a sense of purpose. This girl was in need of help. As odd as it seemed, with bodies strewn throughout the house, he wanted to ignore all of that, find another glass, pour them both a bit of whiskey and get to know her.

"Have you got a place to stay..., where he can't find you?"

"No.

"If you need a place to hide, I've got an extra room."

Smooth, Aki! I am impressed!

"Thanks for the offer. But you don't know me..., or what I'm about."

"I'm a pretty good judge of character."

"I was Hamza's girlfriend. I carry a gun."

"That was yesterday."

Sam came back into the kitchen and joined them at the table. Sitting, he readjusted the towel covering his wound and tightened the other two holding it in place. "Sasi's making the calls. Get ready for a swarm."

"I'm hearing sirens," said Nadya. "Those are sirens, right? It's not just me?"

Aki pointed at the bottle. "I think it's the whiskey."

Sam, sending a text to Kathryn, Paul and Melissa, shook his head. "No. They're real. Don't let him pull your leg."

Pull her leg? What does that mean, Aki?

Nadya, if he's going to pull our leg, I'm going to have something to say about that.

197

His name was Bambang. He was only about five and a half feet tall but his wide shoulders suggested that he was very much into weight lifting or wrestling, probably both, when he was still in school.

Today, unshaven, hot and sweaty and with slightly graying hair, he looked much older. His breath smelled like he'd had a beer along with his garlic infused lunch and his red, watery eyes suggested that he had not slept well the night before.

Gun in hand, he was the first one up to the house. Sam met him on the doorstep and motioned for him to enter. Sasi, opening the balcony windows to let in fresh air, sat in her normal spot at the table while Nadya and Aki placed themselves on the couch.

Seeing the bodies, Bambang crunched over the glass to the kitchen, glanced inside and then did the same with the two bedrooms. Coming back into the living room, he motioned to the next man standing at the door.

"Eddi. Post somebody at the back door. Nobody comes or goes without my permission. Get a photographer in here, coroner, see if anybody's still breathing. Nobody touches anything."

He motioned for Sam to sit at the table with Sasi. "You four must have some story to tell. We're going to record this conversation, so think before you talk." He pointed to Sasi. "Who are you?"

"Sasi."

"You made the call?"

"Yes."

"You're the one that was kidnapped."

"Yes."

"Who was it that kidnapped you?"

"Hamza."

"Is he one of the dead ones?"

"No. He's not here."

"You know where we can find him?"

Sasi pointed to Nadya. "She probably does."

Bambang turned his attention to her. "Who are you?"

"Nadya."

"You know where we can find this guy?"

"Maybe. He's got a lot of hiding spots."

"How is it that you know him?"

"Ex-girlfriend."

"Oh. Just for the record, since when?"

"A few days ago."

"You had an argument?"

"Disagreement."

"OK. We'll get back to that." Bambang turned his attention to Sam. "Who are you?"

"Sam."

"How are you involved?"

"I'm visiting my cousin, Sasi."

"You from here?"

"No. America, California."

"Give me the address. Where are you staying while you're visiting?"

"With Sasi, here at the house."

"OK. I'm coming back to you in a minute. You on the couch. Who are you?"

It suddenly occurred to Aki that he was in an untenable situation. Everyone here knew him as Argo. If he gave his real name and was linked to the firestone, he would be charged with Dimyati's murder.

Bambang was impatient. "What's the matter? Forgot your name?"

"There's more to it than that."

"Give me a name now, just for the record."

"Argo."

"How are you involved?"

"Sam invited me here."

"You two friends?"

"No. He's my sensei."

"Oh. You live in America, too?"

"No. I live here."

"How is he your sensei if you live on opposite sides of

199

the planet?"

"It's hard to explain."

"You don't know your name and you don't know how you got here. I'll definitely be coming back to you."

Bambang turned back to Sasi. "How did you get away from your kidnappers?"

"Sam and Nadya. I don't know how they broke in, but they got the key that unlocked my door and brought me back here."

"Where were you being held?"

"Nadya would know that."

Nadya shifted on the couch. "It's an old warehouse. I can show you."

"What I don't get," said Bambang, scratching his chin, "is how you and Sam hooked up. I don't see a connection."

"I had a run-in with Hamza," said Sam. "I was having a beer with Sasi's brother at a bar when Hamza came in. He was giving Joko, her brother, a hard time. I stepped in."

"That doesn't explain Nadya."

Nadya got up, stepped over the body and joined them at the table. "Hamza got hurt. He wanted revenge. So, he sent a few of us over to kill or capture Sam and Joko last night. Sam was waiting for us."

"Are there more bodies that I'm not aware of?"

"No..., not that I know of."

"OK. So, you join Sam, show him where Sasi is and bring her back here. Have I got that right?"

Everybody nodded.

"Did anyone expect retribution from Hamza?" Bambang, glancing from Sam to Sasi, let his eyes rest on Nadya. "Judging from your looks, all of you did, except Mr. no-name here. I'm wondering why nobody called the police."

Silence.

"Interesting answers, all of you. Which brings me to the next question, Sasi. Why, out of more than a million people in this town, did Hamza decide to kidnap you? Is there a ransom note somewhere?"

200

"According to Joko," said Sam. "She was reported as missing."

"Who's Joko?"

"My brother."

"Where is he now?"

"Parts unknown," said Sam. "He was terrified that Hamza was going to kill him after our encounter in the bar."

"OK. I think I got everything, except for this guy. Argo, you weren't a part of any of this so far, right?"

"Right."

Eddi came into the room with the photographer, coroner and two others.

"Eddi," said Bambang. "See if there's a missing person report on this lady here and run a check on Hamza, whatever his last name is. Put out a warrant for his arrest. Consider him armed and dangerous."

Then Bambang turned back to Sam. "Were you here when she went missing?"

"No."

"Had you already planned to be here at this time?"

"No. I flew in after Joko contacted me."

"You dropped whatever it was that you were doing so that you can fly half way around the planet to help save your cousin? You must be pretty close cousins."

"We'd just recently made contact. I felt an obligation."

"You didn't think the police could do their job?"

"I had no idea. Once I got here, everything happened fast."

Bambang turned to Aki. "Figured out your name yet?"

"Like I said, Argo."

"Let me see some ID. And while you're doing that, the rest of you can fill me in on why Hamza kidnapped you. Everyone's holding back and I don't know why. We'll start with you, Sasi."

The bodies were identified, removed and on their way to the morgue, their chalk outlines on the floor remained. Bullet holes were marked and bullets removed. There was a crowd in Sasi's house, everyone getting fingerprints, collecting evidence for one thing or another. Several reporters and camera crews waited anxiously outside, hungry dogs waiting for scraps of information.

Bambang retired to the small courtyard in back of Sasi's house along with Sasi, Sam, Nadya and Aki. They sat in the shade of the house on the east side next to the fire pit on chairs brought out from the kitchen.

"OK. I've got everybody's story and, according to your versions anyway, I know what happened up to this point. What I want now is to see these firestones. Sasi, go get yours. Aki you say you've got yours with you. Let's see it."

Aki removed the rock from his backpack and handed it to Bambang, who turned it around several times, examining it from different angles. "Looks like a plain old rock to me."

Aki nodded in agreement. "Doesn't look like much, does it?"

Sasi returned and handed her firestone to Bambang. He held one in each hand, compared the weight of one to the other, their different shapes and, standing and moving out into the sunlight, rotated each so he could compare how they reflected or refracted the light.

Coming back into the shade, he handed the firestones back to their owners. "I don't understand. I've got three bodies, two prisoners, a warrant out for Hamza, a shot-up house, you four and a circus news frenzy out front, all over these two rocks. What am I missing? None of you look stupid, so I'm guessing that there are things that you're not telling me. Anybody want to talk?"

While Bambang had most everyone's attention, Sasi was keeping her eye on Nadya and Aki. Aki was controlling it better, possibly because he'd been with the stone's spirit longer, but Nadya seemed to be doing a lot of internal mumbling.

Sasi was not sure how to approach her after all of this hullabaloo died down. Nadya was two people now. Which one would she be talking to? Since she didn't know her well to begin with, how could she compare?

Same with Aki. What was his spirit's name? No way to judge which one is talking. Do these spirits know each other? Are they aware of each other? Just the fact that they're not showing themselves now was proof that their hosts had some kind of control.

What she really wanted was for everyone to go away so that she could sit down and find out what was going on inside their heads. She looked over at Sam to see how he was taking it, but he was busy examining the bandage on his leg.

Bambang reluctantly returned Sam's passport, verified Aki's address and asked Nadya if she needed police protection, which she declined.

"Where will you be staying?"

Nadya shrugged. Hamza had friends everywhere. Surely someone in the police department would have access to her whereabouts. "I'll find an out-of-the-way place and keep in touch."

That wasn't quite satisfactory to Bambang, who wanted to keep everyone under his thumb until this mystery was solved. But these people hadn't actually committed a crime. What they had done, remarkably, was successfully defend themselves against five armed attackers. They were victims, not criminals.

"That will have to do. I've got everyone's contact information. Nobody go anywhere. I still have lots of questions."

When the place cleared out and the door was closed, Sasi busied herself with brewing tea while Aki and Nadya brought in the chairs and seated themselves at the kitchen table. Sam attempted to nail the door frames back into their housings.

When they were all seated at the table, teapot in the middle and a box of cookies opened up, Sasi looked over at Nadya. "So.., how are you and Rools getting along?"

Nadya, whose complexion was normally a golden tan, turned white. "Who?"

"Rools, your new companion. How are you two getting along?"

"I..., I'm not sure what you mean."

"I've been working with Rools for thirty years and I've just recently learned his name. I've been..., maybe too careful. You pick up the stone one time and become possessed. How does it feel?"

"I can help with that," said Aki. "Nadya, how are you doing? Are you OK?"

"I'm going crazy."

"I know what's happening to you."

Nadya smiled, a tight smile to all of them and began to stand. "I'll keep in touch. I think it's time for me to go."

"Please sit," said Aki, reaching out, lightly tugging at her arm. "I can help you. What I have to say may save your life."

"How do I make it go away?"

"You can't. Not until it wants to."

"I can't stand it. My privacy is invaded."

"It's not as bad as you think."

Not as bad? Aki, give me some credit. You're much improved over what you were. Think of all the things we've...,

"Once you get used to..., what's his name? Rools? You'll have a friend."

"Anything that invades my space is not a friend. I want it gone."

Nadya, I did not invade your space. I asked if I could come in and you nodded, yes.

"Now I'm asking you to leave."

I choose to stay. We can either get along. Or, I can make things unpleasant for you. I can be your friend.

"No way."

Sasi and Sam watched this verbal transaction with

interest. Aki could almost hear the conversation.

"Nadya. Would you like some tea?"

A momentary distraction. Nadya, incredulous, stared at Aki. "What?"

"Has he told you that he's chosen to stay?"

"Yes."

"Give him the opportunity to go back. Sasi, can you please give Nadya your firestone?"

"I don't want it. I'll never touch it again."

"That's a mistake. Give Rools a chance to go back. That's the first step."

"He says he doesn't want to."

"Still, offer him the chance. If he doesn't go, you'll have to learn how to live with him."

"Never."

"There was a man named Dimyati who had possession of this firestone before me. He could not accept the idea of someone else's spirit coexisting with him and jumped off of a cliff. I don't want that to happen to you. You're too beautiful of a person to not be here with us."

Aki! I am impressed! My, how you've grown, thanks to me.

Hi Kathryn,

Just to let you know, everybody's fine. I'm staying with Sasi again at her house. Seems a few people turned up dead so I can't leave the country until they clear things up. You all are going to get an earful when I come back.

Say Hi to Melissa and Paul for me. Give Capn a scratch and a plain donut from me. I'll pay you back for the donut when I come home. Please give yourself a hug and my love. I miss you all and am anxious to come home. The first thing I want is to eat your mahi-mahi grilled tacos with a long, cold beer, chips and salsa. OMG that sounds good!

Sam

Kathryn read the text several times hoping to squeeze more information out of it than was there.

A few people turned up dead? How can everybody be fine if some people died? Sam, you can't just leave me hanging like that.

Well, you did. But it's not right.

Give myself your love. What does that mean?

Kathryn went topside and pulled the canopy over the cockpit so that she could sit in the shade. Capn decided to join her when she went below to retrieve her coffee and on her way back up, grabbed a treat for him.

It was not often that she got a Thursday off from work so the ambience was a pleasant surprise. Her neighbors on the dock, most of whom worked during the week, were gone until sometime around four and the weekenders, as they were called, hadn't arrived yet. That noise would begin sometime around four on Friday.

So, the morning was quiet, a sunny morning with hardly a breeze. The water in the marina was glassy and the place was almost hers alone except for the maintenance people coming through to collect trash and the occasional diver passing by to scrub some boat's hull. Capn settled in at her feet and savored the treat for about ten seconds, sniffed around for any crumbs, looked up, saw there was no more coming, so put his head on his paws with a sigh.

Hey Sam,

Got the day off today. The marina sure is quiet when everybody's gone. Paul's in school until two and is busy with his finals. He's getting straight A's. Hard to believe. He and Melissa are talking to each other all the time. I think they're becoming a "thing." That would be nice. She keeps him on his toes and cuts no slack.

I'd love to BBQ some mahi-mahi when you get back. Paul's come up with a spectacular mango salsa to go with it and we've found some better corn tortillas, thin and light. I'm getting hungry just thinking about it. I think I'll see if he and Melissa are up for dinner tomorrow night. Mmm. You lose, buddy. That's what you get for not hanging around.

Missing you, too. Give yourself a hug from me.
xoxo
K

Kathryn debated about the x's and o's for a while. Appropriate? Too suggestive? It's just a sign of affection. Right? People do that all the time.

Deciding that it was OK and that it might, just might, lead into something more, she sent it off.

The vote was two to two. Sasi and Sam wanted Aki and Nadya to stay at Sasi's house. They voted to go.

"We're safer if we stay together," argued Sam.

"This place is a target now," Nadya replied. "If Hamza's looking for me, he'll be looking here."

"He won't come around," said Sasi. "There's a warrant out."

"You don't know him like I do. I'm going to go find some woodwork to crawl into until I know he's in jail. Even then...,"

Nadya trailed off, either hearing some other voice or imagining how far Hamza's wrath might reach, Sasi couldn't tell. She waited for the rest, but when it didn't come, went into the kitchen, retrieved the cloth for the firestone and the box that contained them. Coming back into the living room, she handed them to Nadya.

"You'll be wanting these. They won't do me any good anymore."

Nadya didn't want them either but took them, wrapped the firestone inside the canvas and placed it in the box.

"I'm going to ask Rools to leave every day."

Inching his way to the door, Aki smiled. "I do that, too. But, he knows he's got it too good to leave."

"I'm going to make his life hell."

"Careful. That works both ways."

There were hugs all around at the front door. Sam accompanied Nadya and Aki out to Aki's car, an old gray Suzuki Swift with more than a few dents in it.

"I'm not a bad driver," said Aki. "Some of these dents just happened overnight. I came out in the morning and there they were."

Sam smiled. "That's what they all say. Nadya? You sure you don't want me to call a cab?"

"Any cab I take will deliver me to Hamza. I'm leaving with Aki. He says he'll drop me off wherever."

Aki. How sweet it is! She wants to go with us!

208

"It's not like that."

Nadya tried the handle of Aki's passenger side door but found it locked. "It's not like what?"

"I'm having a conversation with my other half. Sometimes he's an idiot."

"And which one is talking now?"

"Me, Aki."

An idiot? Aki, you know I'm always for you.

Saying good-bye again, Sam watched as they got into the car. "You sure you two won't change your minds?"

Aki shook his head. "I've been gone for way too long. I want to go home."

"How about you, Nadya. You're probably safer here."

"Thanks, Sam. But I want to disappear. I'll call as soon as I know where I'm going to be."

Sam watched as they drove away, his heart heavy. This was not turning out at all like what he'd expected. And if it was ending oddly for him, Sasi must be devastated.

Going back inside, he found her sitting at the table in the living room, cup of tea between her hands as she stared out the balcony window. He sat down across the table from her and poured himself a cup.

"How are you doing?"

"All these years I've studied that stone..., and it's gone in a heartbeat."

"What will you do now?"

"I'm not sure."

"Nadya loved your lectures. Throw yourself into them."

"It's a small crowd, Sam. And a lot of what I discussed was discovered through the firestone. You are right, though. There's a whole lot more that I can talk about. "

"Like?"

"We know so little about what comes next."

"The future?"

"Death."

"Maybe Nadya will convince Rools to...,"

"You don't see Aki losing his partner, do you? I'm beginning to think that they're going to be hosts until they die."

"Hamza's still on the loose. That may come sooner than we think. Let me ask you this. If you have a chance to own the firestone again, would you take it?"

"Too soon to tell. I don't know that I would ever allow another presence inside my head. So, with that in mind, I guess not. It's time to let it go. I would very much like to know how the four of them are going to get along."

"Four?"

"Nadya, Rools, Aki and his visitor. I hope we get a chance to see how they develop."

"They might keep coming back for advice."

"I hope so. When are you leaving?"

"I want to hear that Hamza's caught. I'll stay until then."

"You're watching out for me?"

"Of course, I am."

"I don't think I'm worth Hamza's trouble anymore. You can probably go anytime."

"Not a chance. I like your cooking too much."

Driving away, Aki breathed a sigh of relief, exhaling slowly. "Whew..., glad that's over."

"It must've been quite a shock, walking into that."

"I can't imagine what you went through..., are still going through. How are you handling it?"

Nadya released her seat belt and leaned forward, keeping her profile below window level. "Let me know when you get lost in traffic. No need for anybody to see us together."

"Right. So..., how are you doing?"

"Haven't had time to think about it."

"How is he?"

"Who?"

"Rools."

"I don't want to think about it."

"You're going to have to." Aki turned left, heading toward the main road. "Where do you want to go?"

"With you."

"Me? Back to my house?"

"If that's OK."

"You sure?"

Aki. This beautiful woman wants to go home with you and you're trying to talk her out of it? And you call me an idiot.

"You're right. I have to deal with Rools. You've already been through this. You're the one I need to talk to."

Hooray!

"I just got back into the country. I don't have much to eat at my apartment. Would you like to stop somewhere?"

"No. Maybe pick up some groceries on the way. I've got money."

Aki laughed. "No need for that. What do you like to eat?"

This is important, Aki. Pay attention.

"I am."

"You are, what?"

211

"Missy was telling me to pay attention."

"You always talk like that?"

"We have a constant conversation."

"Doesn't that drive you crazy?"

"It did at first. We've gotten used to it."

"You say, we. You act like you accept her."

"What else can I do?"

"Did that guy really jump off the cliff?"

"Saw it with my own eyes."

"Is this what I have to look forward to?"

"Nadya, I have no idea. So much depends on how you two get along."

"You have arguments?"

"Disagreements. We've learned to compromise."

"What's the biggest problem?"

Aki laughed. "What we're going to eat. I'm all about health. Missy is just the opposite."

"What do you like?"

"Rice, pasta, lots of vegetables. A little bit of fish and chicken."

"And Missy?"

"Beef, pork, lamb, sausages, cheese, eggs, anything that will clog my arteries."

"I'm with Missy."

Aki, she's a keeper! Ask her if she likes wine.

"No."

"No..., what?"

"Missy wants to know if you like wine. I said, no."

"I do like wine."

Does she likes carne asada burritos?

"She won't know what those are."

"What?"

"Carne asada burritos. I said, you wouldn't know what they were."

"What are they made of?"

"Beef, flour tortillas, guacamole...,"

"You're right. I don't know. You know how to make them?

"No. But we can look up the recipe. You like to cook?"

212

Might as well look up cheese enchiladas while we're at it.

"Anything that takes my mind off of Rools and Hamza is good for me. The police should've let me keep my gun."

"It was used in a crime."

"But, Sam didn't even press charges. I helped him find Sasi. If not for me, they'd still be looking. What do you have to defend yourself at your place?"

"Nothing."

"Nothing?"

"I had a calm life until Missy came along. No need for weapons."

You had a boring life before I came along.

Nadya sat up and buckled in. "I guess it's safe now. How far to your place?"

"Twenty minutes. There's a grocery store close to where I live. I'll stop in and get a few things. You can stay in the car if you think that's safer."

"I will. Buy some wine, will you? I need to take the edge off."

"You didn't say what you liked to eat."

"I don't eat much. I snack a lot."

Me, too!

"They sell roasted chickens there."

"Perfect. Maybe get some lunch meats?"

"OK."

Get some cheeses too. How come you don't argue with her about lunch meats?

"It's different."

"What's different?"

"It's a long story, Nadya. You'll get used to it."

Aki, I like this girl. We're going to get along fine.

Nadya and Aki nearly devoured the roasted chicken. Washing it down with wine and some vegetable fried rice, they ate pretty much in silence, preferring the pleasure of satisfying their appetites over conversation.

Afterward, they retired to the other half of the room, sat in the two chairs that faced the television and watched the news. After a minute or two, Nadya got up, went to the kitchenette and returned with another bottle of wine and glasses, which she set on the small table between them.

"You trying to get me drunk?"

"I'm trying to get me drunk."

"Rools will still be there in the morning."

Nadya pointed to the screen. "Looks like we made the news. There's Sasi's house."

"Hmm. They're still looking for Hamza. I don't like that. They got a shot of my car."

"Not the license plate. That's good."

"You think he's looking for you?"

"Oh, yea. But he's in hiding now, too. Not sure what he'll do next."

"What are your plans?"

"Get rid of Rools."

That will not happen, Nadya. Now that the excitement's over, it's time that we get to know each other.

"Never." Nadya stood. "I'll get the firestone."

Aki looked up. "What?"

Sit!

Ignoring both Rools and Aki, Nadya turned to go. For a second, she saw stars, like she'd just been hit in the head, followed by a searing pain behind her eyes. She plopped back into the chair.

"Nadya. You OK?"

"I..., I'm fine. Got dizzy for a second. Must be the wine."

"You sure? What was that about the firestone?"

214

"Rools and I are having a conversation."

"He doesn't want to go back, does he?"

"No."

"Ask him what he wants."

"He says he wants to get to know me."

"I can't help you with that."

"Aki, I can't stand this!"

Aki. Here's a beautiful woman in distress. What are we going to do?

"Nothing I can do."

Of course, there is. Give her more wine. Give her a shoulder massage. Help her relax. Where are your manners?

"It's inappropriate."

Nadya hit the mute button, suddenly making the apartment very quiet. She studied Aki. "What's inappropriate?"

"Missy says to help you relax."

Nadya laughed. "Really? What did she suggest?"

"More wine, shoulder massage."

Nadya. Tell the man, we accept.

"No."

"Oh, well. That's what I told Missy. It's inappropriate."

"Rools says, yes. I was telling him, no."

Aki scratched his head. "I'm confused. Was that a yes or a no?"

"It's a no from me and a yes from Rools. I think, since we're going to have four way conversations, we need to identify who's talking."

Aki opened the bottle and offered to pour. "We can all agree on more wine, though. Right?"

Nadya. Tell him, yes. We agree.

"Right. All four of us can agree on that."

Nadya studied Aki with a puzzled look. "Aki, where is your girlfriend?"

"Um, I don't have one..., at the moment."

At the moment? You haven't had one since forever!

"Oh. Do you like being alone?"

"It has it's advantages."

"Seems like I've always been with someone. What's good about living alone?"

"I get to do what I want."

"But..., no one to talk to when you're lonely."

"I have Missy. I don't know what it feels like to be lonely."

Right, Aki. You have a friend!

"Being with Hamza was a lot like being alone. He never talked much, not to me anyway."

"You've got to be able to talk. Otherwise, it doesn't work."

"We'd talk, but he never really listened."

"A lot of people are like that."

"Good looking guy like you. Seems like you should have a girlfriend."

See, Aki? It's that weight that you've put on. You can thank me for this.

"Someday."

"You have had one, right?"

Aki sighed. "Yeah."

"What happened?"

"We grew apart."

Aki. Tell her the truth.

"Hamza was arrogant and stubborn. And he liked to hurt people. I couldn't stand that."

"How long were you two together?"

"Almost three years. Don't know why I put up with it."

"Is he the jealous type?"

"Always. Anybody look at me for too long or the wrong way and he'd be ready to fight."

216

"So..., you being here with me...,"

Nadya started to get up. "I should leave. I'm putting your life in danger."

Aki, don't you dare let her go!

"Sit down, Nadya. He doesn't know where you are or who I am, much less where to find us. We're safe."

"I don't know why I wanted to come here. I just knew that I didn't want to be in Sasi's house. I felt like she thinks I stole her firestone. I don't want it. I wish she'd take it back."

"We'll call tomorrow and see if they have any ideas. For now, we're the new experts. But neither of us know how they related to the stone without being possessed by it. We all have something to learn."

Nadya nodded quietly. "They know how it works and we know how it feels." She tried to suppress a yawn but it came out anyway. "I've been going since yesterday."

"When you're ready, your room is down the hall on the right. I folded down the couch and put some blankets and a pillow in there."

"Thanks, Aki. Is Missy quiet when you sleep?"

"She doesn't bother me then, but she keeps wanting me to give her my dream time. I won't allow it."

"And when you're awake?"

"Constant, aren't you, Missy?"

Got to keep you on your toes, Aki. Your good fortune is my good fortune.

"She says she has to keep me on my toes and that my good fortune is her good fortune."

"That's one way to look at it. And if it's bad?"

"She'll protect me. Twice, I've been in life-threatening situations and both times she saved me. So, it's not all bad. Just sayin'."

"Doesn't it get tiresome?"

"We have our moments."

"You think of her as an advantage?"

"Depends on the relationship." Aki smiled. "Rools has been quiet?"

I'm taking it all in, Nadya. I want to see what pleases

you before I inform you of what pleases me.

"What pleases you?"

Aki sat up. "What?"

"I'm talking to Rools."

"Oh..., I see."

I like pleasure, Nadya. Things that make me feel good.

"Like..., wine?"

That's one of them.

"It's not just about pleasure."

You choose what's important to you and I'll do the same. Like the man said, it depends on the relationship.

Aki watched with interest. "That must be some conversation you're having in there."

"Aki, did Missy say she wanted you to give me a shoulder massage?"

"Yes."

"Would you mind?"

"I'd be happy to."

"You're so sweet."

"Want me to light a candle, put on some music?"

Excellent move, Aki! You're just too smooth!

"Don't take it the wrong way, Aki. It's not about being romantic. But, sure. Music and candle are fine."

"I guess I already knew that. I'll get candles. What kind of music?"

"Relaxing." Nadya pulled the table away from the two chairs. "How about a blanket?"

"I'll be right back."

Nadya spread out the blanket on top of the throw rug in front of the two chairs and sat down in the middle.

"Where do you want me?"

Aki sat down in one of the chairs and motioned for her to sit in front of him, facing away. "Relax. Let your head fall forward. I'll start with your neck."

Very good, Aki. You're on it!

Aki started with his hands on her shoulders, thumbs working along her spine. "Your neck muscles are tight."

"I wonder why."

"I think I can guess."

"You have strong hands."

"Not because I work at it."

"What do you do for a living?"

"I trade in stocks."

"Do you make any money?"

"A little better than breaking even."

"Are we talking millions?"

"We're talking food and rent and a little extra, most of which I reinvest."

"Your massage feels really good."

"Working down into your shoulders, now."

"You should do this for a living."

"Then I'd be really broke. What do you do for your money?"

"You mean, what am I going to do for money?"

"You're not working?"

"Hamza wouldn't allow it. Said it was below me."

"What do you like doing?"

"Photography, mostly nature."

"And then what? Sell photographs?"

"Maybe. Probably not much money in it. I'll have to get a real job. Hamza discouraged me at everything I wanted to try."

"Just wanted you by his side?"

"All I needed to do was look pretty. Boring."

"Your shoulders are loosening up. If you'd like to lie down, I'll get the rest of your back."

Aki, you are the cat's meow for being smooth.

"You're really good at this. I think you missed your calling."

"I don't want to massage guys. If all of my subjects were as beautiful as you, I'd change my mind."

"Forget the beauty thing. I'm Nadya. I'm running away from an angry, jealous boyfriend. I want a new life and I hope to live long enough to enjoy it."

Nadya, I like how it feels when he massages us. Just letting you know.

"It's not *us*."

"What?"

"I'm talking to Rools."

"Oh. Us, huh? He's settling in."

"No. He's not. I am me and he's not part of that. He's an unwanted intruder."

Nadya, do we have to go through this again? Accept me and I can help you.

"Never."

Aki smiled. "I know what you're going through. What does he want?"

"He said he likes the massage."

"That's nice. How about you?"

"Of course, I like it."

"Then, why argue with him?"

"Because he's referring to me as us, like we're together."

"Aren't you?"

"Whose side are you on?"

"Yours. But I know what's happening. He'll leave when he's ready. Not before."

Nadya pulled away from Aki, moving to the middle of the blanket. "You said you'd massage my back?"

"Love to. Lie down on your stomach."

Much to Aki's surprise, Nadya removed her top. "Don't get any romantic ideas. Massages are better skin to skin."

"I won't argue."

"Thanks. Just so you know, I'll be leaving in the morning."

"You're welcome to stay until you figure out what you're going to do."

Excellent move!

"No. I don't want to put your life in danger."

"I've got that extra room. Just warning you, I'm a boring person to be around."

Aki..., what?

"Boring is perfect. Thanks, Aki. Face down?"

"Right."

When she was comfortable, Aki sat by her side and began rubbing her back, first in long broad strokes and then, using his thumbs, working along her spine from shoulders down.

"You can undo my bra."

Nadya, we agree on some things already.

"Never."

Aki stopped. "What?"

"Talking to Rools. Keep going."

Smiling, Aki returned to the massage, long broad strokes. "Never..., what?"

"I'm not saying."

Aki, I know what Rools is suggesting.

"No, you don't."

"Don't..., what?"

"Talking to Missy."

"Oh."

"Is it going to be a long night, Nadya? Between the four of us, I mean.

"No idea. You're really good at massages."

Nadya, when he's done here, turn over so he can get the other side.

"No."

Nadya?

"No."

221

The following morning Sasi set the table in the living room, fruit, rolls, hard boiled eggs and coffee. She opened the doors to the balcony and looked out over her million dollar view, breathing deeply.

What an odd string of events, kidnapped, rescued, a fire fight in her house, dead bodies, police crawling all over the place, bullet holes in the walls and reporters outside clamoring for a any kind of news.

Sam came into the room. "I just got off the phone with Bambang. They haven't found Hamza yet. I'm worried. We haven't heard from Aki or Nadya."

"Probably sleeping off that whiskey. We shouldn't have let them drive."

"Aki hardly drank. I was watching. He was OK."

"I wonder how Nadya is doing."

Sam, sipping his coffee, smiled. "She's going to wake up with a hangover and Rools. Wonder how that's going to work out."

"We have to talk to them again. We can't let this go without our knowing how it ends." Sasi tapped one of the eggs with her spoon, rolled it around to loosen the shell and, removing them, put the pieces in a bowl set there for that purpose. "All those years I spent studying the firestone, thinking it was the most important thing in my life. Now, it's gone. I feel a great sense of freedom. I never realized how much it controlled me."

"Possessions are like that. You never own them. You're the caretaker until you to die. They're still going to be around and own somebody else."

"You are wiser than your years."

"I have nothing, so I have time to think about things."

"Your life is richer?"

"Not complicated. If I had a lot of money I would be a much busier person. I enjoy what I have."

"Like your family in San Diego?"

"I'm a lucky man."

222

"You've got quite a tale to tell."

Sam smiled, thinking about how inquisitive Kathryn would be when she picked him up at the airport. "I'll be grilled as soon as I get off of the plane."

"I think it's time for you to go home."

Sam split one of the rolls in half, spread butter and jam over the top and took a short bite. "No, afraid not. You're not going to get rid of me that easily."

"Hamza's not after me anymore."

"He doesn't know that you don't have the firestone."

"I'm pretty sure it's not his highest priority anymore."

"You think he'll try to leave the country?"

"No idea," said Sasi, shaking her head. "He might just be looking for Nadya."

"All the more reason to get her back here with us."

"No clue where she went?"

"No. But Aki dropped her off somewhere. We'll give him a call right after breakfast."

Hi Sam,

Got any news to share? Capn was at the bow of the boat last night howling up a storm and tomorrow night, according to the calendar, is a blue moon. There's a fire out in the back country. Off shore winds are bringing the smoke out here and guess what? Blue moon. I hope this is not a bad omen.

Melissa is joining us for dinner tomorrow night. Pizza. I don't think that they're aware of the blue moon thing so I'm going to leave it at that. Don't want to conjure anything up.
Wish you could join us. Too bad, sucker.

Kathryn
xoxo

Hi Kathryn,

Good to hear from you. Save a piece of that pizza for me. I'd love to catch the next plane but I want to stick around until Hamza is caught.

The firestones are out of our control. Aki and Nadya are the new owners and, last I saw, they were together. Not sure where that's heading. Sasi and I hope to track them down and, maybe between the four of us, we can put this whole thing to rest.

If I asked you out on a date, would you consider it? Cheers!

Sam

Kathryn read the message a few times, wondering if Sam was serious. Would she consider it? Of course, she would. How could she not? Would she let it go farther than just a simple friendly date? Maybe. That depended on so many things.

Money wasn't much of a problem anymore. She was making more than she'd ever made, was due for a promotion and, living on the boat, expenses were low, dock fees and utilities.

Paul was wanting a car and if he kept his grades up, she owed him one. It wasn't even an issue anymore. Since they moved onto Spittin' Image, he never looked back. The divorce, living in that old, dingy apartment, needing money, unhappy. That was another life as far as he was concerned and his renewed enthusiasm was bubbling over.

Would she go out with Sam? Sure. Why not? He was, oddly, the safest one to be with. But, didn't he just say that he killed someone in Indonesia? Still...,

Her boss had asked her out several times, jokingly, but serious. Two different girls at work and a male coworker had all asked her out. Nope. Never have an affair with your peers at work.

Melissa's dad, Sal, had asked her out several times. She'd accepted the invites for BBQ as long as Paul was a part of it. The four of them had sailed together several times and that was always fun. But, a relationship with Sal? No. It might work until Paul and Melissa had some kind of spat.

They hadn't taken Spittin' Image out for a long time. That was one of the unforeseen problems with living on a boat. When first purchased, nothing has a permanent place so it's easy to throw all of the loose stuff into a box or some corner that will keep it out of the way until returning to the dock. Over time, things become stationary and it's too much trouble to head out.

Does Sam sail? He'd been on the boat many times. But had he ever been out to sea with them? Kathryn could not remember.

Sasi sat at her balcony window watching a flock of seagulls heading west, back toward the sea, not in any kind of formation. More like everyone taking the shortest route or choosing the best wind conditions and if their peers were not smart enough to see the wisdom of their choices, too bad for them.

A storm was approaching. She'd noticed the cirrus clouds sweeping in earlier in the day and, as the humidity and temperatures rose, could see the incoming cumulous clouds building on the horizon, still four to six hours away if her estimate was right.

Sam was in the shower. As comforting as it was to have him around, she felt guilty about keeping him from going home and insisted every day that he leave. Nope. Not until Hamza is caught.

Sasi longed for her quiet days, a time when weeks passed by with very few visitors, fewer calls, exciting times nevertheless, down in her little makeshift cellar exploring the firestone, an infinite number of realities, structured like a bee's honeycomb, but filled with possibilities. Working with Sam, learning how to transcend time and visit moments embedded in eternity, conversations with Kashif, communicating with Kathryn's dreams, tracking down someone with a sister firestone, bringing the two together.

What was the purpose behind all of those years of discovery, thirty of them, if there was no answer? As Sam said, you don't own things, they own you. How many people before her had wanted an answer to the mysteries of the firestone before they died and then been deprived? Was she merely the next one in a long line?

Suddenly, Sasi was feeling very old. All of those aches and pains that she'd been ignoring while on the trail of the other firestone were now coming back in spades. In one short day, thirty years of dedication flew out the door when Aki and Nadya drove away. Sasi was feeling lost,

226

without purpose, tired.

They don't know anything. They have no idea of the possibilities because both of them are possessed. If only they can somehow free themselves...,

If only they could use the powers of the firestones rather than the other way around. They have to hear about what is possible before they disappear from our lives.

Watching Sasi, Sam paused at the doorway, not wanting to disturb her thoughts. These times would be coming to an end soon and he wanted to keep this memory of Sasi in his mind. Finally, he entered the room.

"Deep thoughts?"

"Nadya and Aki. Any word from them?"

"They're going to be here in a couple of hours."

"Excellent. So..., they're both OK?"

"So far. I talked them into it, but they were skeptical. I was afraid that if we met somewhere in public, we'd be recognized."

"Where has Nadya been?"

"At Aki's..., makes sense. He can relate to her better than anybody now."

"We've got a storm coming."

Sam walked over to the balcony and confirmed her prediction. "You've got a great view from here. That makes this a million dollar house."

"Million dollar view, maybe. The house? No."

"Not with all these bullet holes. I can patch the walls but you're going to have to find someone to fix the woodwork."

"Maybe I'll go buy a saw and do the work myself. Nothing else for me to do now."

"That sounds rather defeatist."

"It's the sound of success, Sam. We've brought the stones together. We've accomplished the impossible."

"I have this feeling that it's not over yet."

Nikko was a small man, one of those people that easily fit into a crowd. He dressed like everyone else, casual, not too sporty or sloppy. He never wore new clothes and he did not wear bright colors. Nondescript. That was Nikko.

He wore wire-rimmed glasses, not too thick but good enough to distort his eyes so that it was hard to tell where he was looking. If someone was asked to recall a face, his would be the one overlooked. Asked how many in a crowd and he would be the one not counted.

On the other hand, Nikko could remember almost everything he saw. He could tell you how many in a crowd, by gender, who was together, which ones were happy, smokers, drinkers, someone looking to do harm.

Nikko loved solving riddles. If he heard something on the news or read something somewhere that did not make sense, he would take the time to figure out what really happened.

Along with his natural skills, Nikko discovered that he had a love of technology, anything to aid in his search for answers to riddles. Voice recorders, hidden cameras, tracking devices, you name it. Nikko either knew of it or was already using one version or another. He should have been a detective.

But there was no money forthcoming from the police department. He did not fit their size requirements, was not healthy enough, did not test well and, even if he did pass, the pay was not good.

Hamza had a great need for such a person. His group of fellow embezzlers, extortionists, crooks and heavy-handed enforcers were only as good as their words at the moment and with all of the usual cliques, families, closed door agreements, all the different things that come together to make money, sometimes things got dangerous.

It was good business to know what his partners were up to. Having reliable information from a quiet, but very knowledgeable source, someone who could come and go

228

without being noticed, that kind of person should be paid very well. Nikko was the man.

Hamza let Nikko know where and when meetings were going to take place. During those times, Nikko placed tracking devices on their cars, took pictures of the owners and built files on everyone.

Sometimes, if the meeting was in a public place, he would sit nearby with a cup of tea, reading the paper, taking notes.

Sasi owned something that Hamza wanted but he wouldn't say what it was. Being a cautious man and wanting to know more about her, Nikko discovered that Sasi had a brother, Joko, who only stayed at the house from time to time.

After she was kidnapped, Nikko placed an obscure motion detector near her front door that would send him a signal whenever someone passed by. When it appeared that someone was living there, he took pictures of Joko and put a tracker on his car.

When Joko picked up Sam at the railway station, Nikko got pictures, called a friend who worked inside, discovered who Sam was, where he was from and, with a bit more snooping, what he did for a living. When Sam rented a car, Nikko was not far behind.

He followed them to a run down seaside bar, placed a tracker on Sam's rented vehicle before he went inside and sat down in a dark corner with a beer, a bag of peanuts and recorded Sam's encounter with Hamza.

Later, after watching the video a few times, he warned Hamza that this guy was a professional and that he'd better step up security around Sasi.

Hamza argued that no one knew where she was and by this time he was not thinking clearly anyway. He wanted revenge. Sam and Joko, as far as he was concerned, were as good as dead.

No one, not even Nikko, expected Nadya to switch sides. She wasn't even supposed to go that night. Hamza was busy with his injuries and didn't want her around. She wanted to see who this guy was.

Aki was the unexpected one. Where did he come from and why? He went into the house right after the shooting, stayed during the whole investigation and left with Nadya later that night, taking with him the tracker that had been placed on his car, leaving behind the pictures that Nikko had taken.

Who was this person? A brother? Lover? Was she having an affair on the side? Some of Hamza's best men had just been killed or captured, but this was the story that needed to be followed.

When they stopped at a grocery store, Nikko did the same. Eating dinner in his car, he watched Aki and Nadya enter into his apartment. Noting the address, he began his search for a name.

The phone rang. It was a different ring tone than what Hamza was expecting so it took a few seconds for him to recognize that the call was for him. The old cell had GPS and, now that he was in hiding, it was a liability.

"It's me."

"Speak."

"Sending you a video of your fight in the bar."

"Why would I want that?"

"Thought you might want to see what you're up against."

"I already know."

"This guy's pretty good."

"There's only one of him."

"I'm not sure that's true. Nadya left with another man last night."

"She didn't stay at Sasi's house?"

"No."

"Where did she go?"

"His place, I guess. I followed them."

"She spent the night?"

"As far as I know. I never saw them come back out."

"Who is he?"

"No idea. I've never seen him before."

"She's still there?"

"Last I saw. I put a tracker on his car. It hasn't moved."

"Would you like to make some money?"

"Doing what?"

"Pick up a package at the warehouse. I'll call ahead and get it ready. Put it underneath the driver's seat of the car. It's magnetic. It'll stick."

"No. Count me out."

"A lot of money for not much work."

"I'm not in that kind of business."

"I need you to do this."

"Get someone else."

"Everyone's kind of busy right now."

There was a long pause in the conversation. Hamza took the time to pick up the homeostatic pencil and apply it to his swollen lip and bloody nose. Touching the raw skin, a burning sensation shot through his nerves like they were on fire, making his eyes water.

"No. I don't have it in me."

"It's your chance to move up."

"Invisible..., that's me. I want to keep it that way."

'Let me put this another way. I need a favor and I'm asking you to do it. If you want to stay employed you'll go to the warehouse and pick up the package. They'll give you instructions. Let me know when everything's in place." Click.

Leaving his flat the night before, Hamza grabbed some of Nadya's make-up on the way out, something he hoped would cover the black and blue welt around his eye on the left side of his face.

Standing in front of the bathroom mirror, he selected the jar that most closely matched the color of his skin, wondering at the same time how he was going to apply it. A pleasant surprise, an applicator inside, one of the first good things to happen since the police got involved.

Nadya and her friend will be dead minutes after they get into the car. It'll blow five minutes after it detects motion. Too bad. She was a good woman.

That leaves Sam. Bullets or a bomb? Hamza tossed the question around for a while and then decided that an explosive device would give no satisfaction. He would die quickly and would never know who did it. Bullets are better. Wound him, make him suffer for a while. Talk a bit and fire another non-lethal shot, watch him bleed to death in insufferable pain.

Sasi was another matter. He had no desire to kill her. Actually, Hamza liked Sasi and wished her no harm. All he wanted from her was the firestone.

Nadya poured cream into her coffee, stirring until it was almost white and then offered the cream to Aki, who returned it to the fridge.

"I could've put it away. I thought you wanted some."

"No. I never put anything in my coffee."

"Why did you buy it?"

"For you, in case you wanted it."

"Thoughtful. But you don't need to do that."

"How did you sleep?"

"Very well."

Aki watched Nadya sipping her coffee, her hair a mess, no make-up, eyes puffy from a hangover, and he loved her even more. They had talked late into the night, each finding the other more interesting as the night wore on.

"You had enough blankets?"

"I don't even remember. Thanks for letting me stay. I don't know where else I would've gone."

"Like I said, as long as you want."

"What time are they expecting us?"

"I told them, after dinner. I don't want to go over there in the daytime."

"I don't want to go, period."

"Me either."

"Then, let's not. What kind of solutions can they offer? We're the new owners."

"I think we're the new victims, unless you've got control of Rools already."

"Hardly. He's been quiet, thank God."

I'm watching and learning, Nadya. I'm letting you be you for now.

"It's appreciated."

I enjoyed last night. How was it for you?

"Go back to sleep."

I never sleep. I enjoyed watching your dreams.

"You can do that?"

I have many talents, Nadya. We're just getting started.

233

Aki smiled a knowing smile. "I shouldn't have mentioned his name. Tell him, hello."

"I will not. You guys want to talk? Get me out of the middle."

"And *this* is why we need to visit Sasi and Sam."

"How long had she owned the firestone?"

"Don't know. Maybe we should make a list of all of the things that we want to ask."

"Number one, how to get rid of Rools."

That won't happen, Nadya. Not until I'm ready.

Aki reached for a pad and pencil. "I'll write that down. It's on everyone's mind anyway. Don't know if you're going to get your wish."

"What will it take, Rools?"

I have to want something more than what I'm getting with you.

"What might that be?"

Show me something.

"Rools says that he'll leave when he wants something more than where he is."

"You got an answer? Missy, how come you never answer that question?"

I hear you, Aki. You think I don't know what's going on?

"What's it going to take?"

Same as Rools. Show me something better. But I have to say that I've come to really like you. I may never leave.

"What's he say?"

"Same as Rools."

"How is Sasi going to help?"

"Don't know. Takes us back to that first question. How long has she had the firestone?"

"Rools, do you know Sasi?"

I know of her.

"What's the difference?"

She and I were never together, like us. She never allowed me in.

"How did she stop you?"

You will have to ask her that question.

234

"How long have you known her?"

I only recently met her. Inside the firestone, there is no time, only places. Visiting them was her passion.

"How did she do that?"

Ask her.

Aki laughed. "I'm falling behind out here. What's going on?"

Nadya took a long sip of her coffee. "There's a lot more to this than what I know. We *must* talk with Sasi."

"Right after dinner."

Nikko did not like what he was being asked to do. He was never a violent man and wished nobody any harm. For that very reason, it was difficult to work for Hamza, who almost always had it in for one person or another. Most of it never came to violence but, used sparingly, information was more valuable than a gun.

Nikko didn't consider that reprehensible. He was merely getting information for his boss. If it came to violence, he wanted no part of it and did not wish to know about it.

Some of his subjects he liked more than others. While observing them, he found it interesting that some tipped generously while others not at all. Some were nice to the people that they interacted with, others arrogant and rude. Some stopped to pet a dog, others just as soon kick them out of the way.

Those he didn't like, he went out of his way to learn more of their secrets and if one of them might cause extra distress, he would pass it on to Hamza. Other secrets, he held back, depending on who his subject was.

Nadya was one of his favorites. Even though she didn't know him, he had learned all about her. Nadya smiled at people holding the door open, always stopped to admire someone's child or pet and treated those in the service sector well, unless she was with Hamza who frowned on all of that. It was impossible to not like Nadya.

Taken a step further, he secretly admitted to himself that he loved her, although he knew that he would never even get to know her. That was part of Hamza's requirement. No one was to know who he was or what he did for his money.

Put a bomb under the car of the one person that he admired most of all his subjects? Better to put one in Hamza's car and be done with what seemed to be the source of all this evil. But, after that, no income.

Nikko was shown how to power up the device and how to input the code, thirteen characters long. He was allowed three attempts. Three failures and the device had to go back to the shop and be reset. That would be one possible excuse for not getting the job done, screwed up.

Maybe..., forget to activate the device after the code was input. The authorization to activate would default back to Off after one minute. Unprofessional.

None of this was good. No matter how Nikko thought of the task, it was something that he wanted no part of. He placed a call to Hamza

"Speak."

"I can't do this."

"You will."

"She doesn't deserve it."

"How do you know she's even going to be in the car?"

"They arrived at his place together. They'll probably leave together."

"So..., what? She's a traitor. You know what I do with traitors."

"You don't know all of the circumstances."

"Some of my best friends are dead, others sitting in a cell while she walks free. What does that sound like to you?"

Nikko did not tell Hamza that he had secretly recorded that conversation, an argument between Nadya and Hamza several days earlier when he first decided to kidnap Sasi. Nadya was dead set against it, Hamza greedy and overbearing as usual. If he'd listened to her in the first place, none of this would ever have happened.

Hamza losing his grip? He's already lost his hit men. Yes, he still had his bankers, brokers, gambling casinos and numerous other shady businesses, but his enforcers were out of commission.

"Nikko, you hear me? Go do what you're paid to do."

Rule number one, no names. Hamza just threw the first rule out the window. The man must be desperate. Nikko cringed at the thought of it. He was now in possession of a bomb with his name attached.

"You know I've got secrets on you, too."

Nikko sighed. Hamza had extended credit many times when he was on a losing streak in one of his casinos. His debt was substantial and Hamza had been both tolerant and forgiving. Also, on one of his many nights spent in one of Hamza's hotels, he'd been recorded, a video of his adventures with another man. If Nikko's wife saw those, the marriage would be over.

"You can't get anybody else?"

"They're dead or in jail. I'm counting on you."

Life can be pure crap at times. You try hard to do the right things, develop a talent so that you can make a bit of money, lead a simple but satisfactory life and then it chops you down.

"Nikko, you get my message?"

"Yes, Hamza. I'm doing this for you."

Ending the call, Nikko felt a bit of satisfaction.

You want to break rule number one? I'll break it, too. And I'll put the blame right back in your lap.

Doing what I just did, probably a death warrant.

Just in case, this conversation, like all of the others, has been recorded and after a preset time if I don't log in, will be sent to some very interested recipients.

Aki and Nadya descended the stairs from his second story apartment together, side by side, taking the same steps at the same time, kind of bumping into each other along the way, laughing when they did. As comfortable as they were with each other, anyone watching would think they were lovers.

Buckled up inside the car, Aki turned the key, started the engine, backed up out of his stall and headed for the driveway. "Nervous?"

"I don't know what to think..., or feel. How long to Sasi's?"

"About thirty minutes."

"What do you think she's going to say?"

"You'd know better than me. I just met her. You went to her seminars. What did she talk about?"

"She talked a lot about what we're really doing when we dream. And she talked about this other world. We can't see it but it's there. You always wonder about stuff like that. Who really knows?"

"The firestone's got something to do with it."

"Probably."

"It's going to be a long night. You ready for that?"

"Yeah. Let's get it over with."

Aki pulled out into traffic and headed for the main road. Seconds later, Nikko released the emergency brake, turned on his lights and followed, not too close. Better to stay at least a hundred feet away.

His guilt was weighing heavily. These two people, whatever their relationship, were going to die in about the next four minutes. It would be fast. They wouldn't feel a thing.

Suddenly, he didn't want any part of it. They didn't deserve it and Hamza had no right to ask him to do it. He pulled over to the side of the road and frantically searched for Nadya's number.

He would tell Hamza that they must've gotten out of the

car seconds before, checked out a burned out headlight, ran out of gas, stopped to get some food, any number of reasons could get them out of the car and he couldn't be blamed for that. Hands shaking, Nikko selected her number. Ringing, no answer.

"I'm getting a call from a number I don't recognize," said Nadya.

"I never answer them."

"Me either. Nadya, where is your firestone?"

"Oh, no! I left it on the kitchen counter. Go back?"

"We have to. I'll make a U."

Going back the other way Aki hit a red light. They were stopped in traffic.

"Whoever this caller is, they left a message."

"Light's green. Come on everyone. Let's go!"

As they were starting to move forward another car, going in the opposite direction, flashed their lights and honked their horn.

"Look at that guy," said Aki. "What's he waving about?"

"Looks like he's yelling at us."

"I've been driving OK. I didn't do anything wrong."

"A lot of crazy people these days."

"Hang on. Here's our turn."

Aki pulled into the parking lot, drove toward his stall but stopped short of going in. "After this is all over, how would you like to join me on a trip to San Diego?"

Aki, you are amazing! Carne asada here we come!

"Let's get through this first."

Aki set the brake, killed the engine and opened his door. "I'll go up with you. I've got to pee."

They got out of the car and were about half way up the stairs when the apartment building lit up like it was daytime. A blast of scalding hot air and resultant BOOM threw Aki and Nadya down into the steps. Shrapnel pelted the area around them. Aki's shirt caught fire.

It took a minute for both of them to realize what had happened. People were coming out of their apartments now, everyone yelling, screaming, calling the police and taking pictures. Aki's car was in flames, windows blown out, car body mangled. Nadya was saying something but he couldn't hear. In shock, they hugged each other, crying.

Sirens wailed in the distance. People were staring from the balcony, crossing the street from all directions to gawk at the flaming hot, burning mess.

And then, while sitting there on the steps, arms around each other, both Nadya and Aki spotted the car driving by, the one with the driver who had been yelling at them. It kept going.

Sam was pacing the floor. Sasi was getting tired just watching him. "You're going to wear a hole in the rug."

"They should be here by now."

"Weren't they going to call before they left?"

"It's getting late."

"Didn't they say, after dinner?"

"How late do they eat? They should at least call."

"They're not answering either?"

"If they were, I wouldn't be pacing. Why don't we have Aki's address?"

"Sam, sit down. We haven't had much time to think about anything. They left by their choice. We have no right to hold them any more than the police. They were victims. We no longer have possession of the firestone. We are out of the picture."

"Not until Hamza is caught. Bambang's not answering either. He's out on some kind of emergency."

"I just told you, we are out of the picture. It's daytime in San Diego, isn't it? Talk to Kathryn. I know that you miss her."

"I know what you're trying to do. And I appreciate it. But, even though I never got to teach Aki much of anything, he was still my student."

"Is he paying you?"

"Sasi, whose side are you on? I'm worried about them."

"So am I. And I've got thirty years of curiosity stored up inside me that needs answers. Yet..., I'm sitting down."

She turned her attention back to the view outside the balcony window, posture straight, the way that Sam would always remember her, hand somewhere near her teacup. She pointed. "Look at those clouds, Sam. Take a deep breath and soak in the night. We're going to get a nice, refreshing rain. Maybe that'll help clear things up."

With the crime scene roped off, Aki's demolished smoldering car in the middle, and after the police told everyone to disperse and after Bambang had finished questioning them and leaving a guard on duty nearby, Aki barricaded both the front and back doors, sat down at the kitchen counter, a place that was quickly becoming his and Nadya's favorite gathering spot, Aki on the kitchen side, Nadya with her back to the living room and TV, and popped open a bottle of wine. Both of them were still having a hard time hearing. The conversation was somewhat loud.

"I have to have a drink. How about you?"

Yes, Aki. We're beginning to think alike. I'm proud of you.

Nadya sat down across the counter. "Pass the bottle."

"I can't believe it. Sam kept telling us to stick together. We should've listened."

"I didn't think Hamza would stoop so low."

"How could he know where we were?"

"Maybe he didn't, just what you were driving."

Aki poured the wine, two stiff drinks. "How could he even know that? Somebody was watching. We must've been followed."

"There were lots of people hanging around. It could've been anybody."

"That guy in the car, yelling at us when we were coming back here. He knew."

"One of Hamza's goons, probably. I've never seen him before."

Aki clinked his glass to hers. "I'll call Sam, let him know what happened and tell him we'll be there tomorrow. It's too late to go anywhere now. And I'm not in the mood."

"Me, either. Mind if I take a shower?"

"I'll be right behind you. Can't believe that my shirt caught fire."

Nadya laughed. "When you're hot, you're hot."

"Normally I would laugh at that."

"Have you got a washer and dryer here?"

"Yeah." Aki pointed toward the back door across the kitchen. "There's a cupboard on your right-hand side. Washer and dryer's in there."

"I have to wash these clothes. I didn't have a chance to pack."

"You want to borrow a shirt and pants?"

"If you don't mind. That would be nice."

"Do you want me to run your stuff through while you shower?"

"I can do it. Thanks."

"I'm going to be sitting here anyway. I'm going to watch the news."

"Would you mind?"

"No problem."

"I'll put my clothes outside the door. OK?"

"Perfect."

As soon as Nadya was out of view, Missy began.

Aki, she's undressing!

"It's a shower, Missy. She has to do that."

In our house.

"It's my house."

Let it go, Aki. What we have is a beautiful woman running around naked in our house.

"You are a pervert. That reminds me." Aki headed for his bedroom. I've got to get her a change of clothes."

Something revealing?

"No."

How about that thin, white shirt you have?

"No."

Stretch pants?

"No. I've got some loose fitting pants with a tie top and a loose fitting pullover."

Low neckline?

"Shut up, Missy. Nadya's my guest. She has to be treated with respect."

This is why you have no girlfriends. You have to...,

"I am who I am. Take it or leave it."

244

You are no fun. What happened to joy in living?

"I am exceedingly joyous to be alive right now. We almost got killed. What happens then?"

Aki waited for the reply. "Missy?"

You said, we.

"So?"

You're finally beginning to accept me.

"It was in reference to our presence together. It has nothing to do with, us."

You call it what you want and I'll do the same. To answer your question. I would've gone back into the rock. It was in your backpack.

"Just like that, you'd leave?"

You don't expect me to hang around with a dead man, do you?

"Well..., if you put it that way."

Aki found the clothes he was looking for and placed them next to the bathroom door. He picked up Nadya's dirty clothes and headed for the washing machine.

Skimpy clothes, huh, Aki?

"I'm not looking. I'm just going to wash them for her."

She'll never know.

"Stop bugging me."

Aki?

Nadya stepped into the shower and pulled the curtain closed. The steady stream of hot water felt like heaven knowing that it might not have ever happened at all. She faced straight into the stream, eyes closed, and let the water rinse away the ash.

Nadya. I think we'll be happy here.

Nadya wet her hair, grabbed the shampoo bottle and began to scrub. "Go away."

Admit it. You like him.

"It doesn't concern you."

Let's look at what we agree on. You like him, right? Don't lie. I already know. I need for you to admit it.

"You're in my space. Get out."

I can make you miserable. Or I can make you happy. You choose.

"You're making me miserable."

Bad direction. Remember the sound in your ears? I can make you want to kill yourself, Nadya. Try for happy. Be honest. Do you like him?

"Yes."

Does he like you?

"I think so."

Is he sincere?

"Why all of these questions?"

We're a team, Nadya. I'm helping you sort things out.

"I don't need your help."

If you're happy, I'm happy. I like being happy. So, if that's the direction you want to go, I'm with you.

"I make my own decisions."

I'm proud of you.

"You are very irritating."

Yet consistent. You like him. You get along. You almost both died together. You've gotten drunk together. I'd say you've gotten off to a pretty good start. Wouldn't you agree?

"I'm ignoring you."

246

Right. That works. Even if I'm quiet, you know I'm here. You don't have a private thought without my knowledge of it. Consider us sisters..., or brothers or brother and sister. I don't care. I just want us to be happy.

"It's not, us."

What else can it be? Did you like that back massage last night?

Nadya finished rinsing her hair, wiped the water from her eyes and began to soap up.

Nadya, I understand your shock that such an event came so close to killing you. My commitment to you is to be more vigilant. I owe you that much, part payment for your hospitality.

"You're offering to pay?"

In ways that I can.

"Show me the money."

I can show you the way.

"Another conscience? I've already got one."

Not like that at all. I'll help you make the best decision.

"Is that why you were asking about the back massage?"

You did like it. I need for you to admit it.

"OK. I did. So..., what?"

I liked it, too. It made me happy. And I don't get a chance to be happy very often. So, I think we should get another one.

"That's taking advantage. I won't do that."

You didn't notice how excited he was to do that? You're doing him a favor.

"It doesn't work like that. I like him. We'll see what develops..., over time."

This time thing is confusing to me. In the stone, there are only opportunities. Forget time. This night is full of opportunities. You may not live to see the morning.

"I won't do anything that I'll regret later."

There's that side of it, too. Compromise. How can we make both of us happy?

"It's not, us. Quit saying that."

Nadya finished up in the bathroom, put on Aki's clothes

and went out to check on her laundry. "I'm all done in the bathroom. Thanks."

"I think I just heard the rinse cycle finish. You can probably throw your clothes in the dryer."

"Thanks

"We made the news."

"Not surprised. They didn't name us, did they?"

"No."

"Give our address?"

"No."

"Catch Hamza?"

"No."

"How about that other guy?"

"There are a million cars out there, just like that one. All we know is that we think the driver had dark hair and we agree that he wore glasses. That narrows it down."

Nadya headed for the dryer. "Yeah, you're right."

"Did you want to watch any of this?"

"No."

Aki turned the TV off and headed down the hallway to get a change of clothes. Coming back, he paused at Nadya's closed door. "Good night."

"Good night, Aki. Thanks, again."

"You don't need to say that anymore."

He continued on into the bathroom and jumped into the shower.

She's imagining us naked, Aki.

"Missy. Don't go there."

You're entitled to that view. I have mine. But, I think you're way off.

Aki finished his shower, put on his pants and, while going through the apartment checking all of the windows, both doors, making sure they were locked and that everything was turned off, put on his shirt. Heading into his bedroom, he crawled into his bed and discovered Nadya already there.

"No sex. OK? I'm just scared."

Aki pulled her in and, cuddling, they went to sleep.

Sasi clicked off the TV, shaking her head. "I didn't think Hamza would ever be so desperate that he'd stoop to using a car bomb."

"We don't know that it was him."

"Who else? Kidnapping, attempted murder, you twice, the four of us, once. Now it's Aki and Nadya. My goodness. What did Aki say?"

"I'm going to pick them up in the morning and bring them back here. Hopefully, we can get all of this worked out."

"Better check your rental before you drive it."

"Right. Don't know what I'm looking for, but I'd guess it would be attached to the bottom of the car since I've kept it locked. Anything new down there and I'll call the police and have them check it out."

"You need to go home, Sam. There's nothing here that's worth your life."

"In good time. My ticket's open-ended."

"Sam, did you know that tonight is going to be a blue moon?"

"Kathryn mentioned it, yeah."

"Doesn't it seem coincidental that the coming together of the two firestones is happening on a blue moon? It's like a gathering."

"Kathryn's worried about it."

"How so?"

"The three of them and Capn, the dog, are all going to be together tonight, having pizza on the boat."

"That's not a normal thing?"

"No. They've been busy with their finals. Now they're celebrating."

"Tonight is the night, Sam. One way or another, we're going to get some answers."

Before Sasi's kidnapping, Nikko had time to fly his remote controlled airplanes, his favorite pastime. He knew that he would never be a pilot, but with these new battery-powered planes he could imagine himself up there. How free it was to spiral and dive and loop to loop, much more fun than putting trackers on cars and documenting uninteresting people.

Along with his desire to fly, Nikko had a fascination with remote control. Before long he had built a robot with three wheels, the front, smaller wheel for steering and maneuvering, and the two back ones for forward, reverse and braking.

At first it couldn't do much. He'd follow it around the house, steering it through doorways and around the furniture. The next big leap was to mount a camera on top so that he could see where the robot was going and what it was going to encounter while he sat in another room with the remote. Add to that a microphone and a speaker and it became a spy. The next addition gave it arms and some primitive means to grab and hold things. After that, truth be told, Nikko wanted it to be able to respond to verbal commands.

Not just anyone's verbal commands, his. He bought a computer and mounted it down inside the framework, loaded it with three hundred of his most commonly used words and attached commands to them. Before long, he had developed enough word strings that he could give Bott, that was his name, complex instructions such as, "Bott, get mail."

Bott knew what the mailbox looked like, stored images, and knew that it was mounted outside the house (yes, he could tell the difference). All that took was a boat sonar mounted upside down. If it saw anything within the first five meters up, it was inside. If the sonar showed anything over that, it was outside.

If Bott detected that it was inside and the command

was to get mail, he would head to the doorway built just for that purpose, press the exit button, its image stored into memory, and roll around the circumference of the house on the boardwalk built just for him until it spotted the mailbox. Getting the mail out was difficult until Nikko mounted a special latch that opened the bottom to let the mail fall into the waiting basket. Bott had not yet learned how to close the mailbox. That was Nikko's next project, until the kidnapping.

Since, everything changed. Knowing that he was the one that would be blamed for planting the bomb, should it come down to that, Nikko decided to take a few precautions.

Using what he knew about voices, he took some of Hamza's words from conversations that he'd recorded over the years and split them up into individual bits of sound. He found an on-line downloadable program that swapped one thing for another and put his words on one side of the program and Hamza's on the other so when Nikko spoke, Hamza's words came out. Speech was a little slow. But if the sentence output was slightly delayed, the computer had time to put all of the words together and it sounded not too bad.

What to say? And how to use it? Seemed like everyone's problems would be solved if Hamza was the one to suddenly die. No loose ends there. History is told by the last person standing.

Wouldn't that be fitting? The voice of the man that has caused all of this trouble was the same one that ordered his own death? How to make that happen? Nikko's cell rang.

"It's me. I need you to drive me somewhere."

"When?"

"Tonight."

"What time?"

"At eleven. I'm sending you the address."

"I've got other plans. I...,"

"I'm counting on you, Nikko. I'll be waiting outside."

Nikko flinched, another flagrant violation of Rule

number one. "I didn't sign up to be your chauffeur."

"*Sometimes we have to do things we don't want to do. That's life.*"

"It's not part of my life. Mine is in order."

"*Is it? If word leaked out that you were the one that planted that bomb, it wouldn't be so good, would it?*"

"It all connects back to you."

"*I've paid you well over the years and I've paid on time. I've loaned you money when you needed it. Requesting a ride is not so much to ask, is it?*"

Requesting a ride was not the issue. Hamza had a warrant out for his arrest. If he was caught with Hamza he would be implicated in everything. Acting as a private detective was one thing. Getting involved in those schemes was quite another.

"*Nikko, you hear me?*"

"I heard you."

"*Well?*"

A long sigh. "I see the address. I'll be there at eleven. Where are we going?"

"*I'll let you know when I'm in the car.*"

Click.

Nikko didn't say what he was really thinking. That could make the difference between life or taking a couple of bullets before Hamza got out of the car. After tonight, he was going to quit. Hamza was a loser, always has been and even though the money was good it was time to move on.

Time to earn a living doing something that did not require guns and killings and extortion and all of the nasty ways to get ahead. How about honest work? Something that had little or no stress. It would be nice to wake up in the morning and feel good about life.

With that in mind, Nikko went to work on his new invention. Everyone can testify against a dead man.

Standing up on the second floor under the roof, Sam kept an eye on his car while Aki and Nadya gathered their things. They were supposed to meet him at the door but the sudden rain caused a fast search for an umbrella. The wind was picking up and gusting hard. It was going to be a cautious drive back to Sasi's.

Inside the car, Aki turned in his seat. "Nadya, you sure you don't want to ride up front?"

"No, thanks. It's easier to stay low back here."

Sam got in, buckled up, started the engine, turned on his headlights and headed out. "It'll be about an hour in this weather."

Aki buckled himself in, grabbed hold of the handle built into the door latch and kept his eye on the road. "This storm was expected?"

"Yeah. Sasi talked about it last night. You two had lunch?"

"Breakfast," said Aki. "We got up late."

"I think Sasi's making something for us to eat. Other than that, both of you OK?"

"Still breathing."

"Any aftereffects?"

"Ringing in my ears," said Nadya.

Aki echoed in. "Low grade headache, body stiffness. I feel like I fell down a flight of stairs."

Nadya shifted to her other side, curling up into the back seat. "More like blown up a flight of stairs."

"I'm curious," said Sam. "I know we should wait until Sasi can hear us talking, but did either of you have any warning from Rools or Missy?"

"Nothing," said Aki. "She's helped me before, twice. But not a whisper this time. I think it has to be immediate and visible for her get involved. It's not like she's protecting me. She's protecting her interests."

"Nadya?"

"No idea. Why?"

"Because there's another world inside the firestones, one that sees these things. I'm surprised that neither of them had any foreknowledge of what was going to happen."

"What do you mean by, a world that sees these things?"

"If you're not possessed, that's what Sasi and I are calling it. It's not meant to be derogatory. It just helps us place where the energy of the stone is concentrated. If the energy is inside the stone, it draws you in. And then you can see what it sees. You can pick where and when you want to go. If the spirit is outside, like with the two of you, that world is cut off."

"How can you know anything before it happens?"

"Those events are already out there. They've always been there. We just don't know which path we're going to take until we get to it. We can go back in time, too. Both Sasi and I have talked with Kashif."

Nadya shook her head. "Don't know who that is."

"I do," said Aki. "That's how Missy and I tracked the firestone to you. But, he died over a hundred years ago. How did you talk to him?"

"Like I said, there's another world inside the stone."

Nadya shook her head, doubtfully. "You can't go back and talk with the dead."

"Not just talk. I've been there. Your firestone, Nadya, has a history that goes back to Krakatoa's eruption in eighteen eighty-three. There's even been a book written about it. A boy named Oskar wrote about his time with Kashif's family. He sailed with them on a ship called..., hmm."

Aki blurted it out. "Nerissa. I read about that. They sailed from Mogadishu."

"You read the story?"

"No. I discovered an old receipt book from a lodge that they had stayed at. The owner recorded when, for how long and how they paid."

"How did you come by that?"

"Doing research for Missy."

Switching to a crouched, sitting position, Nadya

peered out of the rain spattered windows. "Any word on Hamza?"

Sam shook his head. "Not to Sasi or myself. I think Bambang has figured out that we're not part of the equation anymore. He hasn't answered any of my calls."

"We spent half the night with him," said Nadya. "He was the one investigating the bomb."

"That's why. He suspects Hamza?"

"Everybody does. But there's no evidence. You saw the car."

"I did. Maybe they'll figure out who made the bomb."

Sam turned the windshield wipers up to full speed. They whirred and thumped nervously from side to side. "It's really coming down. I'll be glad when we get there."

There was more than one person waiting to ride when Nikko pulled up. Hamza got in the front seat while someone looking like a body builder, wearing a black tight-fitting T-shirt, got in the back. Nikko couldn't identify who it was even though the interior light was on. The man kept his face down and slid into the space behind Nikko who, by watching in his rear view mirror, could only see the man's shaved head.

It wasn't a good feeling from the start. Nikko discovered his hands shaking and kept them on the wheel. There was no greeting from either of his passengers and no attempt to introduce him to the other person riding.

Beyond rude, one of the many reasons that Nikko hated Hamza. Someone else is riding in your car? Introduce them!

On the other hand, maybe it was for his own good that he didn't know. If he did, would he be one of the last victims, the one who knew too much? That kind of summed everything up.

Nikko, feeling like this man could just reach up and strangle him at any time or put a knife to his throat or point a gun at the back of his head, also felt like he was now going to be part of some kind of crime.

"Where to?"

"Sasi's house. You're sure that he picked them up?"

Nikko sighed. "Yes."

"He could've dropped them off somewhere along the way."

"There's no way for me to know that unless I'm actually following."

Nikko wanted to say that he couldn't know because he was on a fool's mission for his boss. Right. He wanted to say that he was a fool for putting so much time and effort trying to get even. With his money he could be heading for South America, Australia, Europe, any place but where the police were looking for him. How stupid is that?

He's going to risk what could be a pretty good life somewhere else for a chance to get even, to prove that you can't mess with him and get away with it. It was going to be Nadya, her friend and the foreigner who were going to pay, each for their own little hurtful incursion into his pride.

"So..., Sasi's?"

"No hurry to get there. We want to make sure that's where they're going and give them a while to settle in."

Nikko knew better than to ask what they were going to do. He saw the bulge in Hamza's jacket There was going to be blood and he was going to play a part in this crime.

He had considered alerting the police. The problem with that was that, sooner or later, Hamza would be back out of prison and he was the kind of man who liked to settle scores. The three of them in the car heading for Sasi's house, case in point.

And what would he do then? Out of prison, Hamza would pick up where he left off. He'd be minus a few of his thug friends, but there were always more, ready to step in and Nikko wondered where he and his family would go then?

Not that his family was a close, loving family. Hardly. His son was gay. Nikko didn't care about that so much as that he never visited, preferring instead to be with his friends. There was very little communication between them.

His daughter worked at a noodle shop, had lots of boyfriends and a darling, but spoiled, four year old daughter who Nikko hardly even knew.

The barrier between Nikko and his children was his wife, Ida. If their son was gay, according to her, it was because his father must be part gay because there was nothing like that on her side of the family. Same with their daughter. No whores on her side. According to Ida, their daughter should've gotten married when she found out she was pregnant.

Ida, with her discriminatory views, could hardly conceal her disappointment in her children and blamed it all on Nikko, poor blood. Naturally, this played out badly in

257

their personal affairs and, other than a hastily cooked dinner most evenings, she was off doing her thing while Nikko was left to fend for himself.

This actually worked out well because she wasn't that exciting or interesting to be around anyway and it left him ample time to play detective and work on his inventions.

So, even though he had little contact with his family, he didn't want them to be targeted if he were the one to turn Hamza in. Prison, if he ever got there, was not going to help Hamza reform and it wasn't going to protect the person turning him in.

Could anyone ever know who it was? Of course. Being Hamza's spy, Nikko knew of a few in the department that were, if not friends, then business associates with the man.

What to do? Nikko had a plan if he lived long enough to implement it.

Hands still shaking? Of course. Add to that high blood pressure, nervousness to the point of having a hard time breathing, ringing in the ears and twitching left eye, being light-headed, just to name a few.

Nikko turned up the windshield wipers and took some comfort in hearing them thump side to side.

Capn climbed the steps, wandered out into the cockpit, sniffed his way around it a couple of times and then headed for the bow of the boat.

Every month Capn felt some distant tugging when the moon was full. There was always a desire to break away, explore, go beyond the day to day. But this was something different. Not since that time spent in the animal shelter had these feelings been this strong.

They were all down below, eating pizza, talking and laughing. There was some kind of celebration going on and, while he could understand that, he could not understand why they didn't feel the darkness approaching.

The moon was not up yet, but it's pull was strong. Spittin' Image tugged at the ropes holding her in the slip. Dark water gurgled by, heading east toward the moon.

"He's howling again," said Paul.

Kathryn added another sip of wine to her glass. "He's very restless tonight. It's going to be a full moon."

"Melissa, can you hand me the peppers?"

Melissa looked over at Kathryn quizzically. "Did you hear something?"

"I heard some kind of mumbling, nothing I could understand."

"That's what I thought. Me, too."

"Melissa, can you hand me the peppers, *please*, before my pizza turns to ice."

"Oh! Hi Paul." Melissa handed him the jar with a big smile. "Nice of you to join the conversation."

"What conversation?"

"About Capn's howling."

"I'm the one that brought it up. You joined in..., somehow."

Melissa served herself more salad, insuring that she had some avocado and an artichoke heart. "Is he howling more than usual?"

Paul, between bites, looked over at his mother. "Did you

259

hear something?"

"What? No. Outside the boat?"

"Here at the table."

"You don't get it? She has to say, please,"

"For what?

"You're asking for something, just like me asking for the peppers."

"That's different."

"How?"

"If you're asking for something physical, you're asking someone to drop what they're doing and help you."

"Oh. And if I'm thinking about something and you interrupt my thoughts with a question...,"

Kathryn smiled, sipping her wine. "Paul, don't be difficult."

"Just trying to define the boundaries. Yes, Melissa. Capn is howling a lot more than usual. Why is that, Mom? Please."

Kathryn sighed. "I wasn't going to say anything. But, tonight is a blue moon."

"It's that smoke from the fires out in the back country. That's what's making it blue."

Kathryn nodded. "That, too. Doesn't it seem odd that we're having a real blue moon on a blue moon?"

"Mom, don't go there. Next thing I know, you'll be back at Higgins's Bookstore looking for the sequel."

"We already know it doesn't exist. But maybe we'll be the ones that write it."

Sasi dished out the rice, hot and steamy, into their bowls, returned to the stove and brought the pan back to the table. Everyone watched in silence as she spooned curry sauce with bits of chicken, onion, carrots, garlic and raisins over their rice.

"Eat. Don't stand on ceremony."

You can never tell by the silence. When something is delicious or terrible, the silence around the table is nearly the same. The only way to really know is to see how much they eat and how fast they eat it.

After several minutes, Sam leaned back in his chair with a sigh. "Sasi, that was great. I want all of your recipes before I leave. At least that one anyway."

She smiled. "Thank you. Did you want more?"

"No. But I think Aki is going to lick the bowl. He might want some."

Nadya laughed. "That's what I was thinking."

Sasi started to get up. "Aki?"

"Sure. It's delicious. Thanks."

Aki, it was better than that. We'll have this one day and carne asada burritos the next! The next day will be for me, wine and cheese.

"We?"

There was a momentary silence around the table, everyone waiting. Nadya was the one to ask. "We..., what?"

"Oh, sorry. Missy was talking, referring to me as, us. I have a problem with that."

Nadya nodded. "Me, too. It's like we're sharing an apartment."

"Roommates," said Sasi returning with Aki's refill. "We won't refer to you as possessed anymore. You are roomies."

"I like that better," said Aki, taking the bowl. "Thanks."

Nadya patted Aki on the back. "Roomies, that's us."

"You two are handling this very well," said Sam. "You

261

act like you've known each other a long time."

"Aki's helping me cope."

Aki looked from Sam to Sasi with a big smile. "And I'm a lucky man."

Nadya stood, gathered Sam's and Sasi's bowls, stacked them into hers and headed for the sink. "Thanks, Sasi. That was delicious."

Aki hurried through his refill and took his dish to the sink. He tried to nudge Nadya out of the way but she pushed back, hip to hip. They laughed.

Watching them, Sasi and Sam made eye contact and shrugged. What to make of this? They looked like two young lovers and anyone watching them would believe that everything was normal.

Sasi turned in her chair so that she could see them without having to twist around. "What are you two feeling right now?"

"Surreal," said Aki. "I feel like I'm living in a dream."

Nadya nodded. "Me, too. The car bomb was real. Yet, I can't believe that it really happened. And I feel like I'm on borrowed time."

"We all are," said Sasi. "Just look at the bullet holes in the walls. Or the doors that were kicked in."

Sam poured himself some tea. "I'll buy the wood tomorrow. You have a saw, hammer and a drill?"

"I've got tools. Just not the know-how. Joko was the handyman when he was younger. He left all of his stuff here."

"It shouldn't be too hard. We can reuse all of the hardware. It's just the wood that was splintered."

"Are the doors safe for tonight? Can we lock them?"

"Locks didn't do any good last time. I've pieced everything back together and pounded in a few extra nails. We'll put chairs beneath the doorknobs."

Nadya started rinsing the dishes. "How about you, Sam? What are you feeling?"

"I'm not in a place where I can do much anymore, except for protection. I'll keep doing that."

Sasi stood and cleared the table, leaving the drinks in

262

place. Returning to the sink, she pushed the two of them out of the way. "Thank you. But this is my house. This is my job. Go get your firestones, put them on the table and see what happens. Let's try to put an end to this."

Nadya started to go but stopped and turned. "Sasi, Rools said that he met you only once. You had the firestone for how many years?"

"About thirty."

"And you never held the stone?"

"I held it many times. But I never let it take over."

"How did you do that?"

"It's better, at least I think it's better, to explore the stone's world rather than the other way around."

"Rools said he met you once. What happened."

"He insisted on sharing control. I wouldn't allow that."

"Then, what?"

"He challenged me to put down the stone, which I did."

"How? I couldn't stop him."

"There are any number of outcomes with any encounter. I chose one that did not include him inside my head."

"Where did you learn how to do that?"

"That's what thirty years of practice does."

Putting the firestones together on the table, they did nothing. It was like Bambang said, just a couple of rocks. The magic was gone and neither Missy nor Rools were ready to go back inside.

Kathryn brought out a sheet, blanket and pillow for Melissa sometime around eleven and went to bed shortly after that. Paul and Melissa retired to the cockpit and waited for the moon to clear the rows of palm trees on the east side of the marina.

Capn stopped howling when they came topside and joined them in the cockpit, making himself comfortable on one of the cushions next to Melissa.

"I think he likes you better than me," said Paul. "And I'm the one that takes care of him."

"I smell better."

"Not funny. I feed him, take him for walks, brush him...,"

Melissa scratched Capn behind his ears. "But I give him love."

"I see. I'm just the caretaker?"

"Right. See how he responds to having his belly rubbed?"

"I do that."

"You're too energetic when you do it. You have to be gentle."

"I'm gentle."

"Like a truck."

"No way."

"Come over here and rub my shoulders."

"Why?"

"I want to prove something."

"Right. You just want a massage."

"See? Already you're acting rough. You're afraid and you're putting up a defense."

"What am I afraid of? It's just a shoulder massage."

"Prove it."

Paul moved to the cushion next to Melissa and started in, fingers and thumbs probing her shoulders. "There's nothing to prove. I am an excellent massager, among other things."

"It's too hard. You're too rough. That's why Capn comes to me."

"What's the matter with this? Your shoulders are tight. I can feel where that is and that's what I'm going after."

"Paul, you're in turbo mode. Slow it down. Relax."

"This is how you get to the root of the problem."

"You're making my muscles tighten. I'm trying to protect myself." Melissa pulled away, turned and faced Paul. "Turn around. I'll show you how it's supposed to feel."

"Right. Like you're the expert?"

"Who does Capn come to? You, or me?"

Paul turned, allowing Melissa to begin. She started gently, slowly, probing with her thumbs lightly. "Your supraspinatus muscle is very tight."

"My, what?"

"Shoulder muscle." She pressed a bit harder, digging with her thumbs. "It's right here."

"Ow. OK. I get it. What causes that?"

"You have bad posture when you study and the mouse should be lower. That way you don't strain it by holding your arm up for so long."

"How do you know all of this?"

"I pay attention, Paul. Turn around, will you please?"

When Paul complied, she kissed him on the lips. "It's a blue moon tonight. Anything can happen."

"I think it just did. What was that for?"

"If you have to question, you're worse off than I thought."

Melissa turned so that she could watch the rising moon, snuggling into Paul's chest and insuring that he was comfortable leaning against the bulkhead, which he wasn't. They found another pillow, piled it against the fiberglass and, having done that, Melissa leaned into him again and pulled his arms around her.

"Finals are over, Paul. What's next?"

"Aki, where was that place that you talked about?"

"What place?"

"In America."

"Oh. San Diego?"

"What's it like?"

Aki, tell her about the food!

"You have to have a car, everything's so far apart. Lots of things to see but I wasn't there long enough to see them."

"How's the weather?"

"Perfect while I was there."

"How about crime?"

Aki laughed. "Not as bad as here. Not once was my rental car blown up. But, I wasn't there very long."

"How are the people?"

"Pretty nice."

Aki, she's looking for excuses to go! Tell about the food, the romance of walking along the beach, carne asada burritos, margaritas, cheese enchiladas. What is wrong with you?

"Does it cost much to go there?"

"You're wanting to escape?"

"That's one reason."

"What else?"

Nadya held up her hand, forefinger and thumb about a quarter inch apart. "We were that close to dying. Isn't that reason enough?"

"You can't stay there. Sooner or later we've got to come back here."

"How about a week? Maybe two. Until they catch Hamza."

"We'll call Bambang first thing tomorrow morning, get an update."

"After that, let's go."

"Tomorrow?"

"Why not?"

"You have a passport?"

"In my apartment."

"Oh..., a problem."

"Hamza?"

"He'll be watching."

What??? Aki, I'm embarrassed. Work with her! Work with her!

"Maybe we can get police protection while you get your things."

That's more like it!

"No. He's got friends in the department. That's why I didn't tell Bambang where I was going to stay. And if he knows that we're trying to leave the country, he'll stop us. We're witnesses."

"We can argue the other side. We're victims. We're fleeing for our lives."

"He'll offer police protection. I don't want that."

"Maybe Sam can help us."

"If I get my passport, you're willing to go?"

Aki rested his hand on Nadya's shoulder and gave her a big smile. "Nadya, you're the best thing that's happened to me in a long time. I'm with you."

Nadya leaned forward and kissed him on the lips. "It's nice to be around someone who doesn't want to control everything."

She went to the other side of the bed and removed her bra without taking off her top and then removed her pants, folded them and placed them onto the night stand before sliding in between the sheets. "I can pay my way. I've got money saved up and I can sell my jewelry. I want to see what another life is like. I feel like I'm stuck."

Aki, trying not to appear too eager, cast several glances in her direction as she undressed. Under the sheets, Nadya pressed up against him.

"Please, Aki. No sex. Not yet."

Nikko put the car into park and set the emergency brake. Killing the engine also killed the windshield wipers and, stopped, it was impossible to see outside. Rain pounded down on the metal roof and other than the bustle of Hamza and friend getting out of the car, that was all he could hear.

Nikko had to drive past Sasi's house and park behind the trees further up the street. He would rather have been allowed to turn the car around so that their escape would be a fast return back into traffic where he could get lost, exactly where he wanted to be while some kind of hit man sat in the back seat completely out of his view.

"Keep it running," said Hamza as he closed the door.

Hamza instructions were to keep the car pointed in this direction, going away from civilization, across winding roads to some distant ferry where he would head out for another island. Easy to get lost on those back roads on a night like this, or killed.

Nikko had a sudden desire to light up a cigarette, not that he smoked. It just felt like the moment had arrived. He did try it once years ago, coughed for half an hour and swore that he'd never do it again. But, if there ever was a time for one last smoke, now was it. Isn't that what they do in the movies?

Depending on Hamza's next few moves, Nikko had a response and other than feeling like he was going to die sometime in the next fifteen or twenty minutes, everything was going to plan.

You want to play hardball? Don't mess with the man that knows all about you, all of your secrets, acquaintances and almost all of the things that go on behind the scene.

Don't mess with the man who has a passion for remote control and voice impersonation, a dangerous combination. Bad things can happen if you're not careful and don't treat your associates well.

Nikko started the engine but kept the wipers turned

off. Don't need any extra noise to draw attention. Given the choice, he would have preferred to keep the engine turned off as well. That kind of said a lot about what Hamza's intentions were.

Minutes passed. Every now and then, the rain paused and an occasional bit of moonlight broke through, casting a dim, blue glow over the otherwise drenched and dreary scene.

Nikko sat in quietly, deep in thought, wondering about the strange twists and turns that life delivers and how events can turn on a dime, waiting for the sounds of gunfire, racing footsteps back to his car and speeding away with pounding heart.

Kathryn stared blankly at the clock on her night stand. She couldn't remember if it was running when she went to bed, sometime around ten-thirty, but this clock was saying five after ten.

Batteries dead already? Seems like Paul had replaced them just a couple of months ago. Was it the salt air that makes them go bad so fast? Everything else corrodes in this salty air. Why not the batteries?

Pulling the covers back, she rolled over to the night stand and retrieved her laptop. Twelve-fifteen and a message from Sam.

Hey Kathryn,

Just wanted to say Hi and see how everyone's doing. How did finals go for Paul? How was the pizza? If you saved me that piece, go ahead and eat it. I was wanting to be home by now. Soon, hopefully.

How about you? Did you get that promotion? Making the big bucks now, are you? What will you do with all of that money?

Anyway, missing you guys. Sasi's given me a couple of good recipes I'd be happy to share. Got enough room for two of us to cook on the boat?

Give Capn a good scratch behind the ears for me, will you? And give yourself a hug. Cheers!

Sam

Kathryn studied the message. Sam was being coy. He didn't offer any information about their progress. He didn't say that anyone was hurt, but he also didn't say everything was fine either. It was not going as well as he was making it out to be. All in all, a depressing message. She pondered answering, but decided to wait until morning.

Walking through the cabin, she checked the companionway door, insured that it was locked and got herself a glass of water. Melissa, sprawled out on her quarter berth with covers mostly off, was turned toward the bulkhead and Paul was semi-snoring in his room. Everything looked normal. Seeing that she was awake, Capn got up from his bed under the steps, followed Kathryn into her room and settled into his usual spot at the foot of her bed.

Was all of this worrying for nothing? Sam can take care of himself, probably better than anybody. So, what was there to worry about? Just because this night has the label of a blue moon, is that so bad?

Not by itself. But, he's on the other side of the world staying with a woman who, like Kashif, had possession of the firestone. Any particular reason to be afraid? No. There was every reason to be terrified. Kathryn crawled back into bed and pulled the sheet up. It was too hot for a blanket.

A minute or two later, after much tossing and turning, she sat up and opened the hatch above her bed. Moonlight, slightly blue but reflecting the power of a full moon, spilled across her bed and cast her cabin into soft shadows and a dim blue light. A cool breeze followed, fresh with the scent of the sea as it pushed the smoke-filled air back toward the east county fires.

Many years before, when Hamza was still a boy, he used to sneak up between the rows of bushes along the walkway on the north side of Sasi's house and spy on her. Even then, he had a great desire to play a bigger role in her life.

Through the various windows around her house he watched her make tea, cook dinner, read endless piles of books and prepare her lectures. Sasi was a continuous source of mystery and fascination.

The bushes had grown over the years but their positions in the ground hadn't changed. Feeling like a kid again, sneaking out in the middle of the night and moving through the bushes in the rain, Hamza was almost gleeful as he pulled his gun out of its holster. He was always giddy when he knew that there was going to be a death.

Nikko claimed that all four were in the house. Who would be sleeping where? He knew the layout. He'd been in it many times. Certainly, Sasi would never change her room. She was stubborn like that. That room, she claimed when they were still friends, was better because it was located away from the street. It was quiet and private.

That leaves Nadya, her new friend and Joko's pal in the bar, the foreigner. Does it matter who is sleeping with whom? Not really.

Pausing below Joko's window, the closest one to the street, Hamza clicked off the safety, checked the window and discovered it locked. The bathroom window would be next. But it was too high and narrow to enter. Next would be Sasi's room. Even with the rain she would have her window open. She liked her fresh air.

Crouching beneath her window, Hamza took a deep breath and signaled for Toni to follow. When he was close enough, he whispered, "Do not hurt the woman in this room. All I want from her is the firestone."

"And the others?"

"Shoot them."

"She's a witness."

And there was the crux of the problem. As much as Hamza wanted to kill the others he did not want to hurt Sasi. He did not want to see her shock at taking a bullet, did not want to see her suffer or bleed and, a private admission to himself, he did not want her out of his life.

The firestone was at the root of all of this. It was the firestone that she talked about, the source of many of her ideas although she never called it by that name.

Hamza had heard her lectures, most all of them, recorded by someone he paid to attend. And the more he heard, the more convinced he became that he should be the new owner of the stone.

She was getting older, feeble and less able to take care of herself. Was the rumor true that she had some kind of incurable disease? Wasn't it time for her to pass it on? Certainly not to the foreigner. Who does he think he is coming into the middle of this? Stay in your own country and let the locals solve their own problems.

Beside himself, who else was more able to control the power of this magical stone? Hamza considered himself young, intelligent, enthusiastic and dedicated to whatever cause he deemed worthy. He knew that he could be successful where all of the others had failed.

And while he was contemplating these thoughts, there was a break in the clouds to the west and overhead, a hesitation in the rain. Sasi's little house, with water dripping off of the roof and gutters catching up to the rain, was cast in the light of a blue moon.

"She's a witness," said Toni, quietly. "We can't leave anyone alive."

Sasi didn't know exactly how it was all going to come to an end but she did know what the ending would be and who caused it. That much she had seen.

If ever there was a night for that to happen, tonight was it. All of the players were in position on both sides of the planet. Sam, mentioning that Kathryn was having pizza with her son and Melissa was the final clue. Everything was in alignment.

The wild card was Hamza. Would he be dependably bad? Sasi was thinking that he would. Earlier on, years earlier, something didn't click right in his head and she couldn't figure out if he had learned that behavior or been born with it.

It was compulsive behavior for Hamza to get ahead at all costs and if anything got in his way, remove it and make sure it stayed removed. Anybody go against him? There was a stiff price to pay for that.

Which is why Sasi stayed neutral. While so many were giving up on him, she maintained that he was just finding his way. Surely, one day, he would see the light and come around. She didn't believe any of that, but figured that it kept her from becoming the enemy.

Dependably bad? Yes. Hamza would arrive tonight and he would attempt to do what he set out to do, kill Nadya, of course, and the man that she spent the night with, and Sam for making him look bad.

But, would he pull the trigger when the gun was aimed at her? She didn't think so. There was also a very compassionate side to the man. He revered loyalty and respect. Sasi knew that Hamza respected her.

After Sam's first visit, interacting with the firestone and using the techniques that they'd learned together, she'd looked ahead to her own death and attempted to see beyond. What she'd learned is that all of her possible paths forward were connected to and dependent upon the events that led up to her death.

Hamza was in the room before Sasi was fully awake. She started to sit up, pulling the covers up around her at the same time. He motioned for her to stay put and signaled, with his forefinger against his lips, to stay quiet.

Hamza went to her bedroom door, insured that it was closed tightly and locked it. Returning to her bed, he sat down beside her and whispered, "The firestone, Sasi. Hand it over."

"I don't have it."

"Where is it?"

"I'm not sure...,"

Hamza raised his gun, threatening, and then checked himself. "Is it here in the house?"

She nodded. "Not sure exactly where, but it is here in the house."

"Who has it? The foreigner?"

"Hamza, do yourself a favor and turn yourself in. You'll get off easier."

"Don't even talk like that."

"All they have on you so far is the kidnapping. I can testify that I was treated well and that it was all a big misunderstanding."

"No. I lost some of my best men. Your foreigner friend is going to pay for that."

"He was defending me."

"You're stalling, Sasi. The firestone."

"As I've said, I don't have it."

"Then..., who? Don't mess with me. You know how I get."

Sasi nodded sadly. "Yes. I know all too well. You're on a fool's errand, Hamza. You don't know enough about the firestone. It will consume you."

"I'll be the judge of that."

"No. Actually, you won't. I've been studying it for thirty years and I've only scratched the surface. The firestone

275

can consume you in seconds. All it takes is a minor mistake."

"The firestone, Sasi. Now. Don't make me have to ask again."

"If I told you where it is, you wouldn't know what to do with it. And that's because you don't know enough about it. I'm doing this for you, Hamza, for your own good. You have to trust me."

"Why should I trust you? You gave up on me long ago."

"You gave up on yourself. You didn't believe that you could get what you wanted without bullying. You had to prove that you were top dog. What has that gotten you?"

"I've gotten what I wanted."

"Have you? There's a warrant out for your arrest. Look at yourself Hamza. I can refuse to press charges for the kidnapping. They'll drop that one. I don't know if you had anything to do with the car bomb."

"I didn't plant that bomb."

"Well, I hope that you have an alibi. My advice to you, and I say this as a friend, go back out that window, turn yourself in and make things right."

"The firestone, Sasi. I'm going to get rough and I don't want to do that to you. But..., I will."

Toni was tired of the whole conversation. It was pointless. She was going to talk until the sun came up and still not give Hamza the firestone. He knew stalling when he saw it. With gun drawn, he started toward the door.

"There are two firestones."

"What?" Hamza motioned for Toni to stay put. "Two?"

"That's always been a problem for you. You're so impatient that you never get all of the facts. Yes. There are two."

"In this house?"

"Yes. But not in the form that you think. The firestones have a spirit. I'm going to give you thirty years of knowledge in the next sentence, or two. Pay attention."

"I'm listening."

"If the spirit is inside the stone, and if you know how to

276

manipulate it, you can go anywhere, see anything. But, it's easy to get lost."

"What does that mean?"

"If you forget where you are, you can't come back."

"If that happens..., what?"

"No idea. It's never happened to me. But I suspect that if you can't come back you would lose consciousness of this world."

"You said, if the spirit is inside the stone. What if it isn't?"

"It assumes half possession of the person holding it. It takes over. It shares their body."

"How do you know?"

Sasi shook her head slowly. This man was never going to learn. If she said that Nadya and Aki, sleeping together in Joko's bed, were both possessed, he would simply go in there and shoot them.

Forget about thirty years of learning. Forget about the history that each of these stones contained, or of the endless possibilities for knowledge to be gained working with them. There would be no more questions asked, no more learning...,

The slap came out of nowhere. Still sitting up in bed, Sasi had been looking down at her knees. Her head twisted toward her right shoulder as the pain filled her cheek. It stung. It stung bad. Involuntary tears rolled down her cheeks.

Hamza's eyes were hard now. Her hesitation to answer he'd taken the wrong way. So, like him.

"Get out of bed, Sasi. Put on a robe if you need to and do it quietly. We're going to have a meeting in the living room."

"You're making a mistake, Hamza."

"That's what you've always said. Do it!"

Sasi retrieved a robe from the closet, put it on and stopped at the door, waiting for Hamza to proceed. Standing behind her, he wrapped his arm around her shoulders and pointed the gun at her head.

"Open it, go slowly into the living room, turn on lights

as you go. Toni. Open the door at the other end of the hallway and bring everybody out. No shooting unless you have to."

Sam was crouched next to the couch, gun aimed at the hallway door when they came through. Seeing Sasi, with a gun to her head, he lowered his.

"That's right, hero. Put it down. Slide it over here."

Toni crossed the hallway and, without bothering to see if it was locked, kicked it open. Light from the hallway cast a light into the room. "Rise and shine, girlies. Any fast moves and I'll start shooting. Move it!"

Climbing out of bed, Nadya and Aki exchanged glances. Toni waited for them to exit and followed them out into the living room.

"Go sit by hero," said Hamza. "Elbows on the table, hands flat. First person to take their hands off of the table gets shot. Nadya, hardly recognized you with your clothes on."

When all four were seated, Hamza smiled. "If you want something done right, you just have to do it yourself. Now that everyone is here, let's talk about the firestones. Sasi says there's two. Who's got them?"

Aki, he cannot take the firestone!

"I know."

Hamza pointed his gun at Aki. So, this is the man that she ran away with? "You know *what*, butterball?"

The barrel of a gun gets much bigger when pointed in your direction. Aki, heart pounding, adrenalin pumping, calculated where the bullet was going to hit, mid chest. It was going to shatter his rib cage going in and take out his spine on the way out. "I know that there's two. I have one of them."

Hamza put the gun to Nadya's head. "Go get it. One wrong move and she's history."

Aki went into Joko's room, retrieved the firestone from his luggage, returned and handed it to Hamza. "Go sit, butterball. Hands on the table."

Aki, I'm really starting to not like this man. Shall we take him out?

278

"No."

Hamza, holding the firestone and turning it one way or the other, didn't seem to notice Aki's word. He finally placed the stone on the table. "Who's got the other one?"

"I do," said Nadya.

"Go get it." Hamza pointed the gun at Aki. "Try anything and lover boy here gets it."

Nadya complied. Coming back into the room, she handed it to Hamza and sat next to Aki at the table.

Hamza studied the stone for a minute or two and then placed it on the table next to the other one. "There's nothing magical about these. They're just rocks."

"As I've stated earlier," said Sasi. "The spirits of these stones is either in the stone or cohabiting with their owner. Both Nadya and Aki are possessed."

"Is that so?" Hamza nudged the two stones toward their owners. "Make the spirits go back inside."

"If we could, we would," said Nadya.

"What makes them go back?"

This was a question that no one wanted to answer. Silence filled the room.

"Answer me!"

"The spirit," said Sasi, answering softly, "has to want to leave. We don't know how to make it go back if it doesn't want to."

"Happy spirits," said Hamza, sarcastically. "Let me think about this. If the host was dead, the spirit wouldn't be so happy anymore, would it?"

Aki? I sense great danger!

Hamza pointed the gun at Aki. "Let's see what happens."

Sam, sitting next to Sasi and across the table from Nadya and Aki, flipped the table up with his feet as Hamza pulled the trigger. The bullet penetrated the wood and shoved the table top into Aki, knocking him down to the floor.

Sam flipped over backward, taking the chair with him and holding it as a shield charged Hamza, who fired twice. The first bullet shattered the chair. The second hit

Sam in his ribs and, falling, he threw one of the pieces at Hamza. It hit him in the face, right where Sam had blackened his eye back at the bar. Wanting to finish him off, Hamza aimed at Sam's head and pulled the trigger.

Sasi stepped in front of Sam and took the bullet. It hit her in the chest with a hefty thud. She fell back into Sam's arms with a groan, her head already limp. Hamza was stunned.

"No! Sasi..., why? Not you! No!"

Toni pulled Nadya off of her chair by her hair with a strong desire to get even for all the trouble she'd caused. Standing her up and spinning her around, he was going to break her nose. He was met with claws across his face and into his eyes, Nadya fighting like a cat. He pulled the trigger. Nadya went down.

Sorry, Aki. This one's mine.

Aki shoved the table into Toni's knees, knocking him over. With speed and agility that only Missy could have, he leaped over the table and kicked Toni's gun out of his hand. When Toni tried to stand, Aki grabbed him, carried him over his shoulders to the balcony and with a yell that came from some place unknown, pitched him through the doors. Hamza fired two shots into Aki's back.

Sam threw another piece of chair at Hamza, knocking the gun out of hand. Standing, much more slowly than he wanted, he charged at Hamza, who turned and ran back into Sasi's bedroom. By the time Sam got there he had already jumped out of the window.

Sasi's face was pale by the time Sam got back to her. Her robe was covered in blood and her breathing shallow.

"Sasi. Sam here. Stay with me. I'm calling for help."

Her voice was hardly more than a whisper. "Don't worry about me. I know I'm dying."

"Don't you believe it."

"Go help Aki and..., Nadya."

"Sasi?"

"It's my time, Sam. Let me go."

"I won't!"

Sasi laughed, coughing and gurgling with the effort, a bit of blood trickling out of the corner of her mouth. "How the hell do I get rid of you? Do I have to die in your arms?"

"That's not going to happen. I won't let it."

"I looked ahead, Sam, after you went home. Everything will be OK."

"I can't stop your bleeding."

"Go..., make sure Nadya and Aki..., are together."

"In a minute."

Sasi reached up and touched his cheek. "Good-bye, Sam. You've been a pleasure."

Sasi's arm fell back to her chest. She closed her eyes with a smile and was gone. Sam, holding her close, felt the tears well up in his eyes. He held her close for another minute, wanting to feel as much of her essence as possible.

There was nothing he could do. He gently put her down and, wiping the tears away, surveyed the room.

Aki, face down and staring at the wooden slats of the floor, was trying to figure out how he got there. Beneath his right shoulder, exquisite pain causing his arms to twitch, hands to clench and he couldn't catch his breath.

Aki! Air! We need air!

"I'm trying, Missy."

We've been hit!

"Feels like ribs are poking into my lungs.

I feel your pain.

"Oh, my God, it hurts! Can't move my legs."

But, we did it!

"Did..., what?"

Threw him through the doors!

"Over the balcony?"

Like a bird, except he couldn't fly.

"I can't move."

Aki, you're heart's going a mile a minute. Hey! I'm finally getting time down. Thanks for that.

"Air, Missy. We need air."

It takes a lot to pick someone up and throw them that far. Whenever I'm out on the kill...,

"You're not a lion."

After I've made the kill, I have to stop and catch my breath.

"Whatever. Missy, I'm fading."

I want you to know that I've enjoyed your company. We've had a good run.

"You're leaving?"

Not yet. I'll wait to see if you make it.

"Just like that. You're gone?"

I've never lied to you about that. I have no use for a dead man.

"You think I'm dying?"

Aki, you said it yourself. You can't get air.

"I..., I'm not ready to go. Where..., where's Nadya?

She got shot.

"Is she OK?"

If you can't see her, I can't see her.

"Nadya? Nadya!"

She's not answering.

"Sam? Sasi? Hello?"

Your body's not working for us.

Sam kneeled beside Aki and put his hand on his shoulder. "Stay still, Aki. Don't try to move. Help is on the way."

"Wha..., what happened?"

"You've been shot." Sam hesitated, fighting back the tears, seeing Sasi's limp body across the room. "Hamza's gone. Sasi's dead."

"Oh, no. Nadya?"

"I'll go check. Stay still. I've called for help."

Sam crawled over to the table and pushed it out from between the two of them, the effort being much harder than expected. His hands were sticky with blood and, examining his wound, he discovered the bleeding was worse than he thought.

He crawled over to Nadya who was flat on her back, hands over her wound, both covered in blood.

"Nadya? Can you hear me?"

Her eyelids twitched, but did not open, her voice faint. "Wha..., what?"

"Nadya, I've called for help. It's on the way. You're bleeding. Don't try to move."

Nadya opened her eyes and slowly turned her head from side to side. "Where's everybody?"

"Hamza's gone. Aki's been shot."

"Is he..., dead?"

"He's alive, asking about you."

Nadya managed a weak smile. "So..., sweet, that man. Sasi?"

"She..., she's dead."

"Oh, no! My fault, all of..., this."

"You didn't shoot anyone. I'm going to try to move you next to Aki. He wants to see you. OK?"

Seeing a slight nod, Sam, now feeling very weak, pulled

her over to Aki's side so they could see each other face to face. Nadya reached over and touched Aki's shoulder.

"It was going to be you, Aki. I was ready to go with you."

In between shallow breaths, Aki smiled. "Let's go."

"Where we going?"

"America."

"I'll have to…, pack."

Aki managed a weak smile. "You…, were right. We should've already gone."

Sirens wailed in the distance, sounding like there were several on their way. With loss of blood, Sam was starting to fade. Sitting next to Nadya, he was wanting to lie down, close his eyes and take a short rest. He put his head in his hands. "I've let everybody down."

Nadya managed a pained smile. "You…, you're the best, Sam."

Groaning with the effort, Aki managed to move his hand over to Nadya's and touched her lightly, wanting to hold her. "First time I saw you," he whispered. "I fell in love."

Nadya returned the effort, putting her hand in his and squeezing lightly. "Me, too, Aki. Me, too."

The sirens were close now, screeching brakes, car doors slamming, lots of commotion outside the walls of Sasi's simple little home.

They were yelling, banging on the door, more sirens in the distance. It was going to be a big day for the people reporting the news.

With great effort, Sam stood, wobbly and faint, for the purpose of removing the blockade at the front door. It wasn't that far away, but before he could get there his world turned black.

Rain poured in through the hole in the wall where the balcony doors used to be, drenching Sasi's tidy little world with a million dollar view.

Hamza jumped into the car and slammed the door shut. "Go! Go! Go!"

Nikko hesitated, waiting for the back door to open. "Where's your friend?"

"He left early."

"What?"

"He's dead, stupid. Go!"

Hamza was just piling one insult on top of another and Nikko was getting mighty tired of it. The man was not worthy of the oxygen he was taking up. Better to save it for the next person to come along. Lost his partner in crime and had no remorse? At least bring the body back! Strike one.

Nikko turned on the wipers and pulled away slowly, not wanting to draw attention. Better to drive as if nothing had happened. Police will be looking for a speeding car.

"Step on it, you idiot!"

Strike two. Nikko glanced over at Hamza and noticed that he didn't have his gun. "Don't want to draw attention to ourselves."

"Do as I say!"

Nikko smiled. Strike three. The man has no redeemable qualities. He drove a little faster, not as fast as Hamza wanted, but in this rain too much faster would be unsafe. He knew this would irritate the man and Nikko was beginning to draw a little pleasure from this trip.

"What happened back at the house?"

"Not your business. Step on the gas!"

Strike four. The man knows no bounds. "Everybody dead?"

"Just drive."

Nikko had studied the route going to Hamza's ferry launch. Google Earth was wonderful for things like that, studying the terrain without actually having to drive the route. There were several sections of the road that were isolated and many places where a wrong turn would take

285

you in a bad direction. These were the areas where Nikko figured that he was going to be killed. But now, with his accomplice gone and Hamza without a gun, the tables were turned.

Earlier, running Hamza's voice through his simulator, he made the call and had another bomb prepared, which he installed on his own car. He needed a new one anyway and this seemed like a pretty good way to get rid of a couple of problems at the same time.

He called Hamza's bookkeeper, ordered him to mail all information on Nikko to a P.O. Box along with a check for a sizeable amount of money and destroy all evidence that connected the two together. Don't ask questions.

Just before leaving for tonight's adventure, Nikko reported his car stolen.

All he had to do was say the words, "I think I'm having a heart attack." That would be picked up by the microphone under the dash. Those words, run through the program he'd created, activated the solenoid that pushed the button to start the timing for the bomb, five minutes.

If it got that far, Nikko figured that there were three possible outcomes. One, if Hamza still had his gun and his accomplice and they were in an isolated area, he would say the words, wait about four and a half minutes and jump out of the car or, if unable to do that, just die with them. Two, if he was being killed, saying the words as he was being strangled or after he was shot. By then it wouldn't matter but he would at least get even. Three, the most preferred, what was happening now.

Driving slowly enough to keep Hamza perpetually pissed off, Nikko drove into an isolated area and made a deliberate wrong turn.

"You idiot! What is wrong with you?"

"I think I'm having a heart attack."

Nikko did not have to feign feeling sick. His palms were sweaty, forehead perspiring, heart pounding and it was getting very hard to concentrate. Four minutes.

Nikko stopped the car and stared at the steering wheel. "I..., can't drive." Three minutes.

"Get out! Go around. I'll drive. You're useless."

Nikko got out, stood in the rain for a moment, enjoying that refreshing feeling and then slowly made his way around the car. As expected, Hamza took off without him. He jammed the car into gear, did a U-turn, fishtailing in the process and raced away. Two minutes.

Hearing his car fade into the distance, Nikko breathed a sigh of relief. Yes, it was still raining. It was going to be a long, wet walk home. No one would miss him. His wife thought he was out on assignment, which he was, and didn't expect him until sometime tomorrow. One minute.

Yes, it was going to be a long walk, but it was going to be pleasant. He'd brought a few snacks and one of those very thin raincoats that fold up into a handy little plastic bag that fits in your pocket. Opening it and putting it on, there was brilliant flash of light off in the distance and several seconds later, a loud boom.

Lightning? Or, something a bit more sinister.

Sasi, entering a windowless room with walls of tapestries lit by candlelight, spotted Kashif sitting at a small table not far away. He busied himself by adjusting the biscuits on the plate, two cups and a pot of tea.

Kashif stood when their eyes met, smiled as she approached, put his hands on her shoulders and kissed her on the cheek. "Welcome, Sasi. I've been waiting."

"Thank you for being so patient."

He motioned for her to sit on the pillow he'd placed on the floor on the opposite side of the table. When they were seated, he filled both of their cups, careful to not spill a drop. "How was your journey?"

Sasi, smiling, watched with interest. "You've been practicing."

"A little. I was never very good at this sort of thing."

"You know why I'm here, don't you?"

"Patience, Sasi. How was your transition?"

"Much better than cancer treatments."

"We all have so precious little time. It seems a shame."

"Your death was slow. I saw that when Sam and I came to visit. It must have been very hard for you."

"I knew better times would follow. That makes everything easier."

"Where do I go from here?"

"As you taught Sam, it is from here that you explore and to here that you must return."

"There's no going back, is there?"

"I'm afraid not."

"It should not have ended with Nadya and Aki dying."

"There's nothing more to do. That time has already passed."

"There were so many choices."

"And unfortunately, the four of you chose the wrong one. I am very sorry. I did not want to see it end like that."

"There's nothing more we can do?"

"Once they possessed the stones and met, their fate was

sealed."

"It's not fair."

"Who said anything about being fair? You choose the path. It becomes your destiny."

"She didn't want the stone."

"That does not count for anything. Nobody does, at first. If you want to save them, maybe there's a time when they were together before they both possessed the stones."

"That would be impossible to know."

"That would seem impossible. They both lived in the same city. Perhaps at some earlier time they crossed paths."

"How long would that take, searching the possibilities?"

"What else have you got going on?"

"What will happen with the firestones?"

"That remains to be seen. Sasi, may I suggest that you enjoy this tea? It has a calming effect and it goes very well with these treats that I've brought just for you."

"I'm sorry, Kashif. I'm so worried about everything. I should've rid myself of the stone years ago and then...,"

Kashif reached across the table and rested his hands on hers. "Those things are past. You cannot regret them any more than you can change them."

Sasi sipped the tea and felt the warmth pour through her soul. Yes, he's right. There is nothing more that can be done with the outcome. It is what it is. "What about Sam?"

"He is at a crossroad."

"How can I help him?"

"Perhaps you can find him in a dream. And on that subject, we both have the same goal."

It seemed like they talked on forever about things that can and cannot be. And, after helping her feel at home, Kashif said good-bye and was gone. Sasi found herself alone in that cloud between here and there, light and dark, everything a possibility.

Nikko was nearing the main road when someone driving up behind him honked their horn. He was hesitant to turn because he wanted no witnesses as to his whereabouts. Better to get lost in the hustle and bustle of the city first and become the invisible man.

Whoever it was, they had slowed down to his walking speed and were coming up alongside. For a moment, Nikko panicked, thinking that somehow Hamza had survived and was now coming back for revenge.

The horn did not the sound like the horn from his car and, glancing out of the corner of his eye, the make and model were not the same. He stopped and waited for the driver to lower her side window, a smooth, whirring sound that cleared the rain from the glass.

"Do you need a ride?"

Nikko smiled politely and shook his head. He kept his glasses on, rain soaked, and carried on with his walk. The car stayed alongside.

"I am trying to get to Sukaraja. Do you know the way?"

Nikko stopped again and studied the woman. It was very bold for her to stop and talk to a complete stranger, much less invite him into her car. But Sukaraja was in the same direction that he was headed. She could easily cut an hour off of his walking.

She didn't look like the police or a prostitute or anyone dangerous. Her hair was thick, rather frizzy and her glasses were thicker than his. Glancing inside, the car was clean and, stepping a bit closer, did not smell of cigarettes.

Nikko nodded. "Yes. I know the way. You don't mind?"

"Please get in."

Nikko removed his coat, shook it out and stuffed it back into its tiny plastic pouch. It felt very good to be in a warm, dry space and he wanted very much to put miles between himself and the burned out pieces of his car, the sooner the better. He also knew he would be without a car for a few days, until someone discovered the burned out wreck. "Thank you for the lift."

The woman waited for him to put on his seat belt and then eased her car back into traffic. "Why are you out in this rain?"

"My partner and I had a big fight," Nikko lied. They never fought. They solved that problem years ago just by not talking. Get rid of that part, eat only a few meals together and don't ask too many questions and the relationship goes along just fine. "Sometimes it helps just to go for a walk."

"You must be from around here?"

"Close by. As it happens, I am going to Sukaraja myself. I have some business there." That business was taking public transportation back to his home further north. Blend in, move around, don't be noticed.

"I was going to an interview," she said. "But they never showed up. I blame it on the storm."

Nikko had this sudden fear that she was a reporter. What are the odds of that? Getting in a car with a fricking reporter. "Interview?"

"Back at the landing. No ferry. He could've called."

"Inconsiderate, certainly."

"He figured neither of us would show because of the storm."

"Turn left at this next intersection."

"You still have to confirm."

"Right. You're a reporter?"

"No, not a reporter."

"What kind of interview? If you don't mind my asking."

"For a job."

Nikko's next problem, what to do now that he had just murdered his employer. He smiled, knowing that he would never get a letter of recommendation. "Hiring or applying?"

"Hiring. I'm making a movie."

"Really. What about?"

"Robots."

Nikko sat a bit straighter in his seat. Someone else is

291

interested in robots? Sitting in the same car? What are the odds? "Robots? How so?"

"The movie? Or the position?"

"Both."

"I'm looking for someone who is passionate about robots, someone who has a good grasp of the technology and wouldn't mind spending long hours building several different prototypes. The pay is not good. We're on a tight budget so I need somebody that can improvise."

"Create things from scratch?"

"Yes."

"What's the movie about?"

"Designing a robot that learns on its own. We'd program it, of course, initially. But, I want to give it a curiosity edge so that it becomes intuitive. I want to give it tools and tasks and see if it can figure out how to do them. I know that sounds like a far-fetched dream, but it's my passion. Know anyone who'd be interested in something like that?"

Nikko settled into his seat and smiled, almost a giggle because it was really hard to contain what he was feeling. "Yes. I know of just the person that you're looking for."

Bambang removed the two firestones from their containers and placed them on top of his desk. They appeared to be the same stones that he had held back at Sasi's house. Same appearance, different feel.

They had a soft glow that they didn't have before. Radioactive? No. It'd be glowing all the time. What is it that can turn on and off like that?

As they were evidence, Bambang was forced to wear gloves. But he just couldn't get a good feel for the differences in these stones through the latex. Is that heat coming from them? Hard to tell.

Closing his office door, shutting the blinds and turning off the lights, Bambang returned to his chair and studied the two stones, turning them this way and that.

There. What is that?

Some kind of split inside the stone making a shadow.

It's inside.

If I turn it just a hair more, it looks like a..., lion's face, long, drawn out nose, eyes..., staring at me.

Strange, being observed by a stone. Unwavering eyes, steady. What is it about them?

Bambang turned the stone away, got up, opened the blinds and turned on the lights. Hypnosis. That's what that was. Felt like he was face to face with a lion, like it was here in the room. He? It has a gender? Odd. It's just a rock, nothing more.

But, three of four people in that party are dead and the foreigner is in critical condition. Somehow, Hamza's involved. Half his men are dead and the others either aren't talking or don't know anything. Other than Hamza, what the hell am I missing?

Pushing that stone to the side, Bambang slid the other one closer. The shapes of the stones were similar, but the internal flaws, cracks, smooth and clouded areas, were different, nothing like the lion.

He closed off his office again, cut the lights and returned

293

to his desk, rotating the stone in a slow counter-clockwise direction. He spotted a flaw deep inside, somewhere close to the middle that, if he tilted the stone just right, looked like a tiny island sitting on the horizon of a vast semi-transparent sea.

Wanting a better look, Bambang retrieved a magnifying glass out of his desk drawer and focused on the flaw. Looking through it, the island looked huge. Moving the glass into and out of his view, it was obvious that something else was going on. The glass did not have that much magnification.

Yet..., it was compelling. The approach to the island is from the east because that long shadow is..., if the sun was just below the horizon..., there, color, a pale yellow coming from somewhere inside...,

Seeping through the gloves, Bambang noticed a tingling sensation, like his fingers had been asleep and were just now waking up, lack of blood, tickling his fingertips, wanting to travel up his arms and...,

He pushed the stone away. Hypnosis. There it is again. They hypnotize their victims. That's the only thing that I can think of. But..., how? And why?

Bambang put the two stones back into their containers and placed them on the corner of his desk.

The day's almost over. I'll wait until everybody's gone so I can study them without gloves.

"*Kashif, is this how death is for everyone?*"

"*Sadly,*" *he shook his head.* "*Death for most everyone is a scattering of their spirit, all of the pieces drifting into something more suitable for their new state of mind.*"

"*And why not you, or me?*"

"*We've had training, Sasi. The firestone allows a glimpse of the future. We already knew that there was more to it than that.*"

"*How long will this state last?*"

"*How long can you keep it going?*"

"*It has been a very long time for you.*"

"*I wouldn't know. Here, nothing is measured by time.*"

"*Nadya and Aki still weigh on me.*"

"*I understand. You can't move on until all of your tasks are complete.*"

As usual, he was right. And in answering he also gave a clue to Sasi about time. It does not exist. There is no leaving a message, taking a call, visiting with friends. Visits are possible, but only in the past. In the future, there are only possibilities.

In between, not yet history and not yet completed, time can be ten minutes, ten weeks or ten years. Sasi could visit Sam's last few moments, but she could not find any path in the future where he had gone, which could only mean that he was in between.

During one of her quiet periods, that's what Sasi referred to them as since there was no day or night, she became aware of someone calling. No sound, just the feeling of being summoned.

Sasi became aware of a dog who was concerned about a woman tossing and turning in her bed. The place, from Sasi's view, was blurry and she had the feeling that she was observing the scene through a fuzzy, fish eye lens.

The room was small, compact and there was little space available for anything more than the bunk built into the bulkhead. Sasi could not see any detail of things in the shadows, but did notice a bit of moonlight shining through some kind of opening in the ceiling, lighting the woman's face. Watching her, Sasi realized that this person was Kathryn.

There was nothing to do but observe. She could not wake her any more than she could touch something in the room. But she did say Sam's name over and over, hoping to get Kathryn's attention and, during those moments when she thought she had it...,

Bambang. Kathryn. Remember the name. Bambang.

"Who..., who are you?"

Bambang. Say the name, Bambang.

"Bambang."

Capn seemed settled by all of this. He went back to the foot of Kathryn's bed, watched for a while, yawned, finally settled into a comfortable position on his side and within a minute or two was fast asleep.

Kathryn awoke to the sound of footsteps overhead. Turning so that she was lying on her back, she noticed a shadow pass by the partially opened hatch cover above her bed, Paul cleaning the deck. A bit of water sprayed through the opening and hit her in the face.

"Hey! Knock it off out there!"

"Rise and shine, Mom. That's what you always tell me."

"I don't throw water on you."

"Oh, you have. Anyway, sorry. I'm being careful."

"I'm all wet!"

"It didn't look like much went in."

"What are you doing?"

"Hosing off the ash before the sun dries it. Can you close the hatch?"

"What time is it?"

"Almost nine. Aren't you going to get up?"

Kathryn groaned. "Yeah, I'm getting up." She closed the hatch, got dressed and made her way into the main cabin. Melissa was washing strawberries.

"Morning, Kathryn. Ready to eat?"

"Coffee. I need coffee."

Melissa grabbed a cup from the cupboard, poured one and handed it to Kathryn. "Black, right?"

"Right. Thanks. How did you sleep?"

"I always sleep good here on the boat. I think it's the salty air. How about you?"

"A shipwreck."

"Worried about Sam?"

"Well...," Kathryn sipped her coffee. "We haven't heard from him. Who made the coffee?"

"I did. Why? Too strong?"

"Paul told you to do that?"

"Right."

"You did good. What time did you kids get to bed?"

"About two, I guess."

"How was the moon?"

"You should've stayed up. Beautiful, blue, just like they predicted."

"I was pooped."

Melissa put the bowl of strawberries on the table along with a cutting board and paring knife. "Paul says you like strawberries on your cereal?"

"Sure. Thanks."

"I was going to wait until after you had breakfast...,"

"Oh, dear, what?"

"I found an English subtitle news station in Lampung. They were talking about a car bomb killing a local gang leader. You'll never guess what his name is."

"I know it. Um...,"

"I'll give you a minute."

"Let me think..., um."

"Hamza?"

"Yes! He's dead? What else did they say?"

"There was only one body in the car. That's good. Police are investigating. Some detective named..., wait. I wrote it down. Here it is, Bambang."

Kathryn's spoon stopped half way to her mouth, spilling her cereal and splattering the milk. "What was the name?"

"Bambang. Familiar?"

"I know that name from somewhere."

"Maybe Sam mentioned it."

"I don't think so. I remember Sasi and Aki. No Bambang. He's a detective on this case?"

"That's what they said."

"Where do I know that name from? Do they have contact information?"

"I just happened to write that down, too."

Bambang set his beer down, stared blankly at the little dish of peanuts in front of him and ignored the general chaos in the room. He didn't normally drink beer, basically didn't like the taste of it unless he could eat something salty and crunchy to go with it.

"Don't eat peanuts. I'm allergic to them."

"Don't listen to her. She complains about everything."

"The doctor said, I'm allergic."

"She just moved in and already she's trying to take over."

"Listen to you. I start swelling up. Even the doctor said...,"

"She doesn't like anything, thrives on it. Sorry, Bambang. She doesn't shut up even if you ignore her. She talks in her sleep. I don't know how this happens. Is there a switch somewhere?"

"I do not talk in my sleep."

"Why do you think I go to the other end of the house? Have you noticed I've been gone?"

"I do not talk in my sleep."

"Both of you. Shut up." Bambang took a long gulp of beer and a handful of peanuts. If he was going to drink a beer, he was going to have peanuts or something else with it, maybe both, that was crunchy and salty. That's one reason to drink beer. The other is to feel good or, in this case, better.

"Not the peanuts!"

"Leave the man alone. He wants to enjoy his beer."

"I'm going to swell up!"

"Bambang, doesn't she just make you want to go away? Hiking in the Himalayas, maybe?"

"Oh, God, he's eating them! I'm going to faint."

"Good!"

Bambang gulped down the rest of his beer, left his money on the counter and said good night. Normally, he did not drink at all and he would never drink and drive.

299

But, right now, he couldn't be with anyone. "Why don't both of you go back into your stones? Neither of you are happy."

"Tempting. Better than this. Imagine, eternal nagging?"

"Because you're always running away from your problems."

"What problems? My only one is you."

"Are you going to drive after you've been drinking?"

"It's just one beer. Leave the man alone."

"I'm going to drive it off the cliff if you two don't shut up."

"Did you hear that? He's insane. Where is the stone?

"He's not insane. You're driving him there."

"Where is the stone? If you're going to drive, I want it available."

"He's not insane. Leave him alone."

"It's in my briefcase," Bambang muttered. "I'll get it out and set it on the seat if you'll just shut up."

"See? I told you he's not insane."

"He hasn't done it, yet."

Bambang opened the trunk, retrieved his briefcase and placed it on the seat next to him. He put on his seat belt and started the engine.

"How do I know it's in there?"

"He's not a liar."

"I want to see it."

"Trust me. It's in there."

"Just in case you get in an accident. I need access."

"It's only one beer. He's not going to get in an accident."

"Has that thing got a lock on it?"

"Of course, it would have a lock. He knows how important these stones are. Bambang, tell her they're safe."

"I don't care if they've been safe. I'm worried about now, what's happening right now. This man has been drinking and is now going to drive. I want to see that stone. Open it up, Bambang."

"I'm driving now. I can't open it."

"You're going to get a headache. Open it."

"You've been giving him a headache since you got here.

300

You need to let the man relax and concentrate on his driving."

"When I'm relaxed, he can relax. Open it up, Bambang. I want to see the stone."

"I'm driving."

The pain started behind his eyes, not enough that it blurred his vision, but certainly enough to interfere with his concentration. He'd already been through this once. She could inflict a lot of pain.

Wincing, Bambang pulled off onto a side street, semi-parked his car and put on his emergency flashers. Taking the keys out of the ignition, he turned on the dome light, unlocked the briefcase and flung it open, exposing the two rocks and their containers.

"See? I told you he's not a liar."

"You never know until you call them on something."

"You should apologize. He was telling the truth."

"Both of you, shut up!"

"See? Now you've pissed him off. Stop nagging."

Honk! Honk!

Bambang spotted the car in his rear view mirror, waved, started his engine and moved along. Noticing that his emergency flashers were on, he pushed the button to turn them off.

"I have an idea. Instead of you two arguing all the time, how about helping me solve a murder mystery?"

"She doesn't have the mind."

"I love murder mysteries. I always solve them before the end."

"You wish."

"Are you going to help me, or not?"

"Give us the facts, Bambang. Just the facts."

"Yeah. We'll ask your opinion later."

"First, some rules. Don't distract me while I'm driving. And no interrupting."

"That won't work for him. His attention span is not that long. He has to ask questions as you go. Weak mind, I call it."

"Ignore her. Keep going."

"It started before the kidnapping…,"

"Oooh. I like it already."

"You two are involved."

"I love it! Audience participation."

"Be quiet. Let him talk."

"In a party of four, three people were killed. The other is in the hospital."

"Is he going to live?"

"Looks like he took a nasty fall and banged his head. The doctors think it happened after he was shot because he'd lost so much blood."

"But, he's going to live?"

"Yes."

"Who did the shooting?"

"Hamza and friends. Most of them are dead and we just learned that he was a victim of a car bomb in a stolen car."

"Oh, the intrigue. Who was the bomb meant for? The thief? Or, the owner?"

"Right. See what I mean? And in the middle of all of this, you two."

"We had nothing to do with it."

"No one's accusing you. Actually, I like this. You're not arguing and I have access to your points of view."

"We discuss."

"She won't stop discussing. You'll get used to it, Bambang. It just seems like forever."

"And I have to ask, why would anyone want these two stones? All of this death for the two of you?"

"We should pick up a couple of more beers so we can think this through."

"You can't think, so you have to drink. Like that'll solve anything."

"I'm looking out for him. If we're going to be stuck with you, we need beer. Right, Bambang?"

"If you two can't contribute, please be quiet. What was it like before you invaded my space?"

Silence.

"OK. Blame that one on me. But, that's not the point.

302

Before you came here, what was it like?"

"That was before. This is now.

"Was there life? Music? Sounds?"

"It can't be described like that. You're in limbo until something comes along and changes things."

"What was it in this case?"

"You."

"I'm going at this wrong. Do either of you know Aki or Nadya?

"Who?"

"Who are they?"

"Two of the murder victims. The ones who had these stones before me."

"Never heard of them."

"Then..., the stones must be a pathway. There is no single spirit inside. Does that sound, right?"

"Don't know what you're talking about. I saw an opening, I went through. If I knew she'd be here, I'd have gone the other way."

"Listen to you. You're helpless without me."

"Happier, too."

"You saw an opening? What does that mean?"

"It's a wall, Bambang. We're enclosed. There's nothing there. We just, are. But, sometimes there's an opening, a place where we can slip through.

"We're home. Ride's over. Let's go inside where we can get to the bottom of this."

"You have beer?"

"I'm sure I have something stronger."

"No peanuts!"

303

He comes out of the hallway with a gun to her head.

I could've shot him. She had cancer. She knew she was going to die. She would've agreed even if it was my bullet that killed her.

I should've shot him.

Sacrifice her to save them?

"I'll take the bullet, Sam, if it stops him. I'm going to die anyway."

"I can't do it."

"Doctors gave me six months. I gave me six years. It's been six, Sam. What are you fretting about? Go home. There's nothing left for you here. Pull the trigger."

"I should've checked the windows."

"If you want to blame someone, blame me. I like to sleep with the window cracked open a bit."

"I should've stayed awake."

"Sam, this is a dark place. You don't need to be here."

He comes out of the hallway with a gun to her head.

"They were relying on me."

"I, too, am sorry."

"They died holding hands."

"You cannot regret the past any more than you can change it."

Her words filtered into and out of his subconscious, their conversation through the dark veil between them.

Sometimes they sat at the table drinking tea, having a quiet discussion, balcony doors open and letting in a million dollar view.

Other times, an unfamiliar collection of sounds, doors opening and closing, voices from some distant hallway, phones ringing, hurried footsteps passing by.

Always it was dark, shadows moving within shadows, life outside of touch, sounds little more than a distant buzz.

"Sam."

That voice..., a drop of rain, parched ground, lands with

304

a thud.

"Sam? Can you hear me?"

More drops. I can smell rain.

He comes out of the hallway with a gun to her head.

I could've shot him. They were standing in the light. I could've taken him out. One shot, that's all I needed, a bullet an inch from her face. She would've understood.

"Sam, can you hear me? It's Kathryn. I'm sitting next to your bed. Sam?"

Kathryn placed her hand on Sam's forehead and rubbed gently. "Sam. Vacation's over. It's time for you to come home."

Home?

He comes out of the hallway with a gun to her head. I should've taken the...,

"I spoke with Bambang, an odd man. He keeps muttering to himself. He found your passport. I've got us scheduled for a flight back to San Diego. It would be a whole lot easier if you were conscious. Work with me. Sam?"

He comes out of the hallway with a gun to her head. Sasi, you could've squirmed around a bit. I could've taken him out.

Maybe she wanted to die. She had cancer. Maybe she was expecting me to shoot. I can't do it. I have failed.

"You banged your head when you fell. The doctors say there was some swelling around your brain. I can't imagine you falling, of all people. They say you lost a lot of blood and that you're lucky to be alive. We're lucky to have you, Sam. Paul, Melissa and me. Capn wants a good scratch behind his ears. We're all waiting. Sam?"

A gentle rain now, coming down like a mist, so soft, silent, refreshing.

Bambang calmly untied the boat from the dock, motored slowly through the marina so as not to leave a wake and, leaving the other boats behind, increased his speed out into the channel.

"*Umm, Bambang. Where are we going?*"

"Fishing."

"*I don't like fish. They have too many bones.*"

"*The man has a right to go fishing. He's a detective. He needs some time off.*"

"*Bambang, do you know how to swim?*"

"*Of course he does. Otherwise he'd be wearing something that floats. Right Bambang?*"

"Right."

"*You didn't answer my question. Do you know how to swim?*"

"Yes."

"*Leave him alone. He knows what he's doing. Right, Bambang?*"

"Right."

"*Where are the stones?*"

"In the cooler."

"*I want to see.*"

Bambang didn't even argue. He slowed the engine to little more than an idle, went to the stern of the boat, picked up the cooler and placed it on the seat next to his back at the wheel. He opened the top and exposed the stones sitting in ice along with several beers and lots of crunchy, salty things. "It's a fishing party."

"*What if the boat tips?*"

"*The boat's not going to tip. He knows better than that. Right, Bambang?*"

"Right." Bambang gunned the engine and headed out to sea.

"*It's too fast. Don't you think?*"

"*He's got everything under control. He's a detective. I keep telling you.*"

"What do you know? Nothing. You can't read his mind."

"I've got everything under control. There. Do you feel better?"

"No. You're going too fast."

Bambang pulled back on the throttle, cutting the boat's speed to little more than half of what it was. "You're right. I was going too fast. It's the journey, right? Not the destination."

"See. I was right."

"Listen to her. She's bound to get one right sooner or later. Right, Bambang?"

"Right." Bambang retrieved a beer from the cooler, opened it and guzzled about half.

"I saw how you acted the other night, drinking that stuff."

"It's whiskey. A man's allowed to have a drink. Right, Bambang?"

"We're in a boat."

"He's right. You're both right. What's the score?"

"What score?"

"It's a man thing. Right, Bambang? We keep score."

"Well, then you should know you're losing."

"Don't let her fool you. She's way behind. How about another sip of beer? Maybe that will help drown her out."

Bambang took another long sip. "Ahh."

"That was too much. How far out are we going?"

"The man knows where he's going. He's a detective."

"It's not far. I used to go out there all the time. Then, work got too busy."

"When you became a detective. Right, Bambang?"

"Right."

Letting go of the wheel, Bambang retrieved a bag of mixed nuts, salted, opened the package and grabbed a handful.

"Are there peanuts in there?"

"Let the man have his nuts. He knows what's good for him. Right, Bambang?"

"Right." Bambang picked out a couple of cashews, ate them and took another sip before he upped the throttle.

Clearing the mouth of the harbor with engine roaring there was little conversation and, before long land was on the distant horizon.

Bambang cut the engine. The sudden silence was both welcome and disturbing with the boat now bobbing up and down with the swells, drifting aimlessly.

Bambang walked forward across the deck to the anchor hold, pulled out the anchor and about twenty feet of chain, returned to the cockpit, grabbed another beer along the way and sat down to attach the chain to the anchor.

"It's not long enough."

"He knows what he's doing. Leave him alone."

"That chain is not long enough. We're going to drift away."

"What's he going to hit? There's nothing else out here. Right, Bambang?"

"You're both right. The chain's too short. I'm going to attach the chain to the rope next."

"See?"

"And...," Bambang took another long swig, from his beer. "We're going to drift but there's nothing to hit way out here."

"I think you've had enough. Don't drink any more."

"He's entitled to relax. Leave him alone. He just solved the case."

"He did not. He let that man go."

"What could he do? He was a victim. No reason to hold him. Right, Bambang?"

"Right."

"What about the car bomb? We still don't know who did it."

"Hamza had a lot of enemies. It could've been any one of them. Whoever it was did me a favor."

"You didn't solve anything. You should be back working on the case."

"He needs time to think. What better way than to go fishing? Right, Bambang?"

"Right."

Bambang gulped down another beer and ate a few more

salty snacks.

"*You're drinking too much. I want you to stop now.*"

"*Don't listen to her, Bambang. She's always been bossy like that. Don't know why I put up with her for so long.*"

"*Put up with me? I'm looking out for us. He's drinking too much. We're too far from shore, if you ask me. And...,*"

"*Nobody's asking you.*"

Bambang finished attaching the chain to the anchor, retrieved the two firestones from the cooler, put them in his pockets and zipped it closed.

"*What are you doing?*"

"*He knows what he's doing. How can he relax when you keep nagging? Give the man...,*"

"*Put the stones back where they were! Then I want you to turn this boat around and head back to land.*"

"*She thinks she owns the place, Bambang. It's better if you just ignore her.*"

Bambang calmly attached one end of his handcuffs to the chain, the other end to his wrist, threw the anchor overboard and jumped in.

Before leaving, Kashif turned and studied her. She seemed a bit confused about how to proceed. "Sasi, there is nothing more that I can do. My tasks are complete."

"What about Sam?"

"He is with Kathryn. He is in good hands."

"He still needs our help."

"We no longer possess the firestone. We cannot redirect the future."

"Where are you going?"

"It's time for me to join my family."

"Will we meet again?"

"You are always welcome to visit. But, as you have told me, there are still tasks that you must complete."

"I will be stuck with them forever."

"Patience, Sasi. All things come to an end. May I suggest that you pick one of your concerns and concentrate on it? If you take on everything at once, you'll feel overwhelmed and..., sometimes resolving one resolves others."

"Where to begin?"

"Sam is alive. He will choose his own destiny. You can watch over him and maybe a suggestion or two from you might make it into his dreams. I suggest that you find the one thing that causes you the most anguish and work on it."

"Anguish is everywhere."

"You cannot know joy without knowing anguish."

"And you have rid yourself of anguish?"

Kashif smiled. "No, certainly not. But I have dealt with the things that I can control and have done the best that I can. In that, I find joy."

It was Sasi's turn to smile. "I understand now. One of your remaining tasks was to usher me in, just as mine will be to do the same with Sam. In the interim, I'm allowed the freedom to explore."

Kashif's smile turned into a grin. "You catch on quickly. It's been a pleasure."

As he disappeared from her thoughts, Sasi realized that, while living, she had seen Kashif once, as an old, dying man. Yet, leaving, her memories of him were of a young man with thick black, shoulder length hair, trimmed beard, eyes dark, narrow, observant, a man in shackles, beaten, bloody, a middle aged, graying man, shaggy, white beard, face wrinkled beyond his years.

Remembering their time together, his guidance, Sasi felt a warmth from his friendship, a bit of joy within a sea of doubts and, along with that, a desire to pick up where he had left off.

Where does one begin?

With Sasi it was the murders that had taken place in her house. All of that destruction in such a short time after so many years of harmony. Unfathomable. And as she thought of these things, she remembered a snippet of conversation between Nadya and Aki at her kitchen table when they first met.

"I feel like I know you from someplace."

"I was thinking the same thing."

What did Kashif say? Once they possessed the firestones their fates were sealed? But, if their paths crossed at some previous time, and if one of them said or did something differently, what then? Is it possible to change destiny?

Sitting in the shade at a table next to a pool, Sam stared at the unfamiliar scene. "I don't know where I am."

Kathryn moved his iced tea out of the way, put her hand on his and rubbed gently. "Of course, you don't. You've never been here before. We're at Melissa's house."

"Why?"

"Her father, Sal, is in Europe for six months on assignment. We're house sitting."

"Oh."

"Sorry for the confusion. With all of the medication you're taking, I didn't want to leave you alone at your studio. We'll go over there today and pick up some of your things."

"My studio. It seems so long ago."

"You've been through a lot."

"Any news from Lampung?"

"Hamza, killed with a car bomb. They think Bambang fell overboard and drowned while fishing."

"Sasi?"

"You already know she died. Same with Aki and Nadya."

Sam grew silent. Over and over he felt uncontrollable pangs of guilt, an endless repeat of those final few moments in Sasi's house.

"I'm sorry. I shouldn't have answered so directly."

"I asked. And I already knew the answer. I'm always hoping for a different ending."

"It is what it is."

"Where Is Paul?"

"Helping Melissa in the kitchen. Are you hungry?"

"A little."

"I'd offer you a beer but the doctors say no alcohol."

"A beer sounds good."

"I could go buy some alcohol free."

"What's the point? Where's Capn?"

"On the boat. Melissa's got three cats and we're pretty

sure they don't want a dog hanging around."

"I'd like to see him."

"We'll stop by the boat on the way back from your studio."

"We're staying here?"

"It's a four bedroom house. You've got your own room. Is that OK?"

"Perfect. Where's my phone?"

Kathryn stood. "It's in your room. I'll get it."

Sam smiled. "Thanks. I feel so alienated."

"No wonder. You were a breath away from death. We're lucky to have you here." Kathryn leaned down and kissed him on his forehead. "I'll get your phone."

Melissa came out through the sliding glass door with a pan of baked macaroni and cheese, slightly charred on top. "Hey, Sam. Hope you like Mac and cheese."

"Looks delicious. You made that?"

"It's my dad's recipe. He taught me how to make it when I was little so I could have it ready when he came home."

"How old were you then?"

"Twelve."

"You like cooking?"

"Yep. I want to know what I'm eating."

"Well, whatever it is, it's working. You're beautiful."

"Thanks. Paul's bringing the salad. I'm going to get plates."

"Thanks. You guys are great."

Seated around the table, all four were quiet for the first few minutes devouring Mac and cheese.

Kathryn finally set her fork down. "I have to slow down. That's delicious."

"Thanks. Anybody want more iced tea?"

"Mom. Can I have a beer?"

"You're too young."

"I got straight A's. I've graduated. I'm on summer vacation. I'm not going anywhere today. Why would I? I've got three cool people here that I like to be with and...,"

"Crimanently. Go get one. Just shut up."

313

"Thanks, Mom."

Sam watched him disappear into the house. "He's growing up fast."

"It all happens so quickly. Before you know it, it's over."

Melissa sipped her iced tea. "I'm glad finals are over."

Paul returned with a beer, smiling. He raised his bottle, motioning for a toast. "To Sam. Great to have you back."

Everybody drank to that. Paul got a couple of glugs in. He looked over at Sam with a smile. "Ahh, that's good! I'd offer you some but...,"

Melissa punched Paul in the shoulder. "Cruel!"

"OK," said Kathryn, reaching across the table. "Give me the beer."

Sam laughed. "It's OK. I've done it to him. He's just getting even."

Paul, keeping his beer away from Kathryn, nodded. "It's a game we play."

"Right."

Melissa dished herself a bit more salad. "Paul, did you talk to your mom yet?"

"Um, no. I was waiting for the right time."

"Talk to me about what?"

"About Melissa's and my plans."

"When was it going to be the right time?"

"Now, I guess."

"And...?"

"We want to go hiking."

"OK. Where? Maybe I'll come along."

"Mom."

"At Zion National Park."

"That's in Utah?"

"Right."

"Oh. I get it. I'm not invited."

"It's not like that. We just want to get away and we both love to hike."

"There's lots of good hiking around here."

"Mom. That's not getting away."

"Hmm. Suddenly I feel very old. Where are you going to

314

stay?"

"My dad's got a tent and sleeping bags. We've got a propane stove, lantern...,"

"All right. I see where this is going. I can't stop you and I wouldn't want to. I'm just surprised that it got this far without my knowing."

"He was supposed to talk with you a week ago."

"I wanted to wait until after finals."

"It's our only chance, Kathryn. We'll be in college in the fall and I still need someone to house sit. Sam, you're comfortable here, aren't you?"

"I haven't been here long enough to know. It's pretty good so far. Are you going to leave us this Mac recipe before you go?"

Kathryn eyed Sam. "You're not helping."

"I was on my own at fourteen. Did I turn out so bad?"

"I'm not worried about them. I'm worried about who or what they'll encounter."

"Well?"

"I guess. I...,"

"Thanks, Mom. You're the greatest."

Kathryn looked over at Sam "What just happened?"

"I think you're on your own for a while, except for me. Sorry."

"Cooking for two is as just easy as cooking for four. We'll just eat it twice as often. If you don't mind my cooking."

Sam blew her a kiss. "I wouldn't have it any other way."

Nadya opened the box, removed the film and searched the body of the camera for the latch that would open the back. Finding that, she puzzled over how to load the film, how to hook it through the spindle on the other side and wrap it so that it didn't keep coming loose. Accomplishing that, she snapped the back closed.

Hamza came into the room. "What are you doing?"

"Loading film into the camera."

"That's an antique. Why do you want to bother?"

"It's for my class."

"I told you to drop that class."

"I like photography.

"It's mostly guys in there."

"So?"

"I don't like how they stare at you."

"Men always stare at me. I can't help what they do."

"I don't like it. I want you to drop it."

"It's one of the prerequisites for my major."

"You don't need to go to school. I'm taking care of you."

"Right. But what happens when I'm old and gray? I need a career."

"You won't make any money in photography."

"Hamza. You're so negative. This is just one class out of many."

"I don't like how friendly they are."

"They're my classmates! Of course, they're friendly. We have to work together. I'm learning so much."

"We'll talk about it later. I've got to be somewhere. Drop the class. OK?"

Nadya, watching him leave, did not answer. She smiled, blew him a kiss and, when he was gone, went back to the camera, anxious to learn all of the different settings. Not like a digital at all. How did they ever take so many wonderful shots?

Drop the class? No. Hamza's short sighted, except for

316

when he's working on money deals or getting even. Being the love of his life today does not mean it will be the same tomorrow.

Find a career. Get to know people. Get connections. Not the kind Hamza keeps. Creepy. That's what they are. All of them.

Nadya read through all of the blurbs, fiddling with the camera at the same time and deciding that, once she found a good subject to shoot, she would do the first half in automatic mode, just to make sure she had a few good shots, and do the second half in manual, just to stretch the limits.

And, something about water. Last night she'd had a compelling dream and even though she couldn't remember exactly what it was about, she did remember that water permeated her seemingly endless visions of the night.

Today was a beautiful day, lots of puffy clouds, broken sunlight. Both shadows and lighting would be good, a wonderful day for film.

Feeling free walking out the door, she also felt the weight of Hamza's words dragging her back in. Was she going to have to fight his stubbornness and jealousy for the rest of her life?

He has no hobbies. We have nothing in common. It's all about making money and being top dog. He likes to gamble and I don't want to know what else he does when I'm not around.

Is that what I want?

Exhaling, as if to rid herself of those thoughts, Nadya closed the door, locked it and headed for the lake.

Reflections always make for good photography.

Aki rolled over in bed and stared blankly at the alarm clock, fuzzy. He closed one eye and then the other attempting to get a read, but the splitting headache behind them was morphing the whole process into more pressing needs, running to the bathroom, heaving, relieving the other end and then finding some aspirin, in whatever order comes first.

He crawled out of bed, started to stand, noticed the walls tilting a bit as the floor moved below and decided to sit on the mattress edge until they straightened themselves out. Head throbbing, he felt like his eyes were crossed.

Eventually he stood, not because he wanted to, but because his stomach had something to say about his behavior the night before and that conversation needed to take place in the bathroom.

Ten minutes later, bottle of aspirin in hand, he stumbled into the kitchen, filled a glass with water, took two and then headed for the fridge.

Greasy, something greasy to save my stomach. Eggs? Hmm. High cholesterol. How old are these things anyway? Never eat them.

He put three eggs in a bowl and set it on the counter.

Cheese? No..., moldy. Whew! Think I'm gonna be sick again.

Three scrambled eggs, two pieces of toast with jelly, and a banana later, he settled into a chair with a cup of strong, black coffee and two more aspirin. Leaning back, staring at the ceiling...,

OK. She's gone. Ran off with my best friend.

Should've seen that coming.

Don't ever want to see either of them again.

Aki took a few more sips and, wincing with the strength of it, set the cup on the floor next to his chair.

Crap.

Gotta go somewhere, take my mind off of things.

Thought they were getting a little too friendly.

318

All their private jokes.
It sucks.
God, I feel like crap.
No more booze.
Time to clean up.
Another sip of coffee.
Right.
Like I'm going to do that.
Aki swirled the liquid around, wanting to see how close he could get to the edge without spilling it, decided better of it and let it rest.
They could've told me.
She could've broken it off, waited a while and then hooked up with him.
I could've handled that.
Behind my back? That sucks.
Aki leaned back in his chair, not wanting to go over the previous night's events, but pouring over them anyway.
There wasn't a fight..., was there?
My God, I think I punched him.
They left hand in hand.
He was holding a handkerchief over his nose.
After that it was a black hole. How many drinks? What does it take to make the pain go away?
Feeling the second two aspirin kicking in, Aki stood and, ignoring the mess in the room, went to the window and pulled back the blinds, squinting with the onslaught of light.
Beautiful..., I think.
I need air.
I have to think about things.
My God, I feel like crap.
Think I'll go for a walk.

After Melissa and Paul came back from their hiking trip, Sam and Kathryn decided to spend a night on Spittin' Image. Taking Capn for a walk, the three of them hiked all the way out close to the end of the jetty. Capn wanted to go all the way to the end but Kathryn didn't want to get soaked from the spray. Sam and Capn braved it all the way to the end where an extra large wave gave them a nice surprise.

The sun disappeared behind the clouds before it reached the horizon, eliminating any chance of a green flash and, feeling the wind picking up, they turned back toward the boat with the wind behind them.

"Feels good out here," said Sam, breathing deeply. "Air's fresh."

Kathryn took his hand. "It's good to see you smiling again."

"I can't change anything. I have to let it go."

Kathryn squeezed his hand and said nothing. Sometimes it helped to talk. Sometimes the subject was best left alone. "Are you drinking tonight?"

"What are we having?"

"Where are you taking me for dinner?"

"Oh." Sam frowned. "I..., I didn't know. Where did you want to go?"

"Would you rather not go out?"

"I was hoping for a quiet evening on the boat."

"Pizza, salad, garlic bread, bottle of wine? Something like that?"

"That sounds perfect."

Kathryn checked her watch. "Good. The pizza guy should deliver in about thirty minutes. We have to meet him at the gate."

"You already ordered?"

She laughed. "While you and Capn were taking a bath."

"You already had it planned?"

"No. But you don't have a change of clothes and they're not going to dry out before dinner. Wouldn't you rather stay in?"

"Perfect."

Kathryn lit a candle for their only light down in the cabin, wind howling around the boat, halyards clanging against the mast.

"I feel like a bug in a rug," said Sam, at last. "There's so much going on out there, but it's so calm in here."

The ate pizza and drank wine and remembered their time on the island, being captured and fighting for Kashif's release. There were a million things they could talk about and they did well into the night.

Much later, long after the wine was gone and shortly after the wind died down, Sam turned over in his sleep and dreamed of Sasi, her face flickering in the light of a candle, her shadow dancing off of the cinder block wall behind.

"Are you doing well, Sam?"

"I can't forget."

"Guilt is an anchor."

"That doesn't change my feelings."

"Their paths crossed before they knew anything of the firestones."

"Even you said that we cannot change the past. How does that relieve me of guilt?"

"They are together."

"They died holding hands."

"They are happy."

"How do you know?"

Sasi, with a twinkle in her eye, *"It only takes a change of heart to change your destiny."*

Aki felt like he was walking into a moment of Deja vu. The feeling started when he was at the beginning of the trail that circumvented the lake, just about the time he noticed the concession stand opening and smelling grilled hot dogs.

He didn't normally eat hot dogs, actually just the opposite. He was more of a health nut when it came to food, definitely preferring vegetables over meat. Feeling that he'd been here before, doing this exact same thing, thinking these exact thoughts didn't make any sense.

Must be the booze. My head is buzzing.

Wait, that must be the caffeine.

Whatever, I'm not doing it again.

No more drinking.

Right. Who am I kidding?

Aki wanted a relaxed stroll. Breathing in the fresh air, watching the clouds roll across the sky and enjoying the scenery, the feeling of Deja vu only got stronger.

When he came around a curve in the trail and saw her at the water's edge, one foot up on the bank and the other on a rock sticking up out of the water, leaning down to get a shot of three ducks swimming nearby, Aki stopped in his tracks.

I feel like I'm watching a movie of me watching a movie.

Having taken several shots, the woman stood and looked slightly off balance, like that foot was going to wind up in about two feet of water. Aki hurried down the bank, grabbed her hand and pulled her back to shore.

Embarrassed, she smiled. "Thanks. Thought I could get back."

"No problem." He turned to go, hesitated.

A chance to meet a good looking woman and you're walking away? Aki, don't be a fool.

"You're shooting with film?"

She nodded. "It's for a class."

"Do you do your own developing?"

"That's the next class."

"Getting any good shots?"

She smiled. "I won't know until I develop it. That's the problem with film, isn't it?"

"I guess." Aki started to leave, hesitated. "Do I know you from somewhere? I feel like I do."

"I was thinking the same thing."

He held out his hand. "Aki."

"Nadya."

"Familiar. But I can't place you."

Nadya placed the lens cover back onto the lens with a snap. "Which way are you going?"

"Counterclockwise around the lake. I'm just getting started."

"Me, too. Do you mind if I join you?

"Not at all."

"You can keep going if I stop for a shot."

"I'm in no hurry."

As they walked along the path, it felt like the door was closing. Whatever moment of Deja vu they had was slipping into the past.

"What school did you go to? Maybe that's where."

Aki shook his head. "I went to school in Hawaii."

"Oh. Do you go to a gym?"

"No."

"Night clubs?"

"No."

"Do you come here to the park often?"

"Sometimes I jog the lake."

"That must be it."

"That doesn't explain why I think I know you."

"Where do you work?"

"Out of my home."

"Oh. Stock market?"

"Yes! How did you know that?"

"Lucky guess?"

"What do you do for a living?"

"Student at the moment."

"And after that?"

323

"Depends what kind of work I can get. Something with photography, if I can."

"Like?

"Nature, different cultures, travel around the world and record what I see."

"That's ambitious."

"Someone once said, you can't get off the ground if you don't aim for the stars."

"You'll need a crew, not to mention funding."

"First I have to get good at what I'm doing. If I make it my passion, people will recognize that. The rest will follow."

"Love your optimism. Just what I needed."

Nadya smiled. "Why? You're depressed?"

"Bad night."

"Drinking?"

"That's part of it. Usually, I don't drink. So, when I do, it hits hard."

"I see. Drinking for happy or drinking for sad?"

"To forget."

"Oh. Sorry. I'm being nosey."

"That's OK. It's good to talk."

"Thanks for keeping me out of the water. My foot was definitely going in."

"Probably would've cut your photo session short."

"Payback. I'll buy you a hot dog when we get to the other end."

"You don't have to pay. Save your money for your new enterprise. I'll buy you one."

"That's not how it's supposed to work."

"I can do my work from just about anywhere in the world. And I'm interested in your project and love your enthusiasm. Talk about it over lunch?"

"Put like that...,"

"I have this feeling that my life is about to change."

"Funny. Me, too."

# # #

324

About the Author

Dave Riessen earned his Associate's Degree in Electronics at San Diego City College and then attended San Diego State University where he changed his major to English and focused on creative writing.

Other novels by D. D. Riessen:

You Gotta Have Wings - young adult fiction

On Standby - adult fiction

Sometime Tomorrow - science fiction

The Other World - fantasy and science fiction

* * * *

Dave's work revels with the fanciful, ponders the inscrutable and enigmatic and examines the human character.

To learn about the history behind the stories, please visit his web site at:

www.ddriessen.com

I appreciate your comments. I always strive to make each story the best that it can be and I love that you take the time to read them.

This is my passion.

Thank you